Pam Lecky is an Irish historical fiction author. Having been an avid reader of historical and crime fiction from a young age, it was inevitable that her books would be a combination of the two. Pam lives in North County Dublin with her husband and three children. She can be contacted through social media or by visiting her website www.pamlecky.com

By the same author

Her Secret War

HER LAST BETRAYAL

PAM LECKY

avon.

Published by AVON
A division of HarperCollins*Publishers* Ltd
1 London Bridge Street
London SE1 9GF

www.harpercollins.co.uk

HarperCollins*Publishers*
1st Floor, Watermarque Building, Ringsend Road
Dublin 4, Ireland

A Paperback Original 2022

1

First published in Great Britain by HarperCollins*Publishers* 2022

ISBN: 978-0-00-846487-5

Typeset in Bembo by Palimpsest Book Production Limited, Falkirk, Stirlingshire
Printed and Bound in the United States of America
by LSC Communications

For more information visit: www.harpercollins.co.uk/green

To Keith with thanks for a lifetime of friendship

1

19th December 1941, The Entertainment Hall, Hursley Park

The Hursley Players' production of *Hay Fever* received a standing ovation. From the wings, Sarah Gillespie and her fellow backstage assistant Vera Taylor, watched the cast taking their bows. It was Friday night and the last performance. Thankfully, the play had gone off with very few hitches, to the relief of all, after a less than satisfactory opening night earlier in the week.

Sarah nudged Vera and flicked a glance at Richard, the director, who was pacing up and down the corridor to the side of their makeshift stage, muttering under his breath.

'I don't think he's happy,' she whispered.

Vera snorted. 'He never is! But do you think Mr Coward would approve of that performance?'

'Let's not push our luck!' Sarah replied with a grin. 'But to be fair, they did far better than I'd hoped after Wednesday's fiasco.'

'Yes, though how Sylvia forgot her line again, I'll never know. She only had one.'

Richard appeared beside them, hands stuck in his pockets, and a scowl on his face, which did not bode well. 'I could wring her stupid neck. Bloody amateur!'

Vera and Sarah shared an amused glance. Richard sported rather grand ideas about his abilities and those of his actors.

'It was just nerves, Richard,' Sarah said to him, but his only answer was a grunt before he slouched off to resume his pacing.

'My God, you'd think we were on the West End the way he behaves,' Vera said with a roll of her eyes. 'I've had enough of the histrionics. I don't know about you, but I need a drink.'

'I'll second that,' Sarah replied, watching her cousin Martin take yet another bow. He was lapping it all up. But he deserved it; Martin had outshone the rest of the cast, in her opinion. She could see Uncle Tom and Aunt Alice in the front row, her aunt beaming up at Martin.

Vera linked Sarah's arm. 'Let us await the thespians in the changing room. They will, of course, be full of themselves, but I suppose that is the lot of us lowly backstage slaves. We do all the hard work but get little credit.'

'Yes, but at least our names appeared on the programme,' Sarah replied.

Vera sniffed. 'Yes, at the bottom of the last page!'

'I guess our dreams of Hollywood must wait.'

'Speaking of travel, I hear you're off to London soon. I'll miss you,' Vera said with a wave of her hand. 'This has been fun.'

'Yep. I leave straight after Christmas, but I don't intend being away too long, Vera. Hopefully only a few weeks.'

'But you will miss the auditions for our next spectacular. Martin told me how disappointed you were not to be on stage for this one.'

'It can't be helped,' Sarah said with a shrug as they entered the dressing room.

There was the small matter of finding her renegade father for MI5, but that wasn't something she could share with Vera, or even her family. Only her manager in Supermarine, Miss Whitaker, a fellow MI5 agent, knew about her upcoming mission. Sarah knew her aunt and uncle would try to talk her out of it if she were to tell them what a dangerous path lay ahead. To them, Jim Gillespie was dead, supposedly killed by the same bomb that had killed Sarah's sister, Maura, and destroyed their home. It was best they believed that to be true. Only Sarah knew what had really happened, that Jim was alive and well, heading up an IRA cell in England and collaborating with fifth columnists. She could not bear to think of her father escaping justice. He had questions to answer – to the authorities, and to her.

Ever since Colonel Everleigh, the head of MI5, had first told her the truth about her father, her mind had been in turmoil. With her grief for her sister, Maura, still raw, to learn that their father had abandoned them to their fate made her livid. Revenge was foremost in her thoughts. Soon enough, she would have the opportunity to put things right, but for now, to be part of the production team for the play had been a welcome distraction. After an eventful couple of months, she certainly needed that. She was lucky to be alive after that awful day in Winchester when a Nazi had nearly succeeded in killing her.

The girls sat down to wait for the cast. Vera produced an apple and offered Sarah a bite. She declined. 'Such a pity Paul can't come down here for Christmas,' Vera remarked between mouthfuls.

The reminder was unwelcome. It had been quite a blow to receive her boyfriend's hastily written letter with news of his imminent departure for America. Worst of all, their plans to spend a few days in London after Christmas were in tatters. She was desperate to see him; desperate for him to know her true feelings. Their recent reconciliation had only been by letter. Not ideal!

'Yes. I was gutted. It would have been lovely to see him before he left for the States,' Sarah said. 'I've only met him once since we both came to England. His flight training was up in Yorkshire.'

'What rotten luck! Where is he going exactly?' Vera asked, her eyes full of sympathy, which almost brought tears to Sarah's eyes.

'Alabama; for further training. Just my luck,' she said with a gulp, 'but he has to go where the RAF dictate.'

Vera raised a brow. 'One of the fly boys, that's impressive. How long will he be there?'

However, before Sarah could answer, the cast trickled in, two of the male actors leading the way.

'Thank God that was the last performance. I could murder a pint!' said one.

'Ha! Just like you murdered those lines, Angus!' said the other, giving him the side-eye.

Angus squared up to him. 'What do you mean by that?'

'Now, lads, take it easy. Richard is on his way.' It was Martin, standing in the doorway, shaking his head at the two men who were eyeing each other up. 'Everyone did just fine, tonight. And, Angus, I'll take you up on that idea of a pint.'

Angus shrugged and turned away. Sarah smiled at her cousin. He had a knack for defusing tricky situations. 'Yes, do hurry up, lads; us ladies are parched!' she said.

Sarah's alarm clock rattled into life, and she awoke to a pounding headache. *That will teach me to carouse with Vera Taylor.* With a groan and her eyes still closed, she slapped down on the bell and savoured the blissful silence of the sleeping house. Twenty minutes later, she woke up again, spotted the time and leapt out of bed.

'Damn, damn, damn,' she muttered as she dragged on her clothes. Why on earth had she agreed to meet Vera so early for the clean-up? With a glance in the mirror, which made her cringe, she pulled a brush through her hair before galloping down the stairs.

'Morning!' Aunt Alice greeted her in a chirpy tone, a pot of tea in her hand.

'Good morning. Sorry, I can't stop for breakfast. I'm running late,' Sarah said as she shrugged into her coat.

Her aunt tut-tutted and shook her head. 'You'll be sorry later. What about a piece of toast? I don't like you going to work on an empty tummy.'

This was typical of Alice; such a mother hen. And for the hundredth time, Sarah wished Maura could have experienced family life with the Lambes. 'I'll grab something in the canteen, I promise. See you at lunchtime,' Sarah said, kissing her aunt's cheek, before making for the door.

She stalled in the open doorway. All was still; that particular silence that comes with snow. Flurries were drifting down, coating everything in white. She breathed in the cold air and her pounding head eased. As she pulled on her gloves, she saw young Edward, the Post Office messenger boy, coming down the path. Sarah waved to him, thinking how smart he looked in his uniform. But he didn't respond as he normally would; instead, he walked up to her, unsmiling, before reaching into his satchel and pulling out a telegram.

'Good morning,' Edward said, not quite meeting her gaze. 'This is for you, miss.'

Sarah went numb, staring at it. Telegrams were never good news. Not these days.

'Who's there, Sarah?' she heard her aunt call out. Seconds later, Aunt Alice was at her side, looking down at the messenger boy. 'Good morning, Edward,' she said. 'How's your mum doing?'

'Much better, Mrs Lambe.' His eyes strayed to the telegram in Sarah's hand. 'Should I wait for an answer?'

Sarah heard her aunt's sharp intake of breath before she pressed Sarah's arm. 'No. My dear, best you come back inside to open that. Run along now, Edward.'

'Very good, Mrs Lambe,' he replied and scooted off.

'Come in, love,' her aunt said, tugging Sarah back into the house and closing the front door.

Sarah sat down by the fire, staring at the envelope. Maybe it was from the colonel in London about her mission, and not something awful. She glanced up at her aunt, whose brows were drawn in concern, a tea towel clutched in her hand. Swallowing hard, Sarah slit open the envelope. It was from Deirdre O'Reilly in Dublin, Paul's sister.

Paul's ship torpedoed Atlantic. Missing, presumed dead.

2

Two months had passed since Sarah had last met Colonel Everleigh, the head of MI5. Now she sat outside his office, on a cold and bleak Friday afternoon, nerves jangling. Everleigh was a manipulative man, though it had taken her a while to realise it. The colonel's revelation that her father was alive had left her reeling, and she had accepted his challenge to work for him in a moment of pure rage and horror – as he had known she would. She had learned her lesson, vowing to be more careful in the future, realising she was just a pawn in this secret war with its obscure rules and shady motives.

The world had stopped turning for weeks after she read that telegram from Paul's sister. She had barely made it through Christmas. Her sorrow had threatened to overwhelm her. Sarah's friend Gladys and her cousin Martin were her greatest support, dragging her out of the house when all she wished to do was curl up in bed and shut out the world. Of course, officially, Paul was missing and with no body found Sarah could hope – but deep down she knew that hope was misguided wishful thinking. And through a haze of grief, Sarah's hatred for the Nazi regime increased so much it frightened her. The need to strike back, in any way she could, became an obsession. Her thoughts returned, again and again, to her father, now collaborating with Germany for his own ends. Jim Gillespie had betrayed her and Maura by abandoning them. The memory of her sister's anguish, in that split second before their home had collapsed around them, continued to haunt her dreams. Only now Paul was present in her nightmares too, reaching out to her in his final moments as the icy water of the Atlantic claimed him forever. She would wake up in torment, thrashing, the sheets twisted around her body. Each time it occurred, it only cemented her determination to strike back.

Ireland might still be neutral, but Sarah Gillespie was not.

The mission to track down her father carried high risk. She was no fool. She knew what she was dealing with, but that didn't matter. Nothing much mattered any more. Without Paul, and without Maura, only revenge was important. Her grief had been tucked away until she completed this mission. Nothing could get in the way. But a tiny voice inside her head poked through every now and again and asked would she be the same person by the end of this? Would working in such a clandestine, though admittedly necessary, job corrupt her morally? It seemed likely when one was dealing in secrets and subterfuge, but war was branding everyone's life, not just hers. The struggle to survive the evil of the times, and the loss and pain, were etched on most of the faces she passed in the street.

And so here she was, ready to do the colonel's bidding. A year before, Sarah would have laughed off the idea as ludicrous, but today her foray into the official world of espionage would begin. Even more incredible for an Irishwoman, it would be for the British Secret Service. But life had been upended so thoroughly since the Luftwaffe had destroyed her world, nothing surprised her any more.

She would remain adamant: she had committed to this one assignment only. If successful, her father would face the justice he deserved. Removing him and his cell of republicans would hurt the very Nazis he was so happy to conspire with. Maura and Paul would be avenged, albeit in a small way, and then she could return to her job at Supermarine. She had been so proud to get the job at the company responsible for the design and build of the Spitfire plane. So much so, that she had made Miss Whitaker promise to keep her position on the tracing team open. She loved the job, taking the engineers' drawings and tracing them out so that the publishers could compile the manuals used to build the planes. Sarah had always found the job soothing. One could forget one's worries as the process demanded total concentration. Yes, a return to Hursley Park and Supermarine would be a return to normal life.

With nothing to do but wait, Sarah watched Miss Abernathy, the colonel's secretary, from the corner of her eye. The young woman tapped away on her typewriter, her red fingernails flashing as they glided over the keys. Sarah caught the odd peek in her direction. There was a hint of disdain fuelling the smile lingering on the secretary's lips.

Despite obtaining her ration book just before Christmas, Sarah hadn't updated her refugee wardrobe. All her clothes were courtesy of the nuns back in Dublin and comprised ill-fitting cast-offs of the most sensible and unfashionable variety. It was bad enough that her friend Gladys teased, but for a stranger to judge her was a bit much. Why were people so quick to draw conclusions based on one's appearance? Though perhaps in the world of espionage, dressing down would be a useful tool to employ when trying to ingratiate yourself or go unnoticed.

'Won't be long now, miss,' the secretary said with a perfunctory smile. With a flick of her wrist, the carriage return swung back across the machine. Ping!

Sarah smothered a sigh and turned her gaze to the window. She'd been waiting for twenty minutes already. What was keeping the man? Changing position, she tried to find a comfortable spot on the high-backed chair and fell to wondering if its design was deliberate, to put visitors at a disadvantage. Out above the rooftops, the view of steel-grey skies promised an icy soaking on her walk back to the lodging house. Discreetly, she rubbed her thigh where it ached. The injuries she had sustained, courtesy of the Luftwaffe, always acted up when the temperature dropped. Since she and Gladys arrived in London it had been bitterly cold. The worst winter in a long time, it was said.

A young office boy entered and plonked a pile of folders on Miss Abernathy's desk just as Sarah heard raised voices coming from Everleigh's office. With a nod, the secretary acknowledged the delivery and kept typing. But the boy was staring at the door to the colonel's office, clearly intrigued and showing every intention of loitering. Miss

Abernathy coughed delicately to get his attention. Still, he did not move. The secretary's finely arched brows rose as the volume of the argument behind the door grew. Sarah strained hard to decipher what was being said. She could distinguish two different male voices, but that was all.

Then Miss Abernathy's patience ran out. Her fingers froze above the keys, and with pursed lips, she trained an icy stare on the office boy. He flinched and scurried out. Sarah smiled, impressed. Perhaps it was a talent she should acquire, for she could envisage many an application for it.

Suddenly, the door to the colonel's office was wrenched open. An elderly man, with an abundance of white hair and cheeks as red as Miss Abernathy's fingernails, stomped out.

'You'll be hearing from me shortly, Everleigh,' he roared over his shoulder, before disappearing out the door. Seconds later, he returned and stood in the doorway, staring at Sarah. 'Ridiculous!' he said with a sniff, and was gone.

The ice-maiden at the desk turned to Sarah. 'You may go in now, Miss Gillespie.'

Sarah stepped through the open doorway to find the colonel standing at the window. He greeted her with a smile and hurried across to shake her hand.

'It's good to see you again, Sarah.'

'And you, sir,' she replied.

'Apologies for keeping you waiting,' he said. 'Please take a seat.' Everleigh waved her to a chair while he closed the door. 'I believe condolences are in order,' the colonel said as he sat behind his desk. 'I was sorry to hear about that young RAF lad. Miss Whitaker wrote to tell me about it and that we would have to delay things a little.'

Sarah squirmed inside. It was too painful to discuss with a stranger. On a fundamental level, she was only here because she believed if she dove into this mission wholeheartedly, it would block out the pain of grief. 'Thank you, sir. I do appreciate your kind words, but I'm eager to start now.'

Everleigh smiled. 'Jolly good. I was afraid your family would persuade you to change your mind and you would stay in Hampshire.' His blue eyes held a challenge.

'With Miss Whitaker championing your cause, you had little to worry about, sir. However, if my family knew the truth, if they knew about my father, I've no doubt they would have done their best to dissuade me, but it is just something I must do,' she replied. 'It is as simple as that, sir.'

'Good, good, excellent, in fact,' he said, relaxing back into his chair. 'Now, I'm sure you have many questions about this operation.'

Sarah's chest tightened. There was no turning back now. 'I do, Colonel. When do I go to Wales? Is there any intelligence on where my father might be hiding?'

'Steady on: it's wonderful that you are so keen, but we need to sort out a few things first.'

'Such as?' she asked, frowning. Surely it was a simple task. Find her father, identify him, and let the authorities do the rest.

'Some training will be necessary before you go out into the field, and you must be fully briefed. We will be sending you into Wales undercover. We must get it right. Every little detail of your new identity is important, but the matter is well in hand.'

This all sounded very formal, making her uneasy. 'How long will all of this take, sir?'

'A week, at most. Now, I must be frank with you and put you on your guard,' Everleigh said.

'Oh?'

'Unfortunately, details of your previous adventure – how you uncovered Captain Northcott as a double agent – have become known throughout the service. Other parties are interested in you. The gentleman who just left is with the SOE.' The colonel shook his head in amusement. 'He is on the prowl, the old goat. They are livid because I recruited you first. They had the idea of nabbing you, too. I'm surprised they didn't send someone down to Hampshire to try to inveigle you to join them. Resist any lures they may throw out, Sarah, I beseech you.'

'I will, sir, but what is SOE?'

'It is part of the secret service. The Special Operations Executive is a band of men and women who specialise in espionage and sabotage, with emphasis on the latter, and generally behind enemy lines.'

'I see,' she said, wondering if she should be flattered. Why would they want her? She couldn't speak any foreign languages and didn't know one end of a gun from another.

'I explained to Sir Douglas that it was out of the question. You are committed to our project,' Everleigh said, with a twinkle in his eye.

'I'll be careful, sir, but you need not worry as I am dedicated to this assignment. It's deeply personal.'

The colonel smiled. 'That's what I told him, but he wasn't best pleased.'

'I'm surprised they would consider me suitable, being Irish.'

Everleigh shrugged. 'But you have more than proved where your loyalties lie. No less than ourselves, they have recruited every nationality you can imagine. They are always on the hunt for talent.' Everleigh grinned at her. 'As am I.' The colonel gazed at her for a moment before lacing his fingers. 'There is something else you need to know, as there is a slight change to our plans. You will be working with a partner on this assignment.'

'A partner? What partner?' Sarah asked, straightening up in her chair. 'Why would I need one? Surely all I have to do is point out my father to your agents and they will do the rest.'

'It is a little more complicated than that, Sarah,' Everleigh said. He regarded her for several seconds, but she could not read his expression.

Sarah dropped her gaze to her hands, clenched in her lap; that uneasy feeling was creeping over her again. Was she being sucked into something far darker than she had been led to believe? When she looked up, she asked: 'In what way, sir?'

'Since last we spoke, I have received further intelligence from one of our agents in Cardiff. A Welsh nationalist and Nazi sympathiser and a known IRA operative were spotted in Pontypool, the nearest town to a munitions factory. Naturally, we are concerned, as Glascoed makes bombs and depth-charges.'

Sarah grimaced; it was an unfortunate reminder of the war at sea and Paul's recent demise. Mind you, a few depth-charges dropped on German U-boats would not be a bad thing. However, in the wrong hands . . .

'Not things you'd want traitors to have access to, sir.'

'Certainly not,' the colonel agreed. 'Glascoed was delib-erately sited in the middle of nowhere in a valley surrounded by hills. It is about thirty miles from Cardiff, deep in the countryside. My fear is the IRA's Welsh nationalist friends may have people on the inside. The enemy within our borders is just as dangerous as those beyond.'

Sarah was surprised to hear Welsh people might be involved. 'These nationalists are pro-Nazi?'

'A tiny but dangerous minority are, yes. The risk is that some vulnerability at the plant has been passed on to the IRA. Our fear is that they plan to break in and help themselves. We need you and your partner to find out what the IRA are planning.'

'And stop them?'

'Of course!'

'And you believe my father is involved?' she asked, already sure what his response would be.

'As I said, one of the people spotted is IRA. We believe she is your father's second in command.'

'A woman! Do you know who she is?'

Everleigh pulled out a file and scanned the topmost page. 'McGrath. Last known address Church Street, Dublin.' He held up a photograph.

Sarah gasped. 'Not Jenny McGrath?'

The colonel's eyes popped. 'Yes! You know of her?'

Sarah nodded, her stomach twisting on a memory. 'Jenny is an old friend of my father. It would be hard to find a nastier piece of work. They courted for a few months after my mother died.'

'I see,' he said, rubbing his chin. 'But they must have stayed in touch.'

'Yes, but I didn't realise she was IRA. Perhaps he recruited her, or they met through a local cell.' Sarah frowned. 'I must admit I'm surprised: in general, my father doesn't hold women in high esteem.'

Everleigh grunted. 'This woman may have hidden talents.'

'Obviously! And she must have followed my father here to work with him.'

The colonel's brows pulled together. 'Possibly, or she was here already, preparing the way. The problem is we don't know when she arrived in this country. We suspect she may have used the IRA's covert route into Fishguard from Cork. We have learned that much since last we spoke, Sarah. Up to now, those using the route have evaded us; their bogus papers have gone undetected. They have experts forging those documents, both here and in Germany. I suspect they have someone in the immigration service in Fishguard working for them as well.'

'How did you discover the route?'

'Ah! We fed the Abwehr false ration card numbers through a double agent.'

'And someone popped up at the port in Fishguard with a card bearing those numbers?' she asked.

'Exactly!'

'That was clever, sir. But at least now you can put a stop to it,' she said. 'Close the route.'

'No, actually. Far better we monitor the activity,' he said. 'It gives us the upper hand.'

'That must take a lot of manpower.'

The colonel grimaced. 'It does indeed. We are recruiting constantly. Now, of equal importance is setting up your job. The fact you know this McGrath woman will make your task more difficult. We may need to change your appearance somewhat. We don't want you spotted first.'

'Yes, she would recognise me straight away. However, if my disguise involves better clothes, I wouldn't say no,' she answered, looking down at her thin cotton dress. The colonel smiled in sympathy, and she pressed on: 'Besides taking on a new identity, what exactly is my job?'

'As we discussed before Christmas, we want you to identify your father. I've already explained our difficulty. He keeps changing his appearance, his name and his location, and he is heavily protected. But we hope you will see through any disguise. Once you identify him, we can arrest him and bring him . . . well, bring him somewhere for interrogation.'

'And trial, I hope?'

'That is not my decision, Sarah.' The colonel cleared his throat. 'I have charged your partner with finding out why the IRA are interested in Glascoed. It makes sense to combine the two operations and it should speed things up if you work together. Your father may not be directly implicated, but if he is as close to this McGrath woman as you say, she may lead you to him.' His tone was almost pleading, but it barely registered. This sounded awfully dangerous. The colonel continued: 'Your partner, Lieutenant Anderson, has recently joined us here from the US Embassy.'

'Oh!'

'Since the US declared war on Germany in December, our unofficial co-operation has been formalised. The Yanks have only recently set up a centralised secret service and want to base it on ours. We've agreed to help train up their chaps, and the lieutenant is the first to become available to MI5. We've given him the codename of Eagle, as a nod to his nationality. Don't be concerned, he has experience in the US Naval intelligence service.'

'Oh, well, that's a comfort.' Everleigh raised a brow. 'Sorry, sir, I don't mean to be sarcastic,' she said. 'I'm sure he will be an asset. It's just I didn't envisage this job lasting more than a couple of weeks.'

'I cannot give you any guarantees, Sarah. But Anderson has quite a reputation for getting his man, as the Yanks like to say. If you work well together, you should be able to wrap this up quickly. It will be down to you both.'

'Have you told him about me?'

'Yes, of course.' The colonel harrumphed.

'There's an "and" or a "but", isn't there?' Sarah asked, her antennae twitching like mad.

'Perhaps. The lieutenant isn't used to working with women, but I'm sure it will work out well . . . once he gets used to the idea. You will have to be fully briefed, of course, and that will begin on Monday. After that, you'll fit right in. You have nothing to prove to me, Sarah, just remember that.'

'Thank you,' she said, wishing the knot in her stomach would ease. The job would be tough enough without having to prove herself to this Yank.

'I'd like to get you both to Wales by early next week, if possible. Our man in Cardiff, Aled Thomas, will set everything up for you and Anderson.' Everleigh smiled. 'I'm told you are quite the actress, so that aspect should be easy for you.'

'Miss Whitaker is your source on that, I assume?' she asked.

The colonel nodded. 'I would be lost without her! Now, shall we introduce you to our American friend?'

3

Sarah followed the Colonel down one flight of stairs and along a dimly lit corridor to the back of the building. Staff chatter, predominantly female, and the clatter of typewriters spilled out from the various offices as they passed. It was wonderful that so many women had the opportunity to do their bit of the war effort, and Sarah wondered if they had requested to work in the service or had been posted to it randomly.

Near the end of the passageway, Everleigh stopped and turned. He drew a deep breath and looked as though he was going to make a comment, but the moment passed and instead he wiggled his brows. The gesture gave her a moment's pause. He really *was* anxious about how she and this Yank were going to hit it off. What was Everleigh not telling her? Yanks were often considered brash, but she preferred straight talking any day. Neither was she an innocent when it came to men, but perhaps Everleigh thought this fellow would intimidate her. With a nod and a smile, which she hoped would quell his doubts, she stepped inside as he held the door open.

The office was small, barely bigger than a broom cupboard. The walls were lined with open shelving units, full to the brim. Lieutenant Tony Anderson of the US Navy sat behind the only desk, his back to the window. Dark brown hair, brown eyes and a square jaw in a tanned face were the first things Sarah noted. That and the fact that he dominated the space. He reminded her of Gary Cooper, the quintessential American hero. And such a contrast to Paul. But she dared not dwell on that; it was too painful. When the lieutenant stood, she reckoned he must be well over six feet. *Not intimidating at all*, she thought as he crushed her fingers in a handshake while Everleigh made the introductions.

The lieutenant's first impression of her was unreadable. Not a flicker: no appraising scrutiny or dismissive glance; totally deadpan. *He's good*, she thought, but she always embraced a challenge. She would reserve judgement and decided upon a cheery approach for now.

'It's good to meet you, Lieutenant Anderson,' she said. 'I'm looking forward to working with you.'

'And I you, Miss Gillespie,' he answered in a flat tone, his gaze flicking towards Everleigh. His voice was low with a slight hint of an accent. But as he was the first American she had ever met, she had no idea where he might hail from.

'Jolly good. I'll leave you two to get acquainted then. Call back to Miss Abernathy before you leave, Sarah.' The colonel smiled at each of them. Then, to Sarah's surprise, he put an arm around her shoulder. 'She may be tiny, Anderson, but she packs a punch, as you Yanks say.' With that, he escaped out the door.

Sarah could have killed the colonel for putting her on the back foot. The colour rushed into her cheeks and Anderson did and said nothing to ease the awkwardness of the situation, but simply continued to stare at her. Desperate to fill the silence, she pointed to the desk and the map that he had been studying as they had entered the room. 'Wales, I assume? Our destination.'

'Sure is,' he replied, returning to his chair, 'Miss Gillespie.'

'Oh, please call me Sarah. After all, we are going to be working together,' she said with a forced smile.

It was wasted on him. Her friendly overtures were crashing and burning.

'OK . . . Sarah, as you wish,' he replied.

She waited. He didn't reciprocate. Sarah smiled harder. 'Perhaps you could show me where Pontypool is? I'd never heard of it until today.'

Anderson twisted the map around and pointed to an area north-east of Cardiff. Sarah leaned closer. Pontypool was only a tiny, shaded strip on the map. 'And the munitions factory?' she asked, glancing up.

The lieutenant's gaze wasn't encouraging. He moved his finger slightly to the east. 'It's situated in the valley here, but for obvious reasons, it isn't marked on the map.' Everleigh had been right about the munitions factory; it was sited well away from any towns.

Sarah flicked a glance at the lieutenant to see if he was being smart. Oh, to be Miss Abernathy and treat him to one of those icy stares. But she had to be content with a raised eyebrow. 'I would have thought we would have access to military maps?'

'It would appear we don't merit such luxuries, Miss . . . Sarah,' he replied, leaning back in the chair and crossing his arms.

'Do you have any theories on why the IRA might be interested in that factory?'

'Worst case, they want to bomb it. Best case, steal from it. Either way, they must be stopped,' he replied.

Sarah nodded, then looked around the room as she straightened up. The only other chair had piles of folders stacked on it and a briefcase on top. The decent thing would be for him to clear it off for her; that was if he had any gentlemanly inclinations, but she was doubting their existence.

After several seconds in which she continued to look at the chair, Anderson drawled: 'Allow me.' He placed the files on the desk none too gently and dropped the briefcase to the floor. The lieutenant returned to his seat. As he passed, she caught the faint aroma of hair oil or aftershave. She wasn't sure which, but it was a pleasant citrus scent. Unfortunately, it appeared to be the only agreeable thing about the man.

'Thank you,' she said, draping her coat over the back of the chair. There was nothing for it but some small talk. 'So, tell me, Lieutenant, where in the States are you from?'

'Illinois.'

'Oh, is that so? I believe I have cousins in Chicago,' she said.

'Most Irish do.' What she suspected was a flicker of amusement flashed momentarily in his dark eyes. 'That's dandy.'

This is going to be a fun afternoon if curt answers are all he will share, she thought, suddenly wishing she were anywhere but here. 'And how long have you been seconded to MI5?'

'I joined a few weeks ago,' he drawled. 'Why do you ask?'

'I'm just curious. It would be good to know each other's backgrounds, would it not? The colonel told me you were attached to the US Embassy up to now. This must be quite a change,' she said.

'It is.' The disdain in his tone was unmistakable.

Was that the issue with this man? That he resented having to work with the British? It wasn't something she was bothered to ask, however, as the man was as responsive as a block of stone. She needed a different tack. Perhaps she could appeal to his sense of camaraderie, as they were both aliens working for the Crown? 'I'm sure you are wondering how an Irishwoman would end up here working for the colonel.'

'I thought it strange, all right.' This was said with a smirk.

Sarah stiffened. So that was it; he had something against her being Irish. She realised he was determined to be obnoxious. *I won't rise to it.* 'And how long have you been in Naval Intelligence?'

'Five years,' he replied, his gaze steady and, if she weren't mistaken, challenging.

'You must have a wealth of knowledge. I hope you will share some of it. As you must know, my experience is limited.'

'Indeed. I've read your file,' he said. 'It didn't take long. You're an amateur.'

How was she to respond to that? God, he was blunt! An image of tumbleweed popped into her head; this relationship was doomed. 'And you take exception to this?'

'It's not ideal, certainly. I can't afford to screw up my first assignment with the Brits.'

'Nor I mine!'

'Neither am I into hand-holding,' he said with a quirk of his mouth. 'You better know what you're doing.'

'They have briefed me,' she lied. *God, this man is infuriating!*

'Really? Now, that is interesting.' Anderson sat forward. 'I wondered who *was* briefing you. How do I know you aren't, in fact, IRA like your father?'

Sarah gasped. 'You cannot be serious.'

With an angry wave which encompassed the building, he sneered: 'I don't understand these British spooks.' He shook his head. 'This place is a breeding ground for double agents. They catch spies and then turn them to work for them. How do you trust people like that? But I'm sure you know all about that little game.'

'No, I do not.'

The lieutenant sniffed. 'You'd hardly admit it, I suppose. How do I know you haven't wangled your way in here for your own ends? Maybe you're gonna supply information to that father of yours.'

'That is outrageous!'

'Don't take me for a knucklehead. My God, you Irish!' He sat back and glared at her. 'I've seen back home how you infiltrate every sphere of life and before you know it, you control everything. If it's not politics, it's the police force. Well, guess what? I don't like the Irish and their goddamn neutrality. That's cowardice in my book, and the likes of your father is the worst kinda scum. How many deaths can be laid at his door?' Anderson waved his hand angrily. 'Not just soldiers, but civilians, too. Do you sleep easy at night knowing that? Anyone who helps the Nazis, or their sympathisers, deserves what's coming to them. I'll be watching you closely. If you don't do your job, I'll make sure that bastard is dealt with.'

Sarah could only stare at him in disbelief, her heart galloping. How dare he speak to her like that; question her loyalties after everything she had been through. Rising slowly, she grabbed her coat only for it to catch. She tugged it free, aware of his mocking gaze. When she reached the door, she turned and faced him.

'I intend to do my duty, Lieutenant, despite being lumbered with such an ignorant and obnoxious man as you. We have no choice but to work together, and hopefully it is for as brief a time as possible, but if you ever speak to me like that again, I shall respond in any way I see fit. I should warn you; I will ask for firearms training, and I am determined to excel at it. Good day!'

Despite the powerful urge, she didn't slam the door but closed it gently. Then she groaned. *That parting shot had been nothing but pathetic, Sarah Gillespie.*

The echo of his laughter followed her back up the stairs.

4

6th February 1942, London

Once Sarah had escaped from Miss Abernathy's office, she left the MI5 building without delay. Wild horses would not drag her back to endure another exchange with Anderson in that pokey cupboard of his. She would not give the man the satisfaction of a rematch until she was good and ready. His animosity had taken her by surprise, but she would be better prepared next time they met.

But as Sarah walked away, despite her best intentions, her thoughts centred on Anderson and his mocking gaze. How on earth was she to work with the man? No wonder Everleigh had been so guarded before the introduction. Had he anticipated how hostile Anderson was going to be and if so, why didn't he warn her? Everleigh was testing her; that was the only explanation. All that talk of trusting her and that she had nothing to prove; maybe MI5 had suspicions about her. Anderson hadn't been afraid to voice it. He feared she was a double agent for the IRA! *Hateful, hateful man!* And how dare he call her an amateur, even if it were true. No doubt he had expected to be working with an experienced MI5 officer, but her lack of knowledge or experience in the field could not be helped. The blasted Yank would just have to accept it.

However, his insinuation that she was working for her father was much more worrying. How could they work together if he didn't trust her? The job would be difficult enough without knowing he would scrutinise everything she said and did. But Sarah was reluctant to go crying about it to Everleigh; she did not want to appear weak. It would be up to her to prove that stupid Yank wrong. She only hoped that his experience would help her find Da promptly, and their association could be ended as quickly as possible.

Now all she wanted was to push any thought of that obnoxious Yank from her mind before the weekend began. He couldn't be more different to Paul, whose gentleness and good humour had been infectious. It only made her miss Paul even more. Irritated that Anderson could live in her head so easily, she did her best to dwell on happier things. She wondered how her aunt and uncle were doing and whether Martin had auditioned yet for the new play. Hopefully Martin would write soon with all the local news. The thought of him brought a smile. She hadn't expected to miss him quite so much, but he was almost like a big brother to her now. With luck, her business in Wales would be over quickly enough to allow her to follow through on her promise to help Vera backstage once more. It was unfortunate that instead of treading the boards in a damp hut in Hursley she would be playing a far more dangerous role in rural Wales. Was she mad? *Best not to think about that.*

Gradually, the tension in Sarah's body eased as she walked along the street, but when she reached a corner, she looked around in surprise as nothing seemed familiar. But it didn't faze her; she just needed to get her bearings. Sarah pulled a street map out of her bag and traced her route from MI5. She hadn't strayed too far north, and it didn't matter, for she was falling in love with the city and wanted to explore every inch while she had the chance.

For the short time she would live here, her plan was to take a different route to work every day. London was still an alien world in many respects and nothing like her native Dublin, which now seemed so sleepy in comparison. Everything about this city thrilled her; she hated to admit it was drawing her in with all the charm of a lover. The mix of old and new buildings, the stories of its past, were fascinating and left her wanting more. But that was nothing compared to the mood of the place. The Londoners' spirit of resistance was palpable in the way they went about their business, determined to keep living and working amidst the ruins. Just as she had experienced in blitzed Southampton, businesses were operating in the direst of circumstances. But it was all done with a smile and a stubbornness in the face of what Hitler had thrown at them, which she found poignant. For that reason alone, she could happily walk around all day simply absorbing it all.

And you never knew who you might meet. One lunch-time, she had even spotted the distinctive tall form of Charles de Gaulle, leader of the Free French, walking along The Strand. The fall of the French had been a devastating blow to the Allied cause. The general had set up a Free French headquarters in London and they were doing everything in their power to help the war effort. As she had watched the Frenchman disappear into the crowd, she wondered if he too felt like an outsider in a foreign land. Luckily, they had both been welcomed with open arms. Except, of course, for that obnoxious Yank!

Setting up in London had been helped greatly by Gladys' presence. Poor Gladys, though. For the last week, while they waited to start their respective jobs, Sarah had dragged her out every day to explore the city. Gladys often grumbled, but anything was better than staying in their cold and damp rented room. Her friend, of course, was totally at home in London, it was the buzz and excitement that attracted her. It had always been Gladys' dream to live and work here. Even before Sarah was lured to London, Gladys had suggested they escape the boredom of the Tracing Room at Hursley Park for the bright city lights. So it had not surprised Sarah when Gladys had declared nothing was going to stop her coming along too when Sarah had revealed her destination.

If Sarah was honest, she was relieved. The notion of living alone in London, even for a short time, had been unsettling. Her cousin Judith had offered her a bed in the flat she shared with her girlfriends, but it would put Sarah in a difficult position. Knowing about Judith's affair with her married boss and having to keep it secret from the family did not sit easy with her as it was. Sarah had no wish to offend her cousin either, so sharing with Gladys was the ideal solution. Luckily, Judith didn't seem to mind as she was well settled, with her own group of friends and a job in the Home Office she loved.

In the end, the only difficulty with their plan to move to London had been Miss Whitaker, their manager at Supermarine. As an MI5 agent, the sprightly spinster had helped persuade Sarah to join the secret service. However, she was not happy to lose Gladys from the tracing team at the same time. But once Gladys had declared her intention of going 'come hell or high water', Sarah agreed to use her influence with Miss Whitaker to make it happen. It had not been easy. Women were expected to take up war work and stick with it. In the end, Miss Whitaker came up trumps and secured a position for Gladys with the London Passenger Transport Board as a bus conductress. The authorities were satisfied once they were assured Gladys would still do her bit for the war effort.

In the distance, Sarah spotted a Lyons teashop and made a beeline for it. A cup of tea and a bun would cheer her and give her a chance to warm up before she set out for her lodging once more. Soon settled at a table and her order taken by a young nippy, Sarah relaxed. Really, she had so much to be grateful for. Although she had lost all close family back in Dublin, and the gut-wrenching loss of Paul was never far from her mind, her family in Hampshire had drawn her into their world so completely, it was as if she had always known them. Even in her despair at Christmas, they had shown nothing but sympathy and kindness. Slowly, after many a long chat with her uncle and aunt, she had begun to accept Paul's death. But there were days when she would let a tiny ray of hope ignite that somehow Paul had survived. After all, they had not found his body. But most of the time, she just felt frozen inside. It was so cruel a blow when they had only been reconciled for such a brief time. It felt like a punishment. Sometimes, she could laugh at that notion, seeing it for what it was; indoctrinated Catholicism. Guilt and nothing but guilt about everything you thought, said or did. Those nuns had a lot to answer for.

Sarah's thoughts turned to her previous life, back in Dublin, as she watched the nippies scooting around the tearoom, serving her fellow customers. How Ma and Maura would have loved to come to this tearoom. The nearest to it in Dublin was Bewley's Café on Grafton Street, but even that had been out of reach for her family when they had been children. Money had always been tight, and treats had been kept to a minimum. Ironically, they had been relatively well off in later years, with three of them bringing in a wage, but the risk of being laid off had cast a shadow, making Da frugal in the extreme. The girls' weekly wage had to be handed to him straight away on a Friday evening. A meagre weekly allowance was all he would let them have. Just another way to control their lives.

Well, at least I don't have him to answer to anymore. Except, of course, he wasn't dead. Jim Gillespie was alive and well and causing trouble. *Blast him! God forgive me, but I wish he were dead.*

Horrified by where her thoughts were leading, she tried to concentrate on the future. But that was futile. MI5 would dictate how the coming weeks would evolve. But chasing ghosts in Wales, now that her first throes of rage had subsided, seemed almost suicidal the more she thought about it. She had always known Da was a hard man, always ready with his fists to settle disputes or, as in the case of her mother, to keep her subservient. A drinker and a fighter and a fanatical IRA man.

But what kind of father abandons his daughters to their fate so easily? The night the bombs fell on North Strand, he had seen it as an opportunity to disappear, even planting his wedding ring on another body to fool the authorities. He didn't check on Sarah and Maura or try to contact them to let them know he was alive. A man capable of that would have no qualms in despatching her if she tried to interfere in his business for the IRA. What if he found her first? She felt her insides churn at the very thought. It was hardly surprising that MI5 wanted him dealt with and his cell disbanded. Facilitating the movement of spies in and out of Britain was abhorrent and that was only the activity they knew about. What else could he be up to? It was well known that the IRA wanted to take advantage of the war to further their own cause. And that usually meant destruction and death.

And as for Jenny McGrath? Now, there was a dangerous woman. Her long, bony face and pale eyes flashed before Sarah, making her squirm in memory. McGrath had appeared in their lives soon after their mother had passed away, and Sarah had suspected the relationship with her father was far from new. Jenny had swanned in, all false praise and outspoken views, pushing the wedge more deeply between the girls and their father. Still grieving and only twelve years of age, Maura had found it difficult to accept Jenny's constant presence in No. 18. Da had lashed out with a slap across the head on the one occasion Maura had voiced her dislike of the woman. While the relationship lasted, the girls had stayed out of the way, up in their room, whenever Jenny called.

Sarah never knew why Jenny had vanished from their lives as quickly as she had breezed in. She had just been grateful to see the back of her. But the realisation that she might have to trace her Da through Jenny made her skin crawl. What was it Miss Whitaker had said? Oh yes: women spies are the worst to deal with.

What would Maura have thought about it all, seeing her big sister tackling traitors and rubbing shoulders with conspirators, even terrorists? Dealing with these people was Sarah's new reality whether she liked it or not. But she was not the same innocent who had been pulled from the rubble last May. The events of the past months had changed her, hardened her, and made her more worldly wise. Her dealings with Captain Northcott had left her flummoxed and unsure of herself. She had been completely hoodwinked by him. For the first time in her life, she had had to question her judgement. But the lessons learned would stay with her. She had grown up.

'Here you go, Miss,' the nippy said, setting down a pot of tea and a plate with her iced bun on the table before her.

Sarah stared at the relative *feast* for several moments, lost in the memory of the last time she had been in a tearoom. It had been in Southampton, last November; the day she saw Paul for the very last time. He had looked so handsome in his uniform, his excitement about joining the RAF lighting up his face as he had spoken about his wonderful and exciting new life. How she missed him!

But Jerry had taken him too. All she had left were memories she barely had the strength to summon up.

Sarah smiled sadly, welcoming back that old bedfellow:

revenge. It was all that was keeping her going. Whatever might happen, she wanted to put a stop to her father's activities, even if it meant her own demise. Anything to hurt the Nazis; to make them pay. And there was little left to lose with Maura and Paul lost forever. Keep smiling, keep busy, and the pain is bearable. *I must keep this hidden, deep down inside,* she thought. It wasn't a feeling she could share; no one could truly understand.

But Sarah found her hand was shaking as she poured her tea, and the highly anticipated delicacy tasted like dust in her mouth.

5

6th February 1942, Paddington, London

With sleet driving into her face, Sarah's cheeks had lost all sensation. She walked as fast as she dared along the slippery pavements. If not for Gladys, returning to Mrs Horgan's domain would have been the final straw in a less than fun day. Gladys always made her laugh. Sarah's frozen fingers curled around the wrapping paper of the parcel she had received from Miss Abernathy. But the paper was wet, and her hand slid right through. She cursed. Would the package hold together long enough for her to get indoors?

There was no welcoming blast of heat as she pushed open the guesthouse door, but the aroma of last night's dinner still lingered in the hallway. Not a pleasant memory. Mrs Horgan's offering comprised turnip, onions, and some dark mysterious lumps, which their fellow guests had speculated were meat. However, no one cared to consider the animal source. When it came to the landlady's cuisine, it was best not to dwell on these things, so Sarah had gulped it down. But now her stomach growled, for all she'd had since breakfast was the bun at the Lyons teashop. She had a sudden longing for hot tea. However, sight of Mrs Horgan, perched at her reception desk, put her off. Any requests were wont to be met with a belligerent stare and a vigorous refusal. Sarah didn't have the energy for an argument this evening. Besides, she suspected the hygiene standards in the woman's kitchen were as poor as the landlady's personal cleanliness. Mrs Horgan glanced up and grunted hello. Sarah stomped past, barely acknowledging her.

As Sarah climbed the three flights of stairs to the attic room she shared with Gladys, she thought longingly of her aunt's house back in Hampshire. The cottage was always cosy and warm, and her aunt's cooking was delicious due to Uncle Tom's efforts in the veg patch. Sarah sighed and kept moving. Life wasn't that bad. Some people had to deal with far more serious inconveniences. Every day as she explored London, she could see the results of the previous autumn's Blitz. Earlier, she had passed a bombed-out block of flats. The front wall had crumbled. High up on one floor, a bathtub dangled precariously over the edge, and in the remains of the stairwell, sets of banisters zig-zagged upwards, hanging suspended in mid-air. With a shiver, she had turned away.

Sarah almost burst out laughing at the sight that greeted her on opening the door. Gladys was sitting in her underwear at the dressing table, one leg resting up on it and her face scrunched up in concentration. Her friend was applying a brown liquid to her leg with a sponge.

'What's tickling your funny bone?' Gladys asked, casting her a quick glance.

'You!'

Gladys shook her head and returned to the job at hand. 'Well, how did it go? Catch any Nazis today?'

'No!' Sarah blew out her cheeks, pulling off her soaking wet coat before slumping down on the bed. 'And it isn't funny. Oh, it was just awful, Glad.'

'Crikey! Well, let me tell you, I'm not going back to Hampshire. No way!'

'I wasn't going to suggest that, but it wasn't the best of starts,' Sarah replied.

'Surely, it can't have been that bad?'

'Trust me; it was not what I was expecting at all.'

Gladys grunted in response, her lower lip caught in her teeth as she concentrated on staining her other leg.

Sarah sniffed the air and cast a glance of distaste at the bottle of gravy browning on the table. 'Did you pinch that from the kitchen?'

'Yep. The old bat went out shopping after lunch.' Gladys looked up. 'Look at it this way; I've saved us having to eat this muck poured over our dinner.' She held up the bottle and shook it. 'There should be some left, if you want to do yours.'

'No, thanks. Could you not use something other than gravy browning? She'll guess it was you.'

'The old bat can't prove it,' Gladys said, flashing her a grin.

'It will be all over the sheets; she'll know.'

'Ah! But she can't prove it was *her* gravy browning.'

'Fair point,' Sarah admitted. 'But do you really want to smell of Sunday roast?'

Gladys stuck out her tongue and continued with her other leg. 'It reminds the boys of home! I have heard no objections so far. Anything is better than milk–bottle legs. Here, be a dear and do the line down the back.' Gladys held out a brown eyebrow pencil. 'And don't go too hard. This pencil has to last me the war.'

'I don't know why you are bothering. Look at that,' Sarah said, pointing out the window. 'Mother Nature is going to rinse it all off.'

Gladys just waved the pencil at her. 'I'll wear my long coat. Come on, hurry up, it's freezing in here. I want to get dressed.'

'OK. Stand up on the stool so I don't have to bend over.'

'Lord, Miss Grumpy! You're in a mood,' her friend replied, clambering up. 'So, spill the beans; what happened?'

'Lieutenant Tony Anderson is what happened,' Sarah ground out.

'Who?'

'My lovely new partner.'

Gladys peered down at her leg. 'That's crooked.'

'Well, keep still then,' Sarah snapped.

'Who is he?' Gladys asked.

'An American naval officer. An obnoxious one to boot, even if he looks like a movie star.'

'Ooh, really? All dark and smouldering?'

'Yes. I'd certainly like to see him smoulder. On a very large fire,' Sarah said.

'Do I detect a smidgen of friction already?' Gladys chuckled.

Sarah scowled up at her, but Gladys just laughed even more. 'Will you introduce me? I like a challenge, even if you don't,' Gladys purred.

'Trust me, you would not thank me.' Sarah straightened up. 'There, that should do. Just don't cross your legs or that will rub off. Where are you going tonight?'

Gladys jumped down and handed her a note. '*We* are going out. This arrived earlier from your cousin Judith. She's taking us out on the town.'

'Brilliant! I could do with some distraction,' Sarah said, scanning the note. She felt her spirits rise.

However, when she looked up, Gladys was giving her one of *those* looks. 'Sarah, you had better borrow something of mine. You can't go out looking like a refugee. It's not a good look.'

'Even if I am one?'

Gladys ignored her and opened the wardrobe, humming under her breath. 'Stop feeling sorry for yourself! Here. My blue dress should fit you reasonably well,' she said, but then she spotted the package Sarah had left on the bed and skipped over. 'Or did you buy something at last?'

'No. It's clothes I will need for the job. My training starts on Monday.'

Gladys picked up the parcel and pulled off the damp brown paper. A pair of sturdy brown boots clunked to the floor. Gladys stared down at them, turning up her nose. 'Classy! Just what a girl about town needs, though I don't believe you'd find Rita Hayworth dead in those.' Then she reached into the parcel and plucked out a green bundle. As she shook out the garment, she burst out laughing. 'Good God, what is this? I've never seen anything so ugly.'

'You know very well what it is. It's a siren suit. Very practical. Come on, you've seen one before.'

Shaking with laughter, Gladys turned it around and tugged at the panel at the back. 'Is this what I think it is?'

Sarah gnawed her bottom lip, trying not to laugh. 'Yes, I imagine it is. How else could you use the bathroom if you're stuck in one of these all day? At least it's a pleasant colour green.'

Gladys made a face and dropped the suit down on the bedspread. 'Well, don't wear it tonight.' Laughing, she ducked around the corner of the bed as Sarah took a swipe at her. 'When I agreed to come to London with you, Sarah Gillespie, I didn't think it was going to be so amusing,' Gladys said.

'Of course, that is my sole purpose in life. Anyway, you *told* me you were coming. I don't think I ever had any say in the matter.'

'I wasn't going to let you have all the fun, now, was I? I was fed up with Winchester, especially since Ruth left.' Her friend looked about the room. 'Mind you, I would have thought twice if I'd known we were going to end up in this dump.'

'I know; I'm sorry. It was the only place I knew, and it's handy for work,' Sarah said, checking through the shreds of the packaging for any more MI5 goodies, only to be disappointed. 'We can ask Judith if she knows of somewhere better.'

'Good. I nearly froze to death here today. That old bat refused point blank to give me anything for the fire. I even contemplated burning some of your awful dresses.'

'You would be doing me a favour.'

'I aim to please,' Gladys said with a bow.

'However, hold off for now. I don't know when I'll have

time to get something new with those coupons. I don't fancy having to queue at a shop for half a day either. It's lucky the job will provide some new clothes.'

Gladys glanced at the siren suit. 'Oh dear! I hope they have something better than that crime against fashion.'

'That's just for training . . . well, I think it is. My boss's secretary took my measurements before I left today. Once they have finalised what role I must assume, they will give me the appropriate clothes. With a bit of luck, I'll be able to keep whatever they provide.'

'Let's hope you're not going undercover as a coal miner. Isn't that what Welsh people do?'

Sarah chuckled. 'You're hilarious, but I suspect you're only jealous.'

This produced a snort from Gladys. 'I don't think so.'

Sarah watched her friend pull on a smart shirtdress with a little envy. 'Don't you start your new job tomorrow? You won't be stuck here all day any more.'

'Yes, thank goodness. Bus conductress is much more up my street.' Gladys stood gazing into space. 'Think of all the lovely fellas I'll get to meet as a clippie. The uniform is pretty snappy, too,' she said, casting another derogatory glance at Sarah's siren suit. 'And anything is better than tracing; it was so dull. It was those old biddies' mission in life to make mine miserable.'

With a smile, Sarah recalled her friend's frequent run-ins with the Tracing Department's supervisor and manager. Gladys could not concentrate for long periods and frequently had to re-do her tracings. 'I'm sure they miss you, Glad.'

'Sure! Miss Whitaker probably cries herself to sleep at night,' Gladys replied with a wink. 'Bags the dressing table first.'

'Sure.' Sarah pulled the blue dress out of the wardrobe and held it up in front of herself before the mirror. It was probably too long, but it was better than anything she owned. A flicker of memory made her catch her breath: Maura in a blue dress, going out to her first dance. She had been so excited, and they had spent ages getting her ready only for Da to arrive home in a bad mood and scupper the whole outing. Feeling the tears well up, Sarah made an effort to distract herself. 'I rather enjoyed the work at Supermarine. Once this assignment is over, I'm going back.'

Gladys waved the hairbrush at her. 'You say that now, but just wait till you have experienced life in London. You won't want to go back to sleepy old Hursley.'

'Maybe.'

Gladys shook her head and set to work with her hairbrush. Sarah loved to watch Gladys do her hair. Her friend could create a look in minutes, whether it was waves or rolls, whereas Sarah was all fingers and thumbs and usually ended up leaving it down. As she concentrated on her friend's demonstration of her skill, she sank down onto the bed. Gladys started by back combing a section of hair held in one hand, then she rolled and pinned it into place with hair grips, forming a lovely high roll of hair to the side. She inserted a pearl clip on the other side.

When finished, she turned and grinned across at Sarah. 'Hey! Why aren't you dressed yet? We have one of Mrs Horgan's gourmet dinners to look forward to before we paint the town red. I have it on good authority it's lobster and champagne this evening. How that woman spoils us!'

'Oh, Lord! If only!' Sarah said as her stomach growled.

She could summon up little enthusiasm for the meal ahead, which she suspected would be last night's leftovers reheated.

'Well, I suppose there is one good thing about this war; there's no danger of us growing fat!' Gladys replied.

6

6th February 1942, The Mecca Dance Hall, The Royal Opera House, Bow Street

Sarah and Gladys pushed their way through the crowds until they reached the edge of the dancefloor. For several minutes, the girls could only stand and take it all in. At one end of the room, a large orchestra was playing on a raised podium, and above their heads the vaulted ceiling rose to a dizzying height. Through the pall of cigarette smoke, Sarah could make out concert boxes overflowing with revellers.

'There must be hundreds of people here,' she shouted to Gladys.

Gladys' excitement was infectious, her eyes popping in wonder as she grabbed Sarah's arm. 'I know. Isn't it a fabulous venue? Nothing like this back in Winchester. Judith chose well.'

'Yes, but how are we to find her in this crush?' Sarah asked, scanning the crowded dancefloor for her cousin's face. But the dancers were moving far too quickly, their faces almost a blur in the dimly lit ballroom.

'Let's skirt around; you look for her amongst the dancers and I'll look around the tables.' Gladys pushed her way along the perimeter of the dancefloor and Sarah followed. It seemed a hopeless task.

A minute later, the band stopped playing and there was a mass exodus of couples from the floor. Sarah felt herself being pushed backwards and away from Gladys, but it was all good-natured and apologetic. It was hard not to smile. There was such a joyous atmosphere in the place. A rush of memories suddenly caught her off-guard. Nights out dancing with Paul until late, sneaking home afterwards and climbing the tree that gave her access to the bedroom window so Da wouldn't know she had disobeyed him, yet again, by meeting Paul. Sarah smiled – she had been so happy then. If only she was here tonight with Paul . . .

'Oh! I'm terribly sorry,' she said, as she bumped into a soldier.

He caught her arm as she was being dragged past. 'Hey, don't disappear!' The young man smiled at her. 'We've only just met. It's a zoo here tonight!'

'Yes, but it's wonderful. It's our first time here,' she replied.

He glanced about, then frowned down at her. 'Did you lose your fella?'

For a moment, Sarah was numb as her vision blurred. But of course, he could not mean Paul; he could not mean his death. Recovering quickly, she said: 'No, my friend Gladys. We're trying to find my cousin and her friends.' She looked about and shrugged. 'With little success.'

The band started up again and the distinctive opening bars of 'Sing Sing Sing' floated across the crowd.

'Guess my luck is in, so. Wanna dance?' her rescuer asked, his eyes full of mischief. He didn't wait for her response but grabbed her hand and pulled her out onto the floor and into the throng.

Her partner had more enthusiasm than skill, but by the end of fifteen minutes Sarah was breathless and laughing, her earlier misgivings about work and a certain Yank forgotten. It was good to be around people again in such a jubilant atmosphere. Sometimes, it was too easy to slip into a sad mood when she was alone. Too easy to let Paul's ghost shape her life.

'Don't be a stranger,' her soldier said with a wink as he walked her off the floor. With a gallant kiss of her hand, he disappeared off into the crowd. Another young man, looking eager to take his place, appeared before her. Sarah put up her hands, laughing. 'Sorry, I must find my friends.'

'Maybe later?' he asked, stepping aside with reluctance.

'Sure.'

As Sarah pushed through the crowd once more, she felt a tug on her sleeve. She turned to find Gladys grinning at her. 'Come on, I found them,' she shouted. 'Would you believe it; they have one of those fancy boxes upstairs.'

The box was on the second level. Sarah hesitated at the door as Judith was the only one of the party she recognised as she peered inside. The gang were laughing and chatting, oblivious to everything. They were seated at a large table, heaving with bottles and glasses. Sarah waved from the doorway to catch Judith's attention.

Judith sprang up to greet her, kissing both her cheeks.

'There you are. How naughty of you to sneak off dancing. Was he handsome? We thought we'd lost you for the evening.' Judith glanced across to the doorway. 'Didn't you bring him along? Oh well, never mind. Come on, have a drink, for goodness' sake.'

As ever, it was impossible to get a word in with Judith.

Judith clapped her hands together to get everyone's attention. 'OK, everyone, this is my dear cousin, Sarah. Newly arrived in London from the depths of Hampshire. We must ensure she has a fabulous evening.' Sarah smiled at the faces now turned to look up at her; a combination of curious and friendly. A chorus of 'Hello' and 'Nice to meet you' ensued.

Judith beamed down at them before tucking her arm through Sarah's. 'And this is Gerald, by the way,' she said, throwing a loving glance at the man she had been sitting beside. As Gerald Pascoe rose to his feet, Sarah could sense she was being scrutinised. She returned the favour, sizing him up quickly. This was her cousin's married boyfriend. She had heard so much about him, though she was the only one in the family who knew of his existence as Judith insisted her parents would be horrified. His appearance surprised Sarah. She had anticipated film-star looks, not receding brown hair, guarded grey eyes behind steel-rimmed glasses, and a hooked nose. Gerald was, however, on very good terms with his tailor; he was dressed immaculately.

They shook hands. 'Nice to meet you, at last, Sarah. What's your poison?' he asked, waving at the bottles on the table. 'Take your pick.'

'Gin, please,' Sarah said, squashing in beside her cousin at the table. Gladys sat down at the other end and immediately struck up a lively exchange with a young man in naval uniform.

Gerald handed Sarah a gin and tonic. 'Plenty more where that came from,' he said, before resuming his conversation with the girl on his other side.

Judith clinked glasses with her. 'Cheers!' Judith leaned in close. 'Thank goodness we got you to London. Much more fun here. Gladys said you started work today. How did it go?'

'Well, thanks,' Sarah answered. Although Judith worked at the Home Office and knew Sarah was now working in MI5, Everleigh had warned Sarah against discussing her job with anyone outside of the office. As it was, she was disobeying Everleigh by telling Gladys a little about her new job, but she knew Gladys was trustworthy.

'If only we could entice Martin to join us here in town. If you suggested it, it might tempt him. I tried to persuade him at Christmas, but he just laughed. That would be jolly, wouldn't it?' Judith said with a wistful look. 'To have him here too.'

'I'm sure he'll come and visit us. But you know as well as I do, he loves his job. Martin will never leave Supermarine,' Sarah replied. 'I must admit, I'm going to miss him while I'm in London. Well, all three of them. Uncle Tom and Aunt Alice have been so good to me.'

'Of course they will miss you, but they understand you need to move on, Sarah.'

'Yes, but I don't intend to stay here for more than a few weeks. As soon as I can, I mean to return to Hursley.'

'No!' Judith looked at her askance. 'You can't be serious? No, no. I won't let you bury yourself back down there.'

Sarah smiled back at her but she was at a loss. She thought she had clarified that her work for the government would be for a short duration only, and certainly not a permanent move to London. But it wasn't the time or place to get into a discussion about it.

'Tell me, who is everyone?' Sarah nodded down the table.

Judith made the introductions, then nudged Sarah with her elbow, her eyes flicking towards her boyfriend, Gerald. 'What do you think of him?' she asked in a lowered voice.

'He seems very nice, Judith,' she replied.

'I hope you two will get to know each other.' Judith sighed. 'He is so lovely, Sarah.' She gave her a searching look. 'I'm so glad you are not one of those judgemental girls. You see, I can't help it; I love him. It's not my fault he is married, now, is it?'

'I guess not,' Sarah replied, suddenly wondering how naïve her cousin was.

'Mum and Dad are so traditional. They would never understand our relationship.'

'But what if they find out? They will be very hurt that you have kept this from them.'

Judith gave her a sharp glance. 'It's unlikely they will ever know, unless someone malicious were to tell them.'

'Judith, I would never do that. But perhaps you underestimate them. If you truly love him, they might accept the situation.'

Judith sighed, picking up her glass. 'You don't know them as well as I do.'

'That is true, sorry. Has he children?' Sarah asked.

'Yes, two. I know; not ideal. And, before you say it, I am well aware he is unlikely to leave his wife. Gerald freely admitted to me from the beginning it was a marriage of convenience. He married her for her money, and she married him because he comes from such a well-connected family. But I don't mind. I get to spend most of the day with him at work and he stays in town with me at least one evening a week. The way I see it, I get the best of him. You would not believe how generous Gerald is.' Judith held out her arm, a diamond bracelet glinting in the light from the table lamp. 'Isn't it fabulous?'

Sarah nodded. Even she could tell it must have cost a fortune. 'It's beautiful.'

'Gerald looks after me very well. Now, we really must find someone fabulous for you too.'

It was on the tip of Sarah's tongue to say she'd rather not follow in her cousin's footsteps with someone else's husband, but she had no wish to hurt her. 'Oh, I'm sure I'll find someone mad enough to take me on, eventually.'

Judith patted her hand. 'What happened was dreadful, but you will get over Paul. You just need time. I could not believe it when Mother wrote to me about it. I don't know how you got through Christmas. We were all very proud of you, though I'm sure you are heartbroken. Such terrible times we live in. So many young men gone. I'm sorry; it must be hard for you.'

'There are many in the same boat. I have concluded it is better not to fall in love when there's a war on. You're constantly worried your man is about to leave and will have to face danger and possibly death,' Sarah replied. 'It's no wonder there is such a buzz here tonight. But doesn't it feel forced? Everyone is laughing, joking and drinking like tomorrow may never come. The sad thing is it may not come for many.'

'That's true, but it's hardly surprising that we all want to make the best of it. Life is so awful at the moment. When we get the chance to let our hair down, we do.'

'Yes, of course. Sorry, I don't mean to be maudlin.' Sarah took up her glass and took a large swig of gin.

Judith squeezed her hand. 'It's OK; I understand. You're missing Paul.'

'And Maura. How she would have adored London.' Sarah sighed and tried to smile. 'And she would have loved it here with all of us. She was happiest on nights out dancing. Da wasn't keen on letting her go, you see. Thought she was too young.' Judith gave her a sympathetic look. Suddenly, Sarah wanted to cry. What on earth was wrong with her? She was supposed to be out enjoying herself, not wallowing in self-pity. *Keep the front up.*

'I realise how lucky I am,' her cousin replied with a gentle smile. 'Gerald is too important at the Home Office to be released for active service. His work there is vital to the war effort.'

'But if things get worse, that might change,' Sarah replied.

Judith's face fell. 'Do you think so? I hope not,' she said, glancing at Gerald.

He turned towards them with a look of surprise. Then he grinned. 'My, but you two are glum. We can't have that! Another drink, ladies? And then I suggest we make use of that wonderful dancefloor.'

It was several hours later before the group broke up. Sarah and Gladys said their goodbyes and headed off into the dark streets to the tube station. Sarah's feet ached from dancing and she longed for her bed, but to her dismay when they reached Covent Garden station, a long queue had formed, snaking down the pavement.

'Should we try another station?' she asked Gladys.

'No point, Sarah, this is the nearest. Look, the queue is starting to move now.' They moved up a few feet. 'That was a great evening, wasn't it?'

'I've never danced as much in my life,' Sarah said with a grin, as they turned inside the ticket hall.

'By the way, your cousin has asked if I want to take her friend's place in her flat. The girl's getting married the day after tomorrow. I gave her a tentative yes, if that's OK. With you heading off into darkest Wales, I don't fancy being on my own,' Gladys said.

Sarah squeezed her arm. 'That's a great idea, Glad, and perfect timing.'

'That's what I reckoned, but I didn't want you to think I was abandoning you.'

'Nonsense! If anything, I'm the one leaving you in the lurch, though I'm hoping the job won't last more than a week or so,' Sarah said.

'That's true and anyway, don't you plan to return to Hursley?'

'Yes!' *If I survive*, Sarah thought gloomily. 'Judith's place has got to be better than Horgan's.'

'Ha ha, there are probably dosshouses better than that place!' replied Gladys. They had reached the ticket booth at last. 'Two for Hyde Park Corner, please,' Gladys said to the clerk.

'Oh no, look, Gladys. The queue for the lift is huge.'

'The only alternative is the stairs, and it takes ages, particularly in these heels,' Gladys said, glaring at her.

'I can't bear enclosed spaces, Glad, you know that,' Sarah replied with a pleading look.

Gladys huffed. 'Oh, OK. At least we're going down, not up.'

The spiral stairs down into the depths of the station made Sarah's head spin, but it was still preferable to being squashed into the lift with strangers. Ever since the bombing, she had a terror of confined spaces. At last, they came out onto the platform and skirted around the air–raid bunks beside the wall.

Gladys stopped about halfway down the platform and rolled her shoulders. 'I hope we don't have to wait too long.'

But Sarah barely heard her. At the other end of the platform, she had spotted a familiar profile. Lieutenant Anderson. But he wasn't alone. On his arm was a stylish young woman, draped in a fur wrap and gazing up at him adoringly. The woman was stunning, with blonde waves peeking out from beneath a fabulous hat.

'Oh, bother!' Sarah muttered.

'What?' Gladys asked turning a puzzled gaze on her.

'My American. He's at the far end. Don't look!'

But it was too late, Gladys was up on her tippy toes, gazing in Anderson's direction. 'Which one is he?' A second later, she twisted back to Sarah, all agog. 'Not the tall, dark–haired god in the blue coat and hat?' Gladys burst out laughing and tugged at her sleeve. 'Come on, introduce us. Though that doll on his arm might not appreciate it. This could be fun.'

'Definitely not! I don't want him to see me. Anderson will think I'm following him around or something,' Sarah said. 'He's loathsome enough as it is.'

Gladys wrinkled her nose. 'Don't talk rot. Why on earth would you follow him? You're not that strange.'

'Oh, thanks very much!'

'Please, Sarah. He's gorgeous!'

'No.'

'You're no fun, Sarah Gillespie,' her friend said, throwing her eyes to heaven.

'Oh, go boil your head!' Sarah exclaimed and turned the other way just as the train pulled into the station.

7

9th February 1942, MI5, St James Street, London

The following few days passed in a blur as her training commenced. In between fittings for some new outfits, Sarah was taught how to read a map properly and the rudiments of Morse code. On the Monday afternoon, she was told to report to Mr Farringdon down in the basement where there was a firing range set up.

However, on entering the instructor's room, she was exasperated to find Anderson already there. She hesitated just inside the door. 'Sorry, have I come at the wrong time?' she asked, looking at the lieutenant. Anderson grinned back at her.

'No, no, Miss Gillespie, do come in and close the door,' the instructor said, holding out his hand. 'I'm Farringdon, by the way. Now, then, what do you know about firearms?'

'Nothing, sir.'

Anderson coughed then treated her to a sardonic smile. She glared at him.

'That's a shame, but never mind,' Farringdon said.

'Really, Gillespie?' Anderson piped up. 'I'd have thought your father would have had you shooting targets from an early age.'

It took a great deal of effort not to snap at him. So far, he had turned up at every training session this week. Sarah was convinced it was purely to goad her. She did her best not to betray it was getting to her: she would not give him the satisfaction. Instead, she ignored him.

Farringdon's gaze flicked between them, clearly curious. 'Well, hmm, let us start with a quick overview,' the instructor said. 'Take a seat.' He picked up a handgun from the table and held it out to her. 'This revolver is an Enfield No 2, which is our standard issue handgun. Simple to use and effective. First of all, I will show you how to clean it.'

Sarah watched closely as Farringdon showed her the different parts of the revolver, followed by a demonstration of cleaning out the chambers and the barrel. All the while, she was conscious of Anderson sitting behind her.

'Have a go, Miss Gillespie,' Farringdon said, pushing the gun towards her. As quickly as she could, she repeated what he had shown her. 'Excellent. Now, how about a little practice session? We have targets set up in the firing range. Come along.'

They entered a long, narrow room, just across the hallway. There were several tables set up and at the far end were the targets, silhouettes of people overlaid with a grid.

'How is your eyesight, Miss Gillespie?' Farringdon asked.

'Fine, sir, as far as I know.'

'Excellent. Now, load up as I showed you,' he said, placing the revolver down on the table along with a box of bullets.

To her annoyance, Anderson strolled into the room. He stood inside the door, leaning back against the wall. She turned away.

I will not let him put me off, she thought as she loaded the six bullets into the chamber and closed it over.

'Very good, Miss Gillespie. Now, stand here where the line is marked on the floor. When you are ready, raise the gun and look along the sight towards the target. Squeeze the trigger slowly and keep as still as you can.'

'Where should I aim?' she asked.

'The heart or the head, Sarah. Your choice,' Anderson drawled.

'As the lieutenant said, though it depends on the situation. You may only want to incapacitate, not kill, in which case you wing them. A bullet in the arm or leg is usually sufficient.' Farringdon stood back.

It was too tempting. In her mind's eye, she superimposed the annoying features of the lieutenant onto the target. Sarah raised the revolver in her right hand and fired. The gunshot startled her, but the recoil wasn't as bad as she had expected.

'OK?' Farringdon asked.

'Yes, sir.'

'Good. Now fire off the rest of 'em.'

When all six shots were fired, Farringdon told her to empty the chamber of the spent bullets. Anderson strolled down the room to fetch the target. 'Well, well, Sarah, not bad for a *first* attempt.' He showed the bullet holes to Farringdon, who nodded in agreement.

'Well done, Miss Gillespie. It would appear you have a natural talent for this.'

Sarah smiled smugly at Anderson.

With a raised brow he drawled: 'Aptitude or practice; I'm not sure which.'

Farringdon threw an impatient glance at Anderson. 'Well, now, Lieutenant, perhaps you'd like to show us how well you can do?'

Sarah had a horrible feeling Anderson wanted to do exactly that to humiliate her. She stood back against the wall to watch, willing him to fail. Farringdon joined her. 'When you're ready,' he told Anderson.

Anderson loaded the gun, raised it and let off the six shots in quick succession. Beside her, Farringdon grunted before heading down the room to retrieve the target.

'That's impressive, young man,' the instructor said, showing Sarah the target. Six head shots almost formed a circle. 'You've had some practice.'

Anderson sniffed. 'A little.'

Sarah turned to the instructor. 'When will I be issued with a handgun, sir?'

Farringdon wouldn't quite meet her eye. 'I'm afraid that has been deemed unnecessary for now as the lieutenant is already armed and you will work as a team.'

It was on the tip of her tongue to ask why they had bothered with the session, but Farringdon had whisked up the revolver and left the room.

'Not too disappointed, I hope, Sarah,' Anderson said. 'But the world feels a little bit safer with you unarmed.' With that, he left.

Staring after him, Sarah had to take several deep breaths to calm down before she felt able to quit the firing range. She made straight for the ladies' bathroom where only the mirror was privy to her diatribe on Anderson's manners.

For most of the week, she tried to avoid him, but she could not steer clear of him entirely. Sarah suspected he knew how much his presence annoyed her. But what could she do? It would be churlish to ask her instructors not to admit him, besides the satisfaction it would give the sod to know she was rattled. However, there was clearly no need for him to do what he was doing, being well versed in the art of espionage already. All she could do was pay no heed to him.

But things escalated on Wednesday morning. As she would be going undercover as an American, she had to practise the accent. Of course, the instructor insisted that Anderson be present to give his opinion. Which he did readily, and sarcastically to the last. After the session, they went back to their cupboard of an office.

Once Anderson closed the door, Sarah spun around. 'I'm heartily sick of you, Anderson. What the hell is wrong with you?'

As she advanced on him, he threw up his hands in mock horror and backed up against the door. 'Whoa, steady on, Irish. I'm unarmed and defenceless!' he said with a sneer.

'As am I, and I have no doubt that is down to *your* interference,' she snarled.

'I'm only thinking of the poor people of Wales,' he replied.

'Just stop it, Anderson! I've had enough of your snide comments, and the constant undermining. We are partners, whether you like it or not.' She emphasised her words by prodding him in the chest with her index finger. Hard. 'Get used to the idea and get over whatever misogynistic notions you harbour in that thick skull of yours. You need to change your attitude. Neither of us will achieve our goals if this continues. Do you want to be the first American working for MI5 to fail, purely because he couldn't handle being partnered with a woman? I think you will agree that would be rather pathetic.'

Anderson's continuing silence enraged her more. Suddenly, she couldn't bear to remain in the same room with him, so she grabbed her coat and bag and stared pointedly at him until he moved away from the door. As she yanked it open, she glimpsed something surprising. A flicker of respect crossed the lieutenant's face.

By the time Sarah and Anderson had their final meeting with Everleigh late on Friday evening, Sarah was unsure how things stood between them. She regretted her outburst, no matter how much she knew he had deserved a good telling-off. The problem was, losing control in front of Anderson made her look feeble. The last thing she wanted. However, some good had come of it as he hadn't shown up at any of her sessions since. Was it possible he had listened to her? Nevertheless, she was still livid with him. What she was facing was hard enough without his constant nit-picking. As she sat there, most of Everleigh's words passed her by while she envisaged multiple satisfying ways of permanently shutting the lieutenant up. In fact, she had indulged similar thoughts all week. Oh yes, she swore that when the first opportunity to teach the man beside her a lesson appeared, she would pounce on it.

Then the colonel broke the news she had been half dreading, and she was fully back in the room. They were to leave for Wales on Monday morning. So soon? The thought filled her with anxiety. Disappearing off with the charming lieutenant was way down the list of things she wanted to do. It even crossed her mind that she might be able to give him the slip once out of London. Of course, that would just feed into his suspicions, and he would go running to Everleigh. No; fate had decreed she was stuck with him.

Everleigh handed them their papers and train tickets for Newport. Sarah could only sit and listen to the remainder of their instructions, the many questions she had longed to ask forgotten as she was suddenly overcome with nerves. Everleigh wished them luck and shook their hands. Sarah suspected he held her hand a little longer than necessary. Did he think she would fail?

After the meeting, Anderson stalked off with barely a goodbye and Sarah was handed over to Everleigh's secretary for the final fitting of her wardrobe. They adjourned to the ladies' bathroom with Miss Abernathy carrying a large box under her arm.

'Do stand still, Miss Gillespie,' Miss Abernathy scolded minutes later, tugging at the back of Sarah's new jacket. She brushed her hands over the shoulders. 'Perfect. They have done an excellent job, I think you will agree?'

'Yes,' Sarah replied, feeling the softness of the pure wool of her suit between her fingers. She had never owned anything so expensive. Such a pity it was a dull grey in colour.

Miss Abernathy returned to the box and began holding up items for Sarah to see. She picked up a white blouse. 'You have two of these and a pale blue jumper as well. One pair of black pumps and, oh yes, a pair of matching trousers and some socks.' There was a pause as a dreamy look came over the secretary's face. 'Gosh, one pair of nylons.' She sighed, caressing the packet. 'What I'd give for a pair of these. You best look after them well.'

'Don't worry; I will. My flatmate will be so jealous. They are like gold dust.'

Miss Abernathy rolled her eyes. 'Don't I know it! Still, if I were you, I'd wear the trousers with that jacket most of the time. No doubt it will be cold in Wales.'

'What about the siren suit?'

'Ghastly, aren't they? Don't forget to bring it with you. I imagine you may need it at night if you are doing surveillance work. Don't ruin these good trousers by getting them wet.'

'I won't. Don't worry, I will take care of all these items. Thanks for your help.'

'Oh, we aren't finished yet,' Miss Abernathy said with enthusiasm, clearly enjoying revealing the box's secrets.

While she turned back to it, Sarah contemplated the weeks ahead. It was Baltic in London and it had been snowing all week. She dreaded to think how much colder it would be up in the mountains of Wales.

'Here is your coat,' the secretary said, shaking it out and helping her to put it on over the jacket. 'A good service-able black. That's a jolly fine fit, too.' She rummaged around again and held up a small plain felt hat, then at last something colourful, a pink and red scarf. 'This will finish it off nicely.'

Sarah nodded. Taking a deep breath, she regarded herself in the mirror above the sink. She would have preferred a bit of colour in the coat too, but her new identity was that of secretary to the lieutenant's US munitions manufacturer, inspecting the Glascoed plant. She had to look appropriately low key. The coat was certainly that. The treacherous thought that Anderson was probably being fitted out with better clothes crept into her head, even if the sod's role required it. No matter; at least she could now dispose of those thin cotton dresses she had come to loathe. Perhaps she and Gladys could burn them after all? A fitting funeral pyre of her past life.

Miss Abernathy cracked a smile. 'And the best of the lot; look at this, Miss Gillespie.' She pulled out a small round box, flipped the lid and drew out a wig. 'Shall we give it a go? You'll need to practise wearing this over the weekend.'

Sarah stared at the blonde hairpiece, surprised at the colour they had chosen, but then they had to ensure Jenny McGrath would not recognise her. The wig would throw the woman off the scent at a distance, but Sarah wasn't sure it would be sufficient at close range. Hopefully, the unlikelihood of her being in Wales at all would help protect her identity. However, she was full sure it would not fool Da for one minute.

She shivered at the thought, but smiled at the secretary through the mirror. 'It's rather a glamorous wig, don't you think?'

'Yes. No expense spared. I understand American ladies are rather fond of the platinum look. It's real hair, see?' the secretary replied, holding it out for her to touch. 'This is much better than bleaching your hair. My older sister tried that and ended up burning her scalp. My mother nearly killed her. We had to have the doctor to her, and she couldn't leave the house for weeks without a hat or scarf. Here,' she handed Sarah a comb, 'smooth down your hair and pin it up, and we will try it on for size.'

Sarah turned back to the mirror and quickly did as she was bid. The secretary slipped a mesh over Sarah's hair before pulling the wig down onto her forehead. 'Hmm, that colour washes you out a bit. You'd better get yourself some pancake foundation if you're to convince anyone you're a Yank. Aren't they all tanned, unlike us poor Brits?'

'Yes, I expect so.' Sarah frowned. 'Where will I find it at such short notice, Miss Abernathy? I thought there was a shortage of make-up.'

'True. Leave it with me. I know someone who works at the Adelphi Theatre who may be able to help as long as you don't mind using stage make-up.'

'Not at all. I've been involved in amateur dramatics and used to it.'

'Excellent. Now, the final touch; put on these glasses.'

Sarah popped the tortoiseshell spectacles on and broke into a grin, staring at the stranger in the mirror.

Miss Abernathy placed her hands on Sarah's shoulders and smiled. 'I have to say I'm a little envious, Agent Snow White. You are all set. The very best of luck.'

Suddenly, it all felt very real. Her new persona, Miss Catherine Cavandish, was born.

8

Sunday was moving day. The taxi pulled up outside Horgan's Guesthouse and Sarah and Gladys piled in, doubled-up with laughter, whilst the taximan shoved their suitcases onto the floor in front of them. Hiring a taxi was an extravagance, but it was the quickest way to get to Judith's flat with all their bags. Behind them, they heard the front door of the guesthouse slam shut.

Gladys giggled. 'Oh, her face! I thought she'd explode.'

'I wouldn't worry about Mrs Horgan. She'll find new tenants quick enough with her low rates,' replied Sarah as the car pulled away from the kerb. 'Wasn't it lucky that Judith's friend got hitched? This couldn't have worked out better. Now you won't be alone while I'm away.'

'But how long will you be gone and where are you off to?' Gladys asked.

'Sorry, I don't know precisely. Hopefully, only a couple

of weeks. Unfortunately, I'm not allowed to tell you exactly where.' Although Gladys knew she was working in the Secret Service, Sarah could not reveal the nature of her mission in Wales.

Gladys suddenly sat up straight, her eyes wide. 'Will you be in danger? You're not going behind enemy lines, are you? Did you make up all that stuff about Wales to put me off?'

'Shush,' Sarah replied, throwing a significant glance at the driver. She would be, in a sense, infiltrating the enemy camp, but she didn't want to alarm Gladys. 'No, don't be silly.'

'And how will I contact you in an emergency?'

'I'm afraid you can't, Glad.' Sarah patted her hand. 'If anything should happen, Judith will know who to contact through her work. If I get a chance, I'll ring Judith's flat to let you know I'm alive and well, OK?'

'You'd better. I will be worried about you.'

'I'll be fine. You, my friend, are going to have a great old time with Judith. I predict you will be out on the town most nights.'

Gladys relaxed back into the seat. 'Yes, and that other girl, Anne, seems nice enough. Guess I'll have to live it up for both of us.'

Sarah was a little envious. Gladys would be living the dream while she was stuck in Wales with that horrible Yank, trying to track down her nightmare of a father. Suddenly, Gladys's job as a clippie looked extremely attractive. She turned to her friend. 'Are you happy with your new job?'

'No regrets,' Gladys said. 'It's the perfect role for me. It's a bit tiring being on my pins all day, but there is always some banter with the troops.' She wiggled her brows. 'You get to meet all sorts.'

'I bet.'

'I'll be doing my first evening shift next week, but don't know which route yet,' Gladys said.

'Maybe not as fun?' Sarah asked.

'Perhaps. I've heard the other clippies talking about it. With blackout you can barely see the coins, which is a pain, and sometimes there's trouble with lads who have been out drinking all day 'cos they're home on leave. Poor blighters: you can hardly blame them for getting pie-eyed.'

'Guess not. But you must be careful, Glad.'

'Don't you worry 'bout me, Sarah. I grew up with three brothers. I know how to protect myself. Why, you will never believe what happened yesterday . . .'

While Sarah listened to her friend's story, she found her thoughts drifting off. .

Now that the departure for Wales was close at hand, her thoughts were turning more and more to Da. Time had tempered her rage, but she still burned to confront him and make him explain his actions. Most nights, as she lay trying to get to sleep, she would rehearse what she would say to him. She wanted to lash out both with her hands and her tongue, to hurt him as much as he had harmed them. And not only for disappearing and leaving them for dead under the rubble of No. 18. For all of it. The years of abuse, her mother's misery and having to grow up in a house of fear. He had blighted their lives. And still he continued; now hurting more people through his IRA activities. But she was going to make him pay – whatever it took.

The tricky bit would be finding him. If Everleigh was to be believed, he was heavily protected and kept moving around. She would have to find Jenny McGrath. It could not be a coincidence that she was now in Wales as well. Hopefully, Jenny would lead her to Da. Dealing with her again was not a pleasant prospect, for she would be a formidable opponent. In fact, Sarah would rather confront Da face to face than Jenny. But perhaps Aled Thomas, their liaison in Cardiff, would have more information. As far as she knew, Thomas was an experienced agent with a wide network of people helping him throughout South Wales. Just as well, for she didn't want to be relying on Anderson to help. To be beholden to him would be unbearable.

'Hey, what are you thinking about? That's one sour expression,' Gladys intruded into her thoughts.

'Sorry, I was imagining the long journey tomorrow,' Sarah replied.

'To?'

'Ha! Nice try, but you won't catch me out that easily.'

Gladys made a face at her and turned to look out the window. 'I hope this snow melts soon. Makes everyone grumpy. The traffic was awful yesterday. It must have added a good twenty minutes to our route. Cold too, I can tell you, when you're standing at the back where it's open to every icy blast of wind.'

'I could always lend you my siren suit. You could wear it under your uniform.'

'I'd rather freeze to death, thanks all the same,' Gladys said with a smirk.

'Don't say I didn't offer,' Sarah replied. The taxi slowed down and pulled in. 'Great, we're here at last.'

* * *

Judith's flat was on the top floor and was surprisingly large. Sarah wondered if Gerald paid her rent. Perhaps he owned it, but it was hardly something she could ask Judith. However, she couldn't see how a secretary could afford such a place without financial help, even with two flatmates.

Judith answered their knock on the door. 'Come on in, ladies. It's good to see you.' She hugged each of them in turn. 'Let me help you with some of those bags.'

'Thanks, Judith. Lovely place,' Sarah said as she stepped into a spacious sitting room. The sun was streaming in through the sash windows. Everything, from the pictures on the walls to the furniture, looked expensive and new.

'We love the place and it's so handy for work,' Judith said. 'Now then. Sarah, follow me. You can store your bags in my bedroom and share with me tonight. Gladys, you will be sharing the large bedroom with Anne, if that's OK. Second door on the left.'

'Super, Judith, this is fabulous. You should have seen the kip we were in. This is heavenly in comparison,' Gladys said as she disappeared off down the hallway.

'I'll second that, Judith. Thanks so much,' Sarah said, following her cousin into the other bedroom.

'My pleasure. It's going to be fun having you here. Put your suitcase up on top of the wardrobe,' Judith said, sitting down on the double bed. 'You look pale; is everything OK with you?'

'Don't mind me. I'm fine. Just a little anxious about this work trip, that's all. My partner is insufferable. I don't fancy being stuck with him for weeks.'

'Oh, dear! Anything I can help with?' Judith asked.

'I wish you could, but I'm afraid not. Unless, of course, you can have American Naval officers seconded to new duties at short notice.'

Judith snorted. 'You must have a very grand idea of what my job entails. Even Gerald couldn't manage that.' Then she patted the bed. 'But a Yank. How interesting.'

'He's not the least bit interesting, I can assure you,' Sarah said with a sniff as she sat down. 'He's anti-Irish and full of himself.'

'That's unfortunate,' Judith said. 'But I'm sure you are a match for him. Now, tell me your news.'

'I don't have any, really, other than preparing for this trip all week. How are things with you?' she asked.

To her horror, Judith's face fell, and suddenly she was in floods of tears. Bewildered, Sarah put her arm around her shoulders and held her as tremors racked her body. Eventually, Judith's tears eased. 'Sorry,' she gulped. She patted her pockets with shaking hands.

'Here, take mine,' Sarah replied, handing her a clean handkerchief. 'What on earth is wrong?'

Judith blew her nose several times, then turned to her with the most forlorn expression. She grabbed Sarah's hand. 'I don't know what to do.' Her face crumpled once again, and her tears fell.

'Oh, Judith! Whatever it is, I am sure I can help. You have only to ask. Tell me what's wrong.'

'You'll hate me!' Judith wailed.

'No, Judith. No matter what it is, I'd never hate you,' Sarah breathed. 'Come on, better you tell me and not bottle this up. It can't be that bad.'

Judith gulped several times, clutching the handkerchief

in her fist against her neck, her gaze fixed out the window. 'Oh, it is! I'm pregnant.'

The implications ran through Sarah's head. This was a disaster. Almost absentmindedly, she rubbed Judith's back. 'Could you be mistaken?'

Judith shook her head. 'I'm never late, Sarah, never.'

'How many weeks?' she asked, glancing down at Judith's stomach. There was no sign of a bulge yet.

Judith snuffled. 'I'm about four weeks late.'

'Does Gerald know?'

Her cousin cast her another anguished glance. 'I . . . no.'

'You will have to tell him. Surely he will want to support you and the child,' Sarah said as her anger grew.

'I don't know! I think Gerald will be furious with me. He'll say I've ruined everything.'

Sarah was shocked. It sounded as if Judith didn't trust this man or know him well enough to know how he would react. 'Have you never discussed the possibility, the risk you could conceive?'

'Not really. The time we have together is fun for him, a chance to relax away from the job and his family. His job is very stressful, you know. From what he says, his wife doesn't care and all he gets from her is nagging about this and that. They don't . . . you know. I don't bother him with anything. He always says how perfect our affair is.'

'What a selfish bastard!' Sarah exclaimed.

'Sarah!'

'No, I'm sorry, it has to be said. Don't you see he's just using you? God, I hate men like that.' Sarah took in her cousin's distressed face. 'I'm sorry. I shouldn't have said that — I don't know him. But please don't let him shirk his responsibility. Gerald should have taken proper precautions.'

'But if I don't keep it, I won't have to tell him and things won't have to change,' Judith said. 'I love him so desperately. I can't live without him.' What colour remained in her cheeks faded. 'What if he were to deny it's his?'

Sarah's heart sank. Her cousin was besotted and terrified to do anything that might upset the mighty Gerald. Fists curling at her sides, Sarah pushed down her anger. Right now, what Judith needed was practical advice. 'Would you not go home and talk to the family? You know they would support you through this.'

A horrified expression on Judith's face was her answer. 'Are you mad, Sarah? They would disown me completely. Good Catholic girls don't get pregnant outside of marriage.'

'Huh! They do if they are taken advantage of.'

Judith's chin wobbled dangerously. 'Why are you being so mean to Gerald?'

'You said yourself he will react badly and all because his *fun* will come to an end.' This set Judith off crying again. 'Look, I don't think your mother and father will disown you, nor Martin for that matter. Of course, they would be shocked at first, but you are their daughter, and they love you.'

'You barely know them, Sarah. Mum is deeply religious.' Judith shook her head. 'It would be impossible.'

'But you can't hide the fact you're expecting forever,' Sarah replied.

'That's just it . . . that's why I think I will have to . . . I've heard about this woman who takes care of these things. She works out of a room in one of the big hotels. So, she must be good. What do you think? She's expensive, though, but I was thinking I have that diamond bracelet. I could sell it.'

'I think Gerald would notice it was missing. Besides, abortions are dangerous, not to mention illegal. Oh, Judith! I'm so sorry. You know I will help you no matter what. I wish I didn't have to leave London just now, but I have no choice. I will promise you that I will get back as soon as I can.' Sarah squeezed her hand. 'Stay calm and do nothing rash while I'm away, please. When I get back, we can talk about the best plan of action, OK?'

Judith nodded and took a long, shuddering breath. 'Oh, Lord! I must look a sight.' She went to her dressing table and repaired her make-up. Sarah remained sitting on the bed. As she watched, she was relieved to see Judith grow calmer. It was strange. Her flawless cousin with her perfect lifestyle, and behind that facade her life was complete and utter chaos. Ironically, it was something they had in common.

But such a dilemma for Judith to have, Sarah thought. How on earth would Judith cope with a child on her own if Gerald reacted badly? But a little voice of envy caught Sarah off-guard. The possibility of having a family and a life with Paul had been taken from *her*, so cruelly. If they had married and had a child together, it would have brought her comfort in her grief.

Some minutes later, Judith turned around, as perfectly groomed as ever. 'Now, I suggest we give you a good send-off. Put your glad rags on and let's go down to The Crown for a few drinks.'

9

16th February, Paddington Station, London

There was no sign of Anderson. Sarah had arrived early and now stood on the platform with her suitcase at her feet. She was self-conscious, despite Gladys' assurances that the platinum wig looked fine. In the station ladies' she had checked it was in position and it was still a shock to see her new image staring back at her. She had pushed the annoying glasses up her nose, wishing she could bin them, but it might look suspicious to do so in a public bathroom. Everyone was eagle-eyed these days, paranoid about spies. *If only they knew.* Smoothing down her jacket, she had to admit, the clothes MI5 had provided fitted very well and suited her role perfectly. She was as prepared as she would ever be. Sarah took a deep breath and straightened up. What she saw in the mirror now gave her a boost of confidence. The only chink in her armour was her American accent. Sarah cheered herself with the thought that it was unlikely anyone in Wales would detect anything amiss. It was rare to meet a Yank in Europe as yet.

Where *was* he? Now and then, the locomotive rumbled and suddenly the platform was engulfed in a swirling ghost of dirt and steam. Sarah peeked at her watch again. Was he going to miss the train? They were due to depart in ten minutes. She smiled, greatly cheered by the thought that there would be a certain satisfaction in reporting back to HQ if he didn't make it. But she instantly regretted the notion; she was becoming petty, but surely that was Anderson's fault for being such an annoying git.

From where she stood, Sarah could see the carriages were already full, the last stragglers rushing along the platform and squeezing on. Just great! It would be standing room only. With growing impatience, she glanced back to the platform entrance, scanning the distant faces, hoping to see the Yank. Should she go ahead without him?

The guard started to pull across the slatted metal grid.

'Hold up!' a familiar voice shouted out.

Sarah turned to see Anderson pushing through and the guard remonstrating with him. Anderson turned around and waved back through the gap. It was then Sarah spotted the same lady she had seen with him at Covent Garden station and couldn't help wondering who she was.

As he walked down the platform, Anderson noticed Sarah and beamed.

Too busy whispering sweet nothings in her ear to be punctual, she thought. But she wouldn't dare say it to his face. She didn't want him to think she was spying on him. His ego was large enough as it was.

'Miss Cavandish, what are you waiting for?' he threw at her as he jogged past. 'You'll make us miss the train.'

Seething, Sarah snatched up her suitcase and chased after him. Halfway down the train, Anderson leapt up the steps and disappeared into a carriage. With a last push of effort, Sarah made it to the door just as the guard blew his whistle.

'Can I help you, miss?' a young soldier asked, looking down at her. He held out his hand.

'Yes, please,' she said, handing her case up to him and climbing aboard. The corridor was crammed, and Anderson had vanished. 'You don't happen to know where the man in the blue coat went, do you?'

The soldier pointed down the corridor. 'He went that way, miss. I'd dump him, if I were you. Leaving you to fend for yourself. That's not proper order.'

Sarah made a face. 'I would if I could, but he's my boss.'

The soldier smiled in reply. 'I'm relieved to hear he's not your boyfriend!'

'And he's American,' she added. She couldn't help herself.

The soldier laughed. 'That explains it all.'

'Thanks for your help,' she said with a grin, taking back her case.

Sarah slowly made her way down the narrow corridor, stepping over soldiers and sailors sitting on the floor or on their kit bags. All the compartments were full as she had feared. At last, she spotted Anderson. He was looking out the window at the far end of the corridor, cigarette hanging from his mouth, as relaxed as you please. When she dropped her suitcase to the floor at his feet, he swung round.

'Good of you to join me, Miss Cavandish.'

'You don't have to keep saying my name,' she snapped.

'I have to get used to it, just like you'll have to get used to mine.' He leaned down and whispered, 'Can't afford any basic slip-ups, now, can we?'

With a sniff, Sarah looked away back down the corridor before answering. 'Heaven forbid, Mr Fisher.'

'Ah, you can call me Dougie. All my friends do.'

'You're too kind,' she replied, staring out the window. The train lurched forward as it moved down the platform. Sarah bumped into Anderson's arm. 'Sorry.'

Anderson's responding chuckle only worsened her mood. He opened the smaller window at the top of the frame, before taking another drag of his cigarette and blowing it outside. 'Best you sit, Catherine, or you'll be mighty tired by the time we reach our destination.'

It would take at least five hours to get to Newport. Sarah didn't fancy standing for the entire journey, but her dilemma was that if she sat down on her suitcase, he would remain towering over her. He seemed to think he was superior to her already; she didn't want to encourage him. Her only hope was some servicemen would disembark further down the line and a seat in a compartment would become available.

To her surprise, Anderson slid down onto his case. 'You planning on staying on your feet?' he asked, looking up at her. *Was he a mind reader?*

'No,' she said. 'Just waiting in case anyone needed to get past us.'

He looked around her and down the corridor. 'They look settled to me.' He rubbed at his chin. 'I don't think you will be disturbed.' His mouth quirked. 'Except by me, of course.'

'That goes without saying,' she answered as she plonked

down onto her suitcase and resigned herself to the tiresome journey ahead.

'Good weekend?' he asked.

Small chat — from Anderson! Sarah flicked him a glance, but he looked innocent enough. 'It was fine, thank you. I moved lodging yesterday.'

'Why?'

'The old one was terrible. My friend and I have moved in with my cousin.'

'I didn't know you had family in London.'

'She's English, Ander . . . Dougie, before you say anything nasty,' she retorted.

'Hey! Calm down, Irish. All I was going to say was that it was lucky to have family around. Mine are all in the States and I haven't seen them in years.'

'Oh!' She could have kicked herself.

Anderson leaned his head back against the wall and blew smoke up towards the window. 'Perhaps we need to call a truce.'

'Are you serious?' she asked, genuinely surprised. Could her angry words the other day have hit home?

'Temporarily, at least.' He patted his chest. 'I'm still recovering from last Wednesday. The bruise on my chest has turned an interesting shade of purple. Would you like to see?' He made as if to unbutton his shirt. Sarah threw him a dirty look and he laughed. 'No? Very effective. I was wondering if it were a new form of interrogation.'

Despite herself, Sarah burst out laughing. 'Shush,' she managed. 'Be careful what you say.'

He looked over her head down the corridor. 'Guess we can't talk shop with all these chaps around.'

'Best not.'

Anderson turned his gaze to her hair. 'Suits you, not sure about the glasses though.'

'Oh, do you have a thing for blondes?' Aghast, she felt the colour rushing into her face. The comment had just slipped out as the image of his glamorous friend flashed into her mind.

He quirked a brow and laughed. 'Did you notice my Clara? Sweet girl. Nothing would do her but to see me off this morning.'

'Sorry, I wasn't prying.'

'It's OK to be curious. Kinda necessary in our job. What about you? Is there some chap waiting for you back in Dublin?'

'No, my boyfriend is missing, presumed . . . Paul is . . . was in the RAF.'

'I'm sorry.' He sounded sincere. 'That's tough.'

'He was on his way to the States. His ship was torpedoed,' she said quietly.

'Bloody U-boats are a menace. Is there no hope?'

'It happened just before Christmas. There has been no further news.'

'He was a pilot. I'm impressed,' he said after a few minutes.

Sarah glared up at him. 'Why? Did you assume all Irishmen were either cowards or republicans?' she snapped.

'Hey, easy, tiger. That's not what I meant at all. I admire anyone willing to get into a tin can and fly. Must take nerves of steel.'

After a calming breath she answered. 'It does. Whereas you Navy chaps prefer the safety of a tin can floating on water.'

Anderson chuckled. 'Sure do.'

★   ★   ★

It was late afternoon. Sarah woke as the train pulled into Newport station and scrambled to her feet, stiff, hungry and cold. She rubbed her neck as they waited in line for their fellow passengers to leave the train. Anderson, standing behind her, was humming a song she didn't recognise. Yet another irritating habit he had.

Suddenly, she felt his hand cover hers and he whipped her suitcase from her. She swung around to protest, but his expression brought her up short.

'Hurry up, Irish,' he said, looking over her head towards the exit. 'I'm starving.'

Once down on the platform, Anderson strode away from her. Muttering under her breath, Sarah followed.

'What's this fella's name, you know, the guy who's supposed to meet us?' he asked, once she drew level.

'Aled Thomas. His codename is Daffodil.'

'Why on earth?' Anderson asked with a snigger.

She scowled back at him. 'Don't be so mean. I assume it's because it is the national flower of Wales. Whoever assigns these codenames is a joker. Anyway, it must be better than leek,' she joked. Anderson wore a bewildered expression. 'You know, the vegetable?' He shook his head. 'It was the previous symbol of the Welsh. Seemingly it was suggested by Shakespeare.'

Anderson hooted with laughter. 'Crazy Brits! Any idea what he looks like?' he asked, scanning the immediate area in front of the station.

'How would I know?'

He grinned. 'You're the secretary. You're supposed to know these things.'

'I'm sure he will make himself known, in due course,' she ground out.

Anderson harrumphed and dropped both cases to the ground, before pulling out a packet of cigarettes and lighting up. He offered her one.

'No, thanks. I don't smoke.'

'Suit yourself,' he said, before taking a drag. 'Sure is cold, here. You missed it, being asleep and all, but the countryside is heavy with snow. Only hope we don't have to be out in it too much.'

'I think snow will be the least of our worries . . . Mr Fisher.'

The sound of a car entering the station forecourt made her turn. A Morris 10 parked up and an elderly man with thick-rimmed glasses and a trilby hat climbed out. He pulled a piece of paper from his pocket and glanced at it. Puzzled, Sarah darted a glance at Anderson. How desperate were MI5 that they had to recruit men in their dotage?

'Mr Fisher?' the man asked as he approached, again consulting the paper in his hand.

'Yes, sir, that's me,' Anderson replied. 'And this is my secretary, Miss Cavandish.'

The gentleman gave Sarah a nod and a charming smile. '*Croeso i Gymru* – welcome to Wales.'

10

16th February 1942, Newport, South Wales

The journey was short and undertaken in silence as Mr Thomas cautiously negotiated the Newport streets. Sarah, sitting in the back, was unsure what his difficulty was, but it was making her nervous. She glanced at Anderson in the front passenger seat and smiled. He was tense, too, with one hand splayed on the dashboard. She suspected Mr Thomas's eyesight wasn't the best as he was perched on the edge of his seat, clutching the steering wheel for dear life. Thankfully, there was little traffic. Sarah stared out the window, mentally mapping their route to distract herself. Her instructor would be proud of her, she thought. *Always know your exits* had been his mantra. Not that she needed to be reminded. Since being pulled from the rubble of her home all those months ago, it was something she checked as a matter of course, particularly when she found herself in crowded spaces.

Ten minutes later, Mr Thomas braked and glided into the kerb. He waved up at the five-storey building across the street. The sign outside proclaimed it to be The Westgate Hotel. 'Here we are,' he said in the same jolly tone as before. 'My son made the reservations for you.'

Anderson turned to him. 'Your son, sir?' he asked, before throwing Sarah a glance laced with confusion.

'Yes, yes, my son, Aled.'

'Ah!' Anderson exclaimed.

'Well, he is at work over in Cardiff, you see, and couldn't leave early to meet you. Asked me to help out.' With that, he opened the door and got out of the car. He groaned as he straightened up.

'That's a relief,' Sarah whispered to Anderson, half laughing. 'I thought *he* was Aled.'

'I'll say!' Anderson remarked as he climbed out.

'I assume you can manage the bags, young man,' Mr Thomas said to Anderson as he pushed his seat forward to let Sarah out from the back seat. 'I'll open the boot for you.'

Anderson looked totally confused. 'What?' he mouthed at her. Sarah waggled her brows at him across the roof of the car. She flicked a glance to the rear of the car. 'Oh, the trunk. I get it,' he said, throwing his eyes heavenwards before joining Mr Thomas. 'Thank you, sir,' he said, pulling their cases out. 'When might we see your son?'

Mr Thomas stood motionless, a deep furrow to his brow. 'Now, let me see.' He tapped the side of his head. 'My memory isn't what it used to be. Oh yes . . .' He shook his head. 'No, that's not it. Ah!' he exclaimed, slapping his hand against his leg. 'He will meet you here in the morning at eight-thirty. Yes, yes, I'm sure that's what he said.' Mr Thomas beamed, but then faltered, frowning down at the road. 'Or was it nine-thirty?'

'Never mind, sir. He can ask for one of us at reception,' Anderson said. 'We will take an early breakfast.'

'Very good, Mr . . . eh . . . *Hwyl fawr,*' Mr Thomas said with a wave as he climbed back into his car.

'I suppose that means goodbye,' Sarah said as they watched him drive away.

She could get used to this. Sitting over a leisurely breakfast the next morning, and blissfully without Anderson's company, Sarah was enjoying the luxury of being waited on. This was the first time she had ever stayed in a hotel. There had never been money for holidays growing up. Not even a trip to Galway to stay with their aunt. Da's excuse had always been lack of funds, but Sarah knew well he hated Ma's family.

'Pardon me, Miss Cavandish?'

Sarah looked up to see one of the hotel staff hovering near her table. 'Yes, that's me.'

'There is a gentleman at reception asking for you.'

'Thank you. Please ask him to join me,' she replied.

A couple of minutes later, a middle-aged man with an angular face and thinning blond hair approached the table. 'Miss Cavandish?'

'Yes. You must be Mr Thomas,' she said, holding out her hand. He was the image of his father. 'Delighted to meet you at last.'

'May I?' he said, pointing to the empty chair.

'Please do,' she replied, placing her napkin on the table, and pushing her plate aside.

'I'm sorry I couldn't meet you yesterday,' he said. 'I couldn't get away. Back-to-back meetings.'

'Don't worry, we were well looked after by your father. Where do you work, Mr Thomas?'

'I'm the manager of a bank over in Cardiff. It gives me a lot of freedom, don't you know. I, eh, travel around quite a bit.' He gave her a knowing look.

Sarah smiled. 'I imagine that is extremely useful in your line of business.'

'Yes, it is.' Aled looked about the room. 'I thought this hotel would suit you best. It's nice and quiet, especially this time of year. Also, it's not too far to Pontypool. This seemed the most appropriate place for an American businessman to stay who wishes to visit Glascoed.'

'Indeed. It's perfect, thank you. The rooms are extremely comfortable. Won't you have something to eat, Mr Thomas?' she asked. 'The firm is paying,' she added, and his eyes twinkled in return. She was warming to him already.

'Thank you, but no. I've just eaten. Will Mr Fisher be joining us?'

'I do hope so, but I haven't seen him yet this morning.'

'Haven't seen who, Miss Cavandish?' It was Anderson. Trust him to materialise out of nowhere. He shook hands with Mr Thomas. 'Aled Thomas, I assume?'

'Yes, indeed.'

'Good to meet you,' Anderson said, sitting down. He flashed Sarah a grin. 'Did you miss me?'

'Don't worry, somehow I struggled through breakfast on my own,' she replied. 'You're allowed to sleep it out one morning, Mr Fisher.'

'Sleep it out, no, no. I was up hours ago. Went for a walk

to explore the town.' He turned to Thomas. 'I would appreciate if you could bring us up to speed.' He glanced at Sarah. 'We are eager to get started, are we not, Miss Cavandish? There's no one in the lounge across the hall. Why don't we adjourn over there, if Miss Cavandish has finished her breakfast?'

They sat around a table at the rear of the room. Everleigh had spoken highly of Thomas to them both before they left London, and Sarah knew he had been an agent for several years. Yet Anderson sat back and made no attempt to hide his scrutiny of Thomas. If anything, Thomas looked amused by the Yank's attitude, but Sarah wanted to kick Anderson's shins under the table for being so rude. Why did he have to be like this with everyone? It was embarrassing.

'I'm not sure how much you know,' Thomas began.

'Tell us everything from the beginning,' Anderson answered. 'Shoot.'

Thomas flicked a glance at Sarah, brow raised, before clearing his throat. 'Well, they recruited me in '37. There were concerns that a local fascist network was growing in numbers, and they charged me with infiltrating it. By sheer stroke of luck, a lad I work with mentioned he was a member of the group. I feigned interest and jumped at the opportunity when he asked if I'd like to go along to a meeting. Turned out the group is affiliated to the Right Club and we were correct to be concerned about them. The branch is headed up by a local landowner by the name of Bennett. He was previously a member of Mosley's crew, the BUF, but left after the Cable Street incident. However, his right-wing leanings didn't wane.'

'What's the Right Club?' Anderson asked.

Had Anderson not read the briefing notes? It felt good to have one up on him at last. 'They are a group of diehard fascists and anti-Semitists,' Sarah explained before turning to Aled. 'But I thought they were only operating in London and the Home Counties.'

'Not any longer,' Aled replied. He looked across at Anderson. 'They spread the word through personal contacts. All very much hush-hush. I guess they are afraid of being infiltrated.' He grinned. 'Their main target for recruitment is service personnel, of course, because their great vision is a military coup d'état.' Anderson's brows rose, but he made no comment. Thomas continued: 'So, I have been attending the meetings ever since and reporting back to London. They are a pathetic bunch for the most part, even though they spout some fairly vile stuff. It's all talk, and I was on the verge of chucking it until one night a woman by the name of McGrath was the guest speaker and was introduced as an IRA member. It was stirring rhetoric, let me tell you. She whipped them up into a frenzy.'

Sarah's heart skipped a beat. She could envisage Jenny McGrath holding forth for she was certainly a woman of passion. The problem was, it was warped and cruel.

'It was the first time we had proof that the IRA were collaborating with these potential fifth columnists,' Thomas continued. 'Naturally, London asked me to keep track of her. Another bloke and I took turns trying to keep tabs on her. We discovered she was working in the munitions factory at Llanishen and living in a boarding house in Cardiff.'

'Is the factory in Cardiff?' Sarah asked.

'Yes.'

'How on earth was that allowed to happen? I thought the Irish were fully vetted before they could work in such places. They'd be high risk for sabotage,' Anderson cut in, looking directly at Sarah. She seethed in silence.

Thomas shrugged. 'McGrath's background check was clean. Until she spoke at that meeting, she hadn't been on our radar at all. Anyway, we notified security at the plant and asked them to keep an eye on her. We were tipped off that she called in sick one day. It was my colleague Nigel's turn to check on her. Sure enough, he saw her leave her lodging, not looking the slightest bit indisposed. She headed into the city centre, but it was obvious she feared she was being followed. She took a circuitous route and kept doubling back. Luckily, he could keep up.' Thomas paused, running his hand through his hair. 'McGrath led him to a park and there she met a man. They spoke for about fifteen minutes and then parted ways. Nigel was a well-trained agent and prepared for any eventuality. He took an entire roll of film of that meeting. Once he looked at the negatives, he contacted me straight away. Neither of us recognised the man with McGrath, so we assumed he could be IRA and should notify London. We were certain they were lurking around Fishguard, running that escape route to Ireland. But from intelligence coming in, we suspected they were running amok up through Wales and into the Irish enclaves up in Liverpool. We just don't have enough men to track them down. Anyway, Nigel said he would send the roll of film to London immediately. Subsequently, they confirmed the man was, in fact, Jim Gillespie, an IRA commander we are anxious to find, as I'm sure you are aware.'

Sarah swallowed hard. It was difficult to sit there and hear her father spoken of in such terms. But she couldn't reveal anything to Thomas. Everleigh had warned her to keep her connection to Jim Gillespie secret. Only Anderson knew. She sneaked a glance at him, but he was leaning forward, listening intently to Thomas. No doubt though that he would be watching for her reactions. He had made it clear he viewed her with suspicion.

'At least, we know who is orchestrating operations here,' Aled was saying. 'Unfortunately, matters didn't turn out too well for Nigel. He mustn't have been careful enough; someone must have spotted him taking those photographs and followed him. The next afternoon, I found him in his back garden with his throat cut and his house turned over. Ruthless bastards!'

Anderson grimaced. 'So now they know they are under surveillance.'

Aled blushed. 'Yes, unfortunately they do.'

'But you got the film to London. That was something,' Anderson said, a note of sympathy in his voice, which surprised Sarah.

'It cost a man his life, though,' Thomas said with a bitterness Sarah could understand.

'Still, at least we still have you on the inside. Your cover is intact,' Anderson said.

Thomas sighed. 'Yes, but I keep a very low profile. I'm just a face in the crowd. I can't draw attention to myself.'

Anderson sat forward. 'That's all well and good, Thomas, but we need to find Gillespie, particularly if he has anything to do with a threat to Glascoed. Is there any way you could find out where he and his cohorts are hiding out?'

'Not without revealing myself. For now, our main concern is the McGrath woman and what she might be up to. She was seen in Pontypool on a couple of occasions. Glascoed is only a stone's throw away. The IRA must have an interest in it.'

'Have you any idea what they might be up to?' Sarah asked.

'Not a whisper at the fascist meetings. I reckon it's a solo IRA operation, though if they are planning something, they will need help. In the meantime, I have put in a request to intercept McGrath's mail. It might throw some light on what they are up to.' Thomas pulled a photograph from his jacket pocket. 'We managed to get this. London panicked when they saw it.'

Sarah took the photo and immediately recognised Jenny McGrath. 'Who is the man with her?' She passed the photo to Anderson.

'Luke Evans. He is a supervisor in Glascoed and a paid-up and rather vocal member of a small nationalist group based here in Newport.'

'Does he attend those clandestine meetings?'

Aled nodded. 'The last few, he's been there, hanging around. We knew about this lad already because he nearly got himself killed a while back. The idiot was one of a small group of protesters who shouted catcalls at parading soldiers in Port Talbot in 1940. The rest of the crowd weren't too pleased, and things got nasty. He and his mates ended up in hospital.'

'Are most Welsh anti-Nazi?' Sarah asked.

'Very much so, but our German friends seem to believe otherwise. Things are bad here, economically, but no one in their right mind thinks Hitler's going to solve their problems. But Jerry assumes the Welsh nationalists are like the republicans in Ireland and are ready to throw their hats in the ring with the Axis. That's why groups like the Right Club have been reaching out to the nationalist groups here in South Wales. They hope their rhetoric falls on sympathetic ears. And, as I said, they are keen to target army and naval personnel.'

'Are they succeeding?' she asked.

Thomas shook his head. 'I've seen very few people in uniform at the meetings. I suspect half of those who attend just want the free tea and biscuits.'

Anderson looked up from the photograph in his hand. 'So, this Evans guy must be their man on the inside in Glascoed. Now, what on earth could they be planning?'

'The IRA usually want guns and explosives,' Thomas said. 'Glascoed is primarily a filling factory. They are about to switch over to heavy bomb manufacture.'

'But they would be handling plenty of explosives,' Anderson said.

'Cordite, TNT, you name it.'

'I assume the place is heavily guarded,' Sarah remarked.

Thomas grunted. 'Not even a mouse could get in there unannounced. The Royal Artillery Anti-Aircraft Regiment are stationed down the lane outside the main factory entrance and around the perimeter.'

'Anti-aircraft; I assume that is standard at all munitions factories. But have the Luftwaffe paid a visit?' Sarah asked.

'Yes. There were a couple of raids in 1940, but nothing since. How they found it is a mystery. The Folly Tower, overlooking the valley to the west, was demolished in 1940 on instruction from the War Office in case Jerry would use it as a landmark.'

'If it's that well protected, how could the IRA hope to gain access? It doesn't make much sense.' Sarah looked to Anderson, who just shrugged.

'That, my friends, is where you two come in. You need to figure out what they are planning. Are they feeding location information to the Nazis so they can bomb the plant or are they considering relieving Glascoed of some of its munitions? I'd risk exposure if I were seen sniffing around there and it would serve no purpose.'

'Agreed. You are far more use playing pals with our fascist friends,' Anderson said.

'That's the way I see it, too. We have cleared your cover with the Royal Ordnance and the plant manager is expecting you this afternoon,' Thomas said. 'The Glascoed staff car will pick you up from here at one o'clock.'

'Does he know we are MI5?' Anderson asked.

Thomas grinned back at them. 'No. You two will have to act your socks off.'

11

17th February 1942, Glascoed Munitions Factory

Before the appointed time, Sarah was waiting in the lobby for Anderson to make an appearance. When he finally did arrive, he had changed into a formal dark navy suit and for a moment, she had to admire how he looked. Anyone would believe he was a wealthy factory owner. If only his manner matched his good looks.

After a slow and deliberate perusal of her boring grey attire, he smirked. 'I'd almost hire you myself!'

Sarah glared at him, before flicking her eyes towards the reception desk. 'Do you want to give us away before we even start?' she hissed.

This earned her an exasperated response. 'Calm down, would you? Jeez, you are a difficult woman to work with.' Before she could remonstrate, he continued: 'Now, once we get into this place, make sure you say as little as possible. You're a secretary. Take notes, observe. Leave the talking to me and don't go asking stupid questions. We will probably only get one chance at this.'

She didn't respond, but with a glare she hoped was on a par with Miss Abernathy's, she walked outside to wait alone for the car, despite the freezing temperature. Really, the man was so damned annoying.

For the entire journey, Sarah had no choice but to smoulder in silence. Unfortunately, he was right; the part she would play required acting a bit dumb. Still, it rankled to have to assume such a passive role. Also, she suspected he enjoyed riling her and was deliberately trying to undermine her confidence. Although she was fuming, she was determined not to let him see how his comments hit home and had to content herself with glaring at the back of his perfectly groomed head.

The route from Newport had taken them along a winding country road with snow banked high on either side, obscuring most of the view. Sarah guessed they must have a team of men keeping the road clear or they would surely be in danger of being cut off in winter. Of course, it wasn't the only means of access. Thomas had told her that all supplies and most of the staff used the railway link. The site was so vast it had two railway stations and a bus terminus.

The car pulled in beside a large building and as they climbed out, a man in a white coat appeared at the door and beckoned them in.

'Good afternoon,' he said. 'Do come out of the cold. You are very welcome to Glascoed. My name is Frank Hughes; I'm duty manager today.' Once the introductions were made, he led them along a corridor to an office. 'Take a seat, Mr Fisher.' He nodded to Sarah and pulled out a chair for her, but she had a feeling she was virtually invisible. All the better to observe.

'Now, sir. I understand you wish to have a tour of our facility.' Hughes glanced down at a letter on his desk.

'Yes, indeed, Mr Hughes, that would be most kindly of you.'

'The Ministry passed on your request to us. I see that you already have a small munitions facility in Chicago, and that you are currently tooling up a larger factory.' Hughes looked up with an expectant smile. 'What brings you to Glascoed in particular?'

Anderson smiled. 'That is correct. We are setting up a heavy bomb plant and the US Government, who are being so kind in helping us with funding, well, they were very keen that we take a look at your set-up. It's supposed to be the best.'

So smooth! Sarah schooled her features; *if only you knew what he's really like, Mr Hughes.*

Hughes beamed at him. 'That's very kind of you to say so.'

'I have a particular interest in the security aspect of your plant,' Anderson continued. 'I assume you have army assistance in this regard?'

'Oh yes, very strict access controls in place at the gates and around the perimeter. Staff must clock in and out. Why don't I show you the overall layout?' Hughes rose and walked over to the far wall where a large-scale map of the site dominated the entire space. Anderson followed him.

'What protection do you have against bombers?' Anderson asked.

Hughes tapped his finger on several places on the map. 'Anti-aircraft guns in these locations. There was a fear that the Folly up at Pontypool could be used as a landmark by the Luftwaffe, so the War Office demanded it was demolished.'

'That was a good idea, Mr Hughes,' Sarah said.

'Oh yes. Once this unholy show is over, it will be reinstated,' Hughes said. 'I know the locals hope so.'

'I suppose your isolated location helps too,' Anderson said.

'Yes. We've had no trouble from Jerry in quite a while. Now, as to general layout. The perimeter fence is eight miles long, would you believe? There are army personnel, here and here.' Hughes pointed to various points around the boundary. 'As you can see, the individual plants are spaced out at regular intervals. We were lucky to find such a large site. A grass embankment encloses each structure. These are twenty feet high to deflect the force of any explosion, and the buildings themselves have extremely thick concrete walls. We are proud of our safety record. Not one major incident since we opened.' He squinted at the plan. 'Now, let me see, what else can I show you? Oh yes, we have underground storage units throughout the site. Here's the hospital unit, fully staffed, and here is the main canteen. This building here is our heavy bomb unit.'

Anderson stood staring at the map. 'I'd be mighty grateful if I could see inside there.'

'We are rather proud of it. Once we are in production, we will make two-thousand-pound bombs for the RAF. That will teach Jerry to mess with us.'

'It certainly will, and we hope to do the same,' Anderson said, turning to Sarah. 'Ain't that right, Miss Cavandish?'

Sarah conjured up her best accent. 'Yes, sir, we sure do.'

'No time like the present.' Hughes grinned. 'And as the unit isn't operational yet, we can dispense with the usual restrictions.'

'And what would they be? I think I should know about them,' Anderson said.

Hughes frowned. 'Why, the same as I'm sure you already have in your existing plant.'

'Absolutely! I just meant what additional measures,' Anderson replied, recovering quickly to Sarah's relief.

'Nothing extra. Occasionally, however, we need to remind the women not to wear jewellery or hair pins or to bring in cigarettes, matches or lighters. Even the smallest bit of metal could cause a spark, as you well know. Protective hats, overalls and overshoes are standard in all our units.'

Anderson nodded. 'Excellent. As I would expect.'

Hughes grabbed an overcoat. 'Jolly good; follow me, please.'

For the most part, Sarah tried to observe everything as if she were IRA. What did they want here? How did they plan to get past the guards at the gate if that was what they were about? Now and then, Anderson would ask her to note something down, which she duly did. He was playing his part well. His questions were pertinent, and they gleaned as much information as they could hope to get. However, it left Sarah more puzzled than ever. It didn't make sense. The plant produced sea mines for the Navy and the heavy bomb unit would be making large bombs suitable for bomber aircraft to carry, not something an IRA man could hide in his pocket then toss at a target and run. Most importantly, no guns were made here.

Sarah trailed after the two men. The site was indeed

vast, almost like a small town. Hundreds must work here, she thought, as yet another group of women passed them, chattering and laughing. All of them were dressed in overalls with their hair tucked under rounded hats. Sarah noticed one girl's hair was yellow in the front. Didn't they call the munitions girls from the last war the canary girls? It was something to do with the chemicals they put into the shells.

If only she could take a look around on her own or ask the girls questions. 'Excuse me, Mr Hughes?' she piped up. Both men turned to look at her. 'Could you tell me where the ladies' washroom is?'

'Certainly, Miss . . .' He had clearly forgotten her name.

'Cavandish,' Anderson supplied, his eyes brimming with laughter.

'Just around to your right in the next block. Follow us back to the main building,' Hughes said before turning on his heel. Anderson shot her a warning look then followed Hughes.

This was her chance to do a bit of sleuthing. But as she turned the corner, she came up short. A few yards away, Sarah spotted the burnt-out remains of a truck. A couple of the factory girls stood close by, looking on as a man in overalls sifted through the wreckage. Sarah sidled up beside them, hoping to ask some questions, but the girls looked at her with curiosity before moving off. Just as she was summoning the courage to interrupt the man, he looked up, a brow raised. She recognised him from the photograph Aled had shown them that morning. It was Evans. Of slender build and sandy hair, his expression was decidedly cross. *Keep calm!* she told herself.

'Oh, dear,' she said, pointing at the truck. 'What happened here?'

'Who might you be?' he asked, coming across to her, wiping his hands in a cloth.

Sarah licked her lips. 'I'm here with my boss. He's building a similar plant back in Chicago. We are doing a tour.'

'Yes?' He looked about before frowning at her. 'But you are on your own.'

'No, Mr Hughes is showing us around. I was heading for the ladies' washroom,' she said, her heart thumping. She showed him her visitor badge.

'Hmm, it's just around the next corner,' he grunted. 'You can't wander around here. We have very tight security.'

'Yes, of course.' She looked across at the burnt-out remains. 'That really does look serious. Was anyone injured?'

Evans cast an annoyed glance at the wreckage and grunted. 'No. Luckily, the driver had just left the cab.' With a sigh he continued: 'Thankfully, only one case had been loaded into the truck, otherwise you would have seen the fireworks from as far away as Cardiff. It was a faulty detonator in a grenade.'

'I didn't realise you made grenades here, too,' she said. 'Mr Hughes did not mention it.'

Evans pointed across to the roof of a building visible above the next embankment. 'Only in a limited way, in that unit over there. Most unfortunate accident. And you would not believe the amount of paperwork something like that generates.' He sighed and walked back over to the remains of the truck. 'Now, if you don't mind, I have a safety report to write up. You hurry along there and get back to Mr Hughes.'

Sarah pretended she was continuing to the bathroom block, then skirted around until she was back at the main building. All the while her mind was buzzing. How come Aled hadn't told them about the grenades? Small and portable, they would be the ideal target for the IRA, and it would appear they were transported by road and not rail like all the other munitions. With a smile, she realised she had one up on Anderson. The day was looking up.

12

17th February 1942, Newport, South Wales

Later that evening, after dinner, Sarah tapped on Anderson's hotel room door. As pre-arranged, Aled was to join them for a debrief. Anderson answered her knock and waved her in. Aled was sitting on the bed. He did a double take when she walked in, staring at her head.

'This is me,' she explained, touching her hair. 'It was a wig.' She made a beeline for the dressing table chair.

'I see,' he said, with a tentative smile. 'That's a good disguise, actually.'

'I doubt it would fool anyone who knows me, close-up,' she replied, then noticed Anderson frowning at her. 'What?'

'One of the hotel staff might have seen you. You should have left it on.'

'Well, you try wearing the stupid thing for a day. Trust me, you'd be jolly glad to take it off.' She glanced at Aled. 'It makes my head itch.'

'You need to take this seriously, Sarah. It's not a game,' Anderson muttered, crossing his arms.

'I checked before I left my room. There was no one around,' she ground out in reply.

'So, folks,' Aled interrupted, his gaze flicking between them. 'How did the visit go? What did you find out?'

'As I suspected, the place is heavily protected. There's no way those guys could get into the site undetected,' Anderson said with a scowl.

'Unless they could pose as staff?' Sarah offered.

Aled shook his head. 'Too risky; it's a tight-knit crew. Most of the workers are local. A stranger would stand out.' He thought for a moment. 'What if they cut through the perimeter fence at night?'

'That's virtually impossible, Aled,' Anderson replied. 'It's patrolled constantly. Besides, the place is huge. They'd have to know exactly where they were going as well as running the risk of being seen by staff.'

'There are shifts covering twenty-four hours,' Sarah cut in.

'I see. Any idea what they are after, then?' Aled asked.

'I'm not sure,' Anderson said with a frown. 'Most of what they manufacture is large, even bulky. They'd have to have a truck to get it out. And what would they want with sea mines or depth charges?'

'Oh, I believe it is the grenades they are after,' Sarah cut in, silky smooth.

'What?' Anderson glowered at her.

'There is a small plant producing grenades. I found it while looking for the bathroom, along with our friend Evans.'

'And you didn't think that was important enough to tell me?' Anderson thundered.

'I'm telling you *both* now,' she replied, returning his stare, wide-eyed.

A rush of colour flooded Anderson's cheeks. Sarah was grateful Aled was present. Perhaps poking a nest of vipers wasn't such a good idea. She turned back to the Welshman. 'Did you not know about the grenades?'

'It wasn't in the report. I knew they used to make them but with the switch over to heavy bomb manufacture I thought they had stopped. That is interesting, though. It would make sense.'

'But the IRA can't get into the facility. How would they get their hands on them?' Anderson asked.

'The grenades are transported by truck, not rail,' Sarah said, keeping her gaze firmly fixed on Aled. 'Perhaps they plan to ambush a truck leaving the plant. Parts of that road are pretty secluded and there are no houses from what I could see.'

'That's a possibility,' Aled replied, 'but any truck would have an army escort for protection.'

'Exactly! A foolish idea, Sarah,' Anderson scoffed.

'Actually, I don't agree,' Aled said. 'Sarah could be right. If you caught them at a narrow point, it wouldn't be impossible. And grenades would be perfect for their needs. I wonder how Evans ties into this.'

'He must work in the grenade unit. When I came across him, he was inspecting a burnt-out truck so he could draw up a safety report. There had been an accident with a faulty detonator.'

Aled's eyes widened, but he made no comment.

'Is there any way we could find out more about him, his role?' Anderson asked into the heavy silence that followed.

'Yes. A cousin of mine lives in Pontypool where the majority of the workforce live. She may be able to get some information for me.'

'I bet Evans has access to the plant logistics,' Anderson said. 'If their plan is to ambush a truck, they'd need to know dates and times.'

'Why not just watch the place to see what the routine is?' Sarah asked.

'Too risky, Sarah, and I'm sure it keeps changing anyway. No, I think Anderson is right. Evans is going to help them do it. He'll tip them off.'

'So, what do we do now?' she asked.

'I will talk to the army commander up at Glascoed and get the information on upcoming shipments. I'll have to warn them, of course, so they are prepared. But we want the shipment run to go ahead so we can catch them in the act. As soon as we have a date, we can plan.'

'We can ambush the ambushers!' Anderson smiled, rubbing his hands together. 'It would be good to see some action. All this playacting is well and good, but it doesn't achieve much.'

'On the contrary, Anderson, we learned a lot today. Brains are just as valuable as brawn,' she said, with a defiant stare, feeling quite smug. 'Wouldn't you agree, Aled?'

'Hmm,' he muttered, eying both of them in turn. 'There's usually room for both in these types of operations.' Anderson grinned across at her, and she felt her heckles rise once more.

'I'll contact my cousin tomorrow and ask her to do some discreet digging about Evans,' said Aled, breaking the tension. 'Well done, you two. Some progress at last. I'll pass this back to HQ.'

'Thanks, Aled,' Anderson replied. Then he stooped down and opened his bedside cupboard. He pulled out a bottle of whisky and some glasses. 'Fancy a tipple?'

An hour later, they said their farewells and Aled walked down the hall with Sarah as far as her room.

'I'll be in touch as soon as I have more information,' he said. 'Hopefully, we can close this operation of theirs down quickly and round them up.'

Sarah touched his arm to stall him, then scanned the corridor to check there was no sign of Anderson. 'Could I have a word? In private? It will only take a minute.'

'Certainly,' he replied. Although he looked puzzled, he followed her into her room.

She pulled down the blackout curtain and turned on the bedside light. She crossed her fingers behind her back. 'The thing is, Aled, we could be kicking our heels for days waiting for this information and I'm keen to get moving on our other mission.'

'Ah! This Gillespie fellow. You need to be patient. It will be like looking for a needle in a haystack. We have no intelligence on him at all.'

'What do you know about this covert route into and out of the country?' she asked.

'We know they are using the small ferries in and out of Fishguard, possibly fishing trawlers as well.'

'I see. The colonel explained how you discovered it. And

the people moving in and out; what do you know of them?' she asked.

'Fascists and Nazi sympathisers. If they are leaving here, it is because they have failed, and with luck we can trace them back to wherever the Abwehr planted them. If we are lucky, we can find their chums and possible co-conspirators. If they are entering the country, it enables us to track them to see what they get up to.'

'But what happens in the other direction, when the fifth columnists escaping from here get to Cork?' she asked. 'How do they get to Europe?'

'They all have new identities and papers, courtesy of the IRA network. The Irish police and G2 had suspected nothing as a result. However, they are now in the loop.'

'What is G2? I've never heard of it.'

'Irish Army intelligence.'

'They co-operate with MI5?' she asked in surprise.

'Yes, and MI6, but on a limited basis as they are deeply suspicious of us.'

'Hardly surprising, given our history,' she replied.

Aled's lips quirked, and he nodded. 'We are doing our best to mend the relationship, and that is why we have tipped them off about this route. They are happy to monitor it for us at their end. When the *special* passengers arrive in Cork, the IRA bundle them onto fishing trawlers that eventually end up in Portugal. Lisbon is barely neutral, with a large contingent of Gestapo and Abwehr agents ready to receive them with open arms. From there, it is easy to get to Germany.'

'I see. But this Gillespie fellow, has he been sighted at all?' she asked, trying to keep her tone neutral, despite her thumping heart.

'Far too clever to act out in the open. He's like a ghost,' Aled replied with a grimace. 'He won't be easy to locate.'

'Yes, I know it won't be easy. But, from what you've said, our only link to him is Jenny McGrath. Is there any chance that she might attend another meeting?' Aled shrugged and Sarah pressed home: 'You see, I was wondering if I could accompany you some evening. I might recognise someone or hear something? It is possible Jenny isn't the only member of their unit going to the meetings.'

Aled frowned at her. 'Well, I don't know. Sounds kind of risky. What if they recognise you?'

'I'll be disguised,' she said, grabbing the wig from the dressing table and holding it up. 'Besides, if I'm with you, they probably won't be too curious. You could say I was your girlfriend or a work colleague.'

Aled raised a brow. 'How's your Welsh accent?'

Sarah smiled and tried it. 'It might need a bit of work, you see, but I'd stay low-key, just like you. I'll follow your instructions to the letter. What do you think?'

'Not bad, Sarah, but listen closely to the staff here in the hotel. I'm not sure you'd pass muster as it is.'

'That's a good idea; I'll do that,' she answered. Luckily, she had a good ear and could usually pick up an accent easily, despite what his lordship Mr Anderson thought! It helped that she liked the musicality of the Welsh accent.

'I suppose Anderson would want to come along as well?' he asked.

That was the last thing she wanted.

'No, no, he wouldn't have any interest in this and is happy for me to pursue it. His only concern is the Glascoed issue, and that is his primary mission. As the first Yank loaned to MI5, he wants to make a name for himself. Chasing an elusive IRA man could be doomed to failure. I'm keen, however. I want to see that operation closed down.'

'Anderson does seem ambitious, certainly,' Aled said.

'Anyway, would it not be good to have two sets of eyes on these people? I might notice something useful,' she replied, hoping she had said enough to coax him. He was still frowning at her.

His expression cleared suddenly. 'Very well. There is a meeting tomorrow evening in Cardiff. Hop on a bus and I'll meet you at Cardiff General . . . the train station, around seven.'

Sarah beamed back at him. 'Thank you, Aled, and don't worry; you won't regret it.'

13

18th February 1942, Newport, South Wales

Much to her disappointment, Anderson was already in the dining room when Sarah came down to breakfast the next morning. She had hoped to avoid him for the entire day, but as she entered, he glanced up from his newspaper; there was no escape. He greeted her unsmilingly before returning to the news. How lucky she was to have such a charming companion, she thought. How different he was to Paul. In all the time she had known him, he had always acted like a gentleman and would never have spoken to a woman the way Anderson spoke to her. Such a pity it wasn't Paul sitting across from her now.

Anderson appeared to be in a sour mood, but why? For a moment, she wondered if he knew about her plan for that evening. Her heart sank. Could Aled have told him about the meeting after all? No. If Anderson knew, he would not be holding back just because they were in a public dining room. He would berate her with pleasure. Perhaps he wasn't at his brightest and best in the morning.

Sarah gave her order to the waiter, then looked about the empty restaurant. She hated silence, and the compulsion to make small talk was too much. 'I'm surprised this place is open this time of year.'

The top of the paper was twitched downwards. 'Lucky us.' Up went the barrier once more. Sarah made a face at it.

After a few minutes, he folded the newspaper with a sigh. 'There's no word from Thomas yet this morning. I guess we are going to be kicking our heels until he finds out when that next shipment goes out. Have you plans for today, Irish?'

'I wish you'd stop calling me that.'

He shook his head, all wide-eyed innocence. 'It's a term of endearment!'

With a withering glare, she continued: 'We are undercover as Americans. If anyone were to hear you—'

'Oh, lighten up, will you, *Miss Cavandish*.'

Seething inside, she said: 'I intend to keep busy today. I have to write up my report for Everleigh and write some letters to my family.' The waiter arrived with her tea and toast.

'That will take all day?' he asked, with a smirk.

'No, of course not. I may catch a film this afternoon. That will kill a few hours.'

'I might point out that we are a team. You should be running your plans by me,' he said. 'Everleigh doesn't pay us to go to the picture house. Best you stay here and wait for the information from Aled.'

'And what about you?'

116

'I have my own plans,' he snapped.

'What happened to *"we are a team"*? You are such a hypocrite, Anderson!'

The lieutenant merely quirked his mouth, enraging her even more.

'Well, I don't see why I should do as you say,' she said. 'Besides, an American visitor would likely sightsee or go to a film. They wouldn't just sit in their room. Have you not considered that we may be under observation?'

'In this backwater? I very much doubt it,' he said with a sniff.

'So, how *do* you propose to be productive today?' she demanded.

Anderson folded his arms. 'I intend to do some reconnaissance. All standard operational stuff. But of course, you would not be aware of that.'

'Oh, I see!' Sarah exclaimed. She could really do with seeing how it was done in the field but her plan to meet Aled would be compromised. *Well, mister, you're keeping me at arms' length; that suits me just fine as I am going to do the same to you,* she thought. But best to pretend to be put out. 'You're leaving me out – very cooperative! And where are you going, or am I not allowed to ask?'

'That road up to Glascoed. I need to figure out where an ambush would most likely succeed so we can be prepared. Aled has arranged for a couple of the local police to come out with me this afternoon.'

Much as she yearned to go, too, she couldn't risk being late getting to Cardiff. 'They will know the road well. I assume you will fill me in when this covert operation is completed. I don't see what you can achieve by this. Surely there could be several spots that would be perfect for staging an ambush on that road. More importantly, how on earth would we cover them all?' she asked.

'We can't, obviously, but it will be good to be prepared; to know the likely locations.'

'Even if Aled could pull in additional help, we'd need a lot of people. This sounds like a big operation for the republicans. They will have a large group of men, particularly if they are getting help from the local fifth columnists. They'd need the numbers if they hope to stop the truck and the escort and overpower them all. Would it not be more sensible for us to ride with the army escort rather than hunting down their ambush party which could be anywhere on that road?'

Anderson's cheek twitched. 'Possibly.'

She raised a brow in surprise. 'Now that wasn't hard.'

'What?' he scowled.

'Admitting I might have a good idea.'

His mouth twisted and his eyes glinted, possibly with humour. 'Either way, the army will be forewarned by us and will be prepared. I'd imagine they will have more men in the escort than usual.'

It all sounded a bit vague to Sarah, but she was the most junior member of the team. Hopefully, Anderson and Aled knew what they were about. But she couldn't resist another poke. 'Have you considered the ambush might happen somewhere else instead?' she asked.

'Of course, though there is nowhere else on the route as suitable or as isolated. We may have to wait until your father's friends make an appearance. That's unless they are warned by someone and abandon the scheme altogether.'

'What's that supposed to mean?' Sarah glared at him.

'I think you know . . . sweetheart.'

Her fingers curled into her palm. How she would love to slap that smug face of his. 'I have nothing to prove to you, Anderson. My focus is on finding my father and turning him over.'

Anderson laughed. 'You haven't a hope in hell of finding that man. A waste of time and resources, if you ask me.'

'I didn't! I have more reason than most to want him to answer for his actions. You can think what you like.' She drained her tea and rose. 'Go on; you go and play soldiers with your friends this afternoon. I intend to do something much more worthwhile.'

'What are you up to?' His eyes narrowed as he stared up at her.

Much as she would have liked to impress him with her plan for that evening, there was a great deal of satisfaction in keeping him in the dark. She gave him a long, hard look. 'My job.'

As Sarah made her way through reception, the young woman behind the desk called out to her. 'I have some post for Mr Fisher, Miss Cavandish.'

'Thank you.' Sarah said. It must be from MI5 in London with instructions, but the receptionist handed her a letter in a pink envelope. Puzzled, she stared at it, curious as to who could be writing to Anderson here. The receptionist looked at her expectantly. Sarah handed it back. 'I'll leave it for Mr Fisher to pick up himself. This looks personal,' she explained with a smile.

'Very good, miss.'

Although it was tempting to open Anderson's letter, she would not stoop to his level. But she was incredibly curious. It had a London postage mark, and if she wasn't very much mistaken, it was from a woman. The letter had a distinctive perfume. Now, why was Anderson receiving billet-doux when on assignment? Had he let his girlfriend know he was going undercover and his undercover identity? Tut-tut. Everleigh would be extremely interested in such a break with protocol. She would file that as future ammunition. Greatly cheered, she skipped up the stairs to her room.

14

18th February 1942, Cardiff

Sarah jumped down from the bus. With half an hour to spare before she was to meet Aled Thomas, she decided to ring Judith to check on her. Her cousin's distress on Sunday had really touched her heart. But above all, Sarah was afraid Judith would do something rash and dangerous and follow through on her idea of getting rid of the baby. Sarah was no innocent. She knew what the dangers and consequences could be. There had been whispers enough amongst the girls at Supermarine. What if Judith went unaccompanied? What if it went wrong? The family would never forgive her for letting Judith face such a thing on her own.

There was a public phone box outside the station. Sarah peeked at her watch again as she entered; Judith should be home from work by now and there was no sign of Aled yet. She put the call through.

'Hello!'

Sarah didn't recognise the voice – it had to be one of the other tenants in the building. 'Hi there, may I speak to Judith Lambe, please?' Sarah asked.

'Hold please; I'll see if she's in,' the voice replied.

'Thank you.' Sarah waited, conscious of the phone call limit of six minutes ticking by.

At last: 'Hello?' It was Judith.

'It's Sarah,' she said. 'Have I caught you at a bad time?'

'Hi, no, I'm in from work since six.' Judith sounded weary.

'Are you feeling unwell? You sound a bit down in the dumps,' Sarah said.

'Just tired. How are you?' her cousin asked.

'I'm fine. But I'm concerned about *you*.'

There was a pause. 'No change here,' was the reply.

'Have you told Gerald?' Sarah asked.

'Not yet. We are going out for dinner on Friday evening. I was going to do it then.'

Sarah could detect the anguish in her cousin's voice. 'He might take it better than you anticipate. Either way, best to get it out in the open, Judith.'

'I know. But I'm positive he will not take it well, which is why I've decided to do it when we are out in public.'

Crikey! What kind of reaction was Judith expecting? Now, she was even more worried. 'Look, maybe talk to Gladys. She's a good egg. You could invite him around to the flat and she could be there, as moral support, when you tell him.'

Again, a pause. 'Thank you, but that is probably not a good idea, Sarah.'

'Or wait until I'm back in London?'

'But it might be weeks before you return. He may have spotted something by then. I might begin to show.'

'Hopefully it's too early for that, Judith. I'm sorry, I don't know when this job will be over,' Sarah said, deeply frustrated. 'But I hope it won't be more than a few weeks.'

'This is hanging over me, every waking minute, Sarah. At this stage, I just want to get it over with. He's already noticed something is wrong: he keeps asking if I'm well.'

'That's a good sign, isn't it? That he's concerned about you?'

'Perhaps.' But Judith didn't sound convinced.

Through the window of the phone box, Sarah spotted Aled's car driving into the station forecourt. 'Just remember you have my support. Have you said anything to Gladys or Anne?'

'No. You're the only person who knows.'

'I understand, though I can vouch for Gladys; as I said, she is utterly trustworthy if you need someone to talk to,' she replied. 'Anyway, I hope all goes well on Friday night, Judith. I'll be thinking of you. My lift has just arrived so I must go, but I'll ring again later in the week. Please take care.'

'You, too.'

Sarah was thankful she didn't have to find The Red Rose pub on her own. As a native of Cardiff, Aled knew the city well and had been to meetings in the pub before. He parked on a side street close to the docks, and they went on foot the rest of the way. Aled said little as they walked along, and Sarah wondered if he regretted agreeing to this. She was nervous enough as it was; she knew the risk she was running. Deceiving Anderson wasn't ideal either, but he had made it clear that he thought the search for her father was futile. If her luck held, some clue to her father's whereabouts could materialise this evening. She might recognise the face of one of his old cronies or hear him mentioned. Anderson didn't need to be here. She could handle this on her own. To the forefront of Sarah's mind was the hope that she could find Da quickly and get back to her old, comfortable life in Hursley.

Breakfast that morning had been particularly trying. But it was prudent to be seen together to keep up the pretence of being travelling companions. Even if it was a strain on her temper. There had been no further attempt by Anderson to find out what she was doing for the day. He must assume she was staying in Newport. What he didn't know wouldn't hurt him, she thought. Sarah had avoided him all morning but had seen him getting into an unmarked car just after lunch. She smiled, thinking about Anderson and his police buddies traipsing around in the snow. It all seemed pointless to her.

Situated down a back street, it was near impossible to see The Red Rose's entrance in the blackout. They hurried through the smoke-filled bar, which stank of alcohol and unwashed clothes. She was self-conscious. There were no other women, only men sitting over their pints, talking in low voices. There was a group of sailors at one table. They all turned around and looked her up and down. She was careful not to make eye contact and was glad she had worn her Miss Cavandish glasses. Something to hide behind. She shoved Aled in the back and hissed at him to hurry.

Aled led her out into a tiny hallway with a flight of stairs heading up into the gloom. She kept her gaze fixed on Aled's back and followed him to a large room on the first floor. It too reeked of beer and smoke. Drab grey walls were plastered with fascist posters and the room was lit by bare lightbulbs dangling from the rafters. It was freezing. Uneven rows of battered chairs had been laid out and, by the looks of it, in a hurry. Aled had told her the meeting locations were rotated between five or six pubs that had sympathetic owners. They were paranoid about spies, he had told her with a grin.

Three men stood at the top, deep in discussion, their backs to the audience. Sarah and Aled sat close to the back of the room and watched as the seats slowly filled up. To her surprise, the group of sailors from the bar appeared and sat up the front. Soon the place was full. Sarah reckoned there were between twenty-five and thirty people. There were no familiar faces, except one. Evans was one of the men at the top of the room. Thank goodness, at the last minute, she had left the blonde wig at the hotel, instead relying on a woolly hat covering her head. Hopefully Evans would not remember her from their brief encounter at Glascoed. Sarah slid down a bit in her seat and waited, her heart beating fast.

Eventually, the crowd fell silent and two of the men at the top sat down. The remaining man stepped forward.

'That's Bennett,' Aled whispered to her.

'Welcome, comrades, and thank you for coming out on such a cold night. Your dedication and loyalty are much appreciated.' A murmur rose from the audience, and he nodded. 'As I have said many times before, our struggle is hard because we are fighting for something great. A Britain we can be proud of. I urge you to endure what is to come.

Loyalty to the cause and to your fellow fascists is paramount and the qualities of a true Briton.

'Never forget the destiny of this great nation lies solely upon our shoulders. Remember, a flame has been lit that the ages shall not extinguish.' The audience cheered. Aled looked at Sarah from the corner of his eye as he clapped. She couldn't believe the crowd were lapping up such bluster. It was all hot air.

'Now, comrades, it gives me great pleasure to introduce Mr Garadice, who has come all the way from our branch in Bristol to speak to you this evening.'

The cold seeped into Sarah's bones as she sat through the two speeches that followed. She longed to get up and stretch; it felt as though her posterior was frozen to the seat. Both speakers were pro-Nazi, spouting a lot of fascist nonsense, which made her stomach churn. She could almost sense Aled's discomfort too, for he fidgeted constantly. Yet the crowd around her were lapping it all up. However, to her disappointment, no IRA speaker was announced. It looked like her little rebellion and solo run were in vain.

By the end of an hour, she was itching to leave, thinking longingly of the warm bed back at the hotel. But she had to wait, and above all, not draw attention. Beside her, Aled shifted on his chair before leaning over and whispering: 'Nearly over.'

Bennett rose and thanked the last speaker. 'Now, Luke Evans is going to pass around the jar as usual. Please give what you can to the cause. We will let you know the location of next month's meeting in due course. We hope to have news you will find uplifting. We have an operation planned that will shape the future of this organisation. The powers that be will have to sit up and take notice of us, once and for all.' This was met by loud applause and a wolf whistle. 'Thanks again for your support, comrades.'

Sarah flicked a knowing glance at Aled. Could Bennett be referring to the Glascoed plot? Aled nudged Sarah as Evans got up from his seat a few rows ahead. Slowly, he made his way down the centre of the room, collecting funds. Sarah's heart began to race. When he got to their row, she kept her eyes down, her chin almost buried in her scarf, terrified he would recognise her. Despite the chill of the room, she broke out in a sweat. The jar was passed along and Sarah and Aled popped some coins in. Evans received the jar back with a grunt and moved on. He hadn't even glanced in her direction.

As the meeting ended, no one looked eager to linger, except for Bennett who remained near the door. Luke Evans stood behind him at a table, counting out the coins from the jar. As the audience filed past, Bennett nodded to each person. A handful were spoken to briefly. Aled and Sarah had to hang back and wait their turn. Sarah grew anxious. What if he spoke to her; wanted to know who she was? There hadn't been many women in attendance; she might stand out. She slipped her hand through Aled's arm, squeezed it, and smiled up at him. He nodded, reading her gesture correctly by the look on his face. With relief, she knew he would assume the role of boyfriend if that was what was required. She would follow his lead.

They were almost the last to leave, but by the time they had reached the door, Bennett had turned away and was talking to Evans. As much as she would have loved to hear what they were discussing, she was relieved to get out into the corridor. But they could go no further. They had to linger at the top of the stairs, waiting for the people ahead of them to get out the narrow doorway at the bottom. Aled gave her an encouraging smile.

At last, the crowd moved and Aled could step down onto the stairs. As Sarah watched from behind him, a couple appeared in the doorway below, trying to enter the pub. The man stepped back outside to let people out, but the woman, swamped in a huge, knitted scarf and hat, forced her way in to stand in the tiny hallway. *How rude*, Sarah thought. The woman clearly had no patience. She stood, tapping her fingers on the bar door as people brushed past her. A couple of people murmured apologies as they squeezed past, but the woman remained silent. Just as Aled and Sarah neared the bottom of the stairs, however, the woman unwound the scarf from around her face.

Sarah almost tripped on the last step.

It was Jenny McGrath.

15

18th February 1942, Cardiff Docks

As soon as they were clear of the door of the Red Rose, Aled strode away down the alleyway. Sarah had to run to match his pace. 'Hey! Slow down, Aled,' she cried out.

'Keep walking,' he hissed. 'You do know who that was?'

'Yes, of course; I recognised her.'

'We need to put as much distance as possible between us and them,' he said, increasing his speed.

Sarah reached out and grabbed the sleeve of his coat. 'No. Wait, please.'

He came to a stop and turned; his face barely visible in the dark laneway. 'Are you mad? We can't stay here. It's too risky.' He glanced past her towards the pub. 'Let's hurry,' he urged, his tone angry, perhaps even a little scared.

'But we can't just walk away. The fact she has appeared, and Bennett and Evans are still here, means they must be going to discuss their plans.'

'Oh, and what are we supposed to do? Sneak up the stairs and listen at the keyhole? That place is crawling with their sympathisers. Seriously, Sarah, you've been reading too many spy thrillers.'

'It's a golden opportunity,' she said.

'Yes; to get caught!' Aled threw up his hands.

'I don't agree! Not if we are careful.'

Aled shook his head vigorously.

'No, please listen,' she said. 'This is too good a chance to pass up. I can pretend I left something behind if anyone discovers me. Anyway, neither Evans nor McGrath recognised me.'

'Yet! Perhaps they didn't have an opportunity to look at you closely,' he ground out. 'If you go back in there—'

'Well, I'm not negotiating, Aled. Either you are with me, or you are not,' Sarah snapped. She heard him gasp and curse as she turned on her heel and headed back down the alleyway.

Outside the Red Rose, Sarah scanned the area. No one around. She removed her scarf and left it on the window-sill before slipping inside. Through the bar door, she could hear the hubbub of conversation, but the hallway and stairwell were empty. She squinted upwards into the darkness. The door to the meeting room was shut but the light was on. She hesitated. Was she mad? What if she were caught? But if she didn't at least try to get some information, the evening would be a total write-off. Too many deaths of people she loved would be in vain if she did not try.

As she put her foot on the first step, she heard the door to the street creak open behind her. Aled. His face livid, he gestured frantically for her to come back outside. Sarah shook her head and climbed the stairs.

A few steps from the top, she stopped. She could hear Bennett's distinctive voice, followed by a burst of laughter. She'd know that cackle of a laugh anywhere. McGrath. With a sigh of frustration, Sarah moved up another step. They were speaking too low for her to make out what they were saying.

'Sarah!' Aled hissed from the bottom of the stairs.

She didn't even turn around but waved her hand at him dismissively and heard the door close again. Hopefully, he would wait outside because she would never remember the way back out of the warren of alleyways if she had to make a run for it.

The voices from inside the room rose and fell but still she could not make out what was being said. Dare she go closer? Sarah climbed up onto the last step and leaned towards the door just as it swung open. She gasped and stood back but not before she caught a glimpse of the inside. McGrath and Bennet were sitting at a table. Evans, however, was looming large and glaring down at her from the doorway.

'What you want?' he demanded. Then his eyes narrowed, and his brows snapped together. 'I know your face.'

Heart in her mouth, Sarah replied in what she hoped was a good Welsh accent: 'I was at the meeting just now, see. I'm sorry, but I think I left my scarf behind. My mother made it, see, so she would be awful cross if I came home without it.'

'What is it?' Bennet called out. Beside him, McGrath lit a cigarette, leaned back, blowing smoke up towards the ceiling.

'Some girl who was at the meeting left her scarf,' Evans said, continuing to glare at Sarah. Then he grunted. 'All right,' he said, at last. 'Wait here and I'll check.' He stomped off, leaving the door ajar.

'You do realise timing will be crucial,' Sarah heard McGrath said 'We can't afford any cock-ups.'

'Have we ever let you down before?' Bennett answered.

Unfortunately, just then, Evans returned and whatever McGrath said was drowned out by Evans's growl. 'Nothing here. You must have lost it somewhere else.'

'That's a shame. Thanks for looking anyway. Sorry to have disturbed you,' Sarah replied. The door was slammed shut.

Shaking, Sarah walked down the stairs, her mind in turmoil. Seeing McGrath again was disturbing. Such a shame she hadn't heard more of the conversation. Reluctantly, she slipped outside. Aled was waiting in the shadows.

'Well, what did you hear?' he demanded, grabbing her arm.

'Nothing really. Evans came to the door too quickly,' she replied. It was so annoying, and she'd hardly get another golden opportunity to eavesdrop.

'Are you satisfied now?' he hissed. 'What did you gain, eh? Bloody amateur!'

'Hey, that's not fair,' Sarah said. She wrenched free and scooted over to the windowsill to retrieve her scarf. When she rejoined him, she said: 'If Evans hadn't come to the door, I could have heard a lot more.'

'Well, you didn't. Now we need to get out of here,' Aled said, glancing back at the pub door before taking off and setting a fast pace.

Miffed, Sarah said, trying to keep up with him: 'Evans wasn't suspicious. McGrath and Bennet were in there and continued to talk while I waited. I heard her mention timing. It must be to do with a possible attack.'

'We don't need to risk listening at doors to know that, we know they are planning something. Unless you managed to hear a date and time, that little stunt of yours was a waste of time.' He glared at her. 'I've worked too hard to have my cover blown by undertaking an unnecessary risk tonight. It has taken me years to build up my network. I'll not risk it so that you can play heroics. No doubt to impress Anderson.'

Sarah gasped. 'I only want to do my job. I don't give a toss about Anderson.'

Aled shook his head angrily and began to walk away. Sarah grabbed at his coat sleeve. 'Stop a moment. We could still learn something. Should we not at least keep watch for a while? This alleyway is dark and gives us good cover.'

'You cannot be serious!'

'What if Gillespie should turn up?' she asked.

'That is highly unlikely. He never has before.'

Behind them, they heard the pub door open, the noise from inside spilling out into the laneway.

'Bloody hell!' Aled muttered and grabbed her arm. 'Get walking!' Aled maintained a rapid stride until they had turned several corners. Then he stopped for a moment, breathing hard. To her dismay, Sarah could hear footsteps echoing, getting closer. Aled gestured for her to be quiet and to follow him. A few yards further down the dark laneway, he stepped into the recess of a doorway. Sarah squeezed in beside him, her heart thundering like a runaway train in her chest. She held her breath. The footsteps stopped at the end of the laneway and time seemed to stand still. Sarah squeezed her eyes shut as she was overcome with guilt. Her impulse had put them in terrible danger. For what seemed like an eternity, the silence dragged on. Then, just as Sarah thought she couldn't stand it anymore, the footsteps resumed and faded away.

'Quick now,' Aled said, taking her hand and pulling her in the opposite direction. A few minutes later, they exited the rabbit-warren of back alleyways. They walked on in silence, at normal speed, until they reached his car.

'I'm sorry, Aled,' Sarah said with a weak smile. 'I got carried away.'

'You certainly did! Look, I know you're new to this and keen, and that's laudable. But sometimes it is more prudent to exit to fight another day. Come on. I'll drive you back to Newport. Just be thankful that woman didn't recognise you.'

'Thank you,' was Sarah's contrite reply.

16

18th February 1942, Newport, South Wales

By the time Aled dropped her off at the hotel, Sarah was exhausted and longing for her bed. Her expectations for tonight had been high. But she had learned nothing. No dazzling piece of information to wow Anderson with or even a clue to where her father was hiding out. She was disappointed and hoped that Aled wouldn't reveal her recklessness to Anderson or Everleigh. She'd never hear the end of it.

Of course, it was typical of Da to stay in the shadows and let others take all the risks. But how was she to find him when she didn't have a single lead? Perhaps she should try following McGrath herself? She would have to wangle the woman's address from Aled somehow. Judging by his earlier reaction, that might be a bit of a challenge. He'd barely given her a polite good night. Perhaps she could go to Cardiff and watch for McGrath leaving the factory where she worked. But how could she explain her absence to Anderson? Hopefully, a better plan would come to her in the morning.

As she passed the front desk heading for the stairs, the receptionist called out to her. 'Miss?'

Sarah sighed and retraced her steps. 'Yes?'

'Mr Fisher asked if you would join him in the guest lounge.'

That was all she needed. She peeked at her watch: it was a quarter to twelve. It was tempting to ignore the summons. Whatever he wanted, couldn't it wait until morning? It was likely he wanted to impress her with his findings from his little excursion that afternoon.

Anyway, how dare he throw out instructions as if he were in charge. Only Aled had the right to boss her around. She started for the stairs, then stopped and clenched her fists. Ignoring Anderson would only make matters worse; he'd be unbearable tomorrow. Grumbling under her breath, she retraced her steps and headed for the lounge.

Anderson was sitting beside the fire, a glass of spirits on a table beside him. As she approached, he looked up from his book, his gaze flinty. 'Where have you been?'

'Good evening to you, too, Mr Fisher,' she replied, sitting down.

'I asked you a question.' He closed his book with a snap and continued to glare across at her.

'And I choose not to answer it,' she replied, 'besides, I already told you I was going to the cinema.'

'Do you expect me to believe that is where you have been since lunchtime?' Sarah shrugged and his gaze intensified with what she guessed was anger. But she didn't care. 'We are supposed to be working together,' he said.

'And yet you were happy to leave me out of your little excursion today. You're extremely selective about co-operation; so don't dare lecture me! Now, if that's all, I'm rather tired.' She stood and looked down at him. 'I don't need another father figure trying to control my life. The last one I had was a bit of a dud.'

'Well, I am sorry to hear that, but might it not have occurred to you I was concerned for your safety?'

Sarah laid her hand over her heart. 'Really? I'm touched by your concern, Anderson, and how gallant of you. Unfortunately, I don't believe it's out of a sense of chivalry, more that you consider me an amateur. You are afraid that I will mess up your mission because you assume I can't look after myself. Well, let me tell you I may not be as experienced as your good self, but I'm no novice.'

'Perhaps not entirely, but you are letting your feelings towards me colour your actions,' he said, his voice low. 'We don't have to do everything together, but we need to work as a team if we are to succeed, and that includes knowing what the other is up to and where they are. There has to be some level of trust.'

Sarah burst out laughing, drawing the attention of the couple on the far side of the room. She shook her head at him. 'Trust! You are unbelievable. And let me tell you, the only *feelings* I have for you are of the negative variety.'

'I am well aware of that . . . Irish,' he drawled.

Now, her anger was bubbling up; she couldn't stop herself: 'And as for teamwork, that is laughable coming from you. In fact, presumptuous beyond anything. No, no, don't you dare talk to me about collaboration. You have done nothing but put me down since we first met. You make decisions and give me orders. That's not my idea of a partnership.'

'Are you quite done?' he asked, his eyes ablaze. 'Let me give you a warning, Irish. If I find you have been in communication with the enemy, I will not hesitate to hand you over to Everleigh,' he growled at her. 'And I hope they throw the book at you.'

So that was it! Anderson assumed she had met up with her father this evening! She almost laughed aloud, but her instincts saved her. She had misread his mood. He wasn't angry, she realised now, he was absolutely furious, the knuckles of his hands white where they lay clenched on the arms of his chair. Underestimating him wasn't clever. If he thought she was up to no good, he would act and ruin any chance she had of confronting her father. Her anger drained away.

'And if I were doing as your warped mind believes, then yes, I wouldn't blame you,' she said, her voice wavering. She sat down again and took a couple of calming breaths. 'My father left me and my sister for dead so that he could run off to play soldiers with his chums here in Britain. I have no doubt he is planning no end of havoc to further the republican cause. He is a dangerous man with a deep-seated hatred of the British. I believe he is capable of great evil. He won't just stop at helping spies escape. Any damage he can inflict on Britain's war effort, that furthers the Irish cause, he will have no compunction in carrying out. He was a brute who never thought twice about using his fists on us or my mother. For that reason alone, I want him brought to justice.' She clamped her mouth in anger for a moment, unable to continue. 'I hate him,' she said at last, 'so, please don't question my motives any more. I wasn't meeting my father tonight. I give you my word and that will have to be good enough for you.'

The fire in Anderson's eyes died, but he remained silent. It was disconcerting. She needed to escape. 'Enjoy the rest of your evening, Anderson,' she said, and quit the room, close to tears.

Sarah woke to a knock on her door. The room was in darkness. Bleary-eyed, she grabbed her dressing-gown, pulled it on and ran her hand through her tangled hair. Half-asleep, she couldn't be bothered to turn on the light and tidy herself up. Grumbling about the inconsiderateness of some people, she opened the door a crack and peeped out. It was Anderson, looking disgustingly wide awake and cheerful.

'Morning, sleepyhead,' he greeted her.

She blinked at him. 'What do you want? What time is it?' she asked. 'It's the middle of the night, surely?'

'You do talk nonsense. Let me in. We can't talk out here,' he replied, looking up and down the corridor.

With some reluctance, Sarah stood back, and he walked past her. He strode over to the window and yanked back the curtains. As the daylight flooded in, she squinted. Where he stood, Anderson was silhouetted against a sky streaked with red and orange.

'It's almost eight-thirty,' he said, frowning at her. 'Late night carousing doesn't suit you, Gillespie.'

She pulled the cord on the dressing gown tight. The room was chilly but that wasn't why she was shivering. Anderson was buoyed up; she could almost feel the energy he was emitting. It was disturbingly attractive. She shivered again and wrapped her arms around her body.

'You know very well I wasn't carousing. Now, what do you want?' she asked.

He held up a telegram. 'This just arrived from Thomas. There is a shipment going out from Glascoed this evening at six.'

'Oh, so that's why you are so disgustingly chirpy at this ungodly hour,' she said, sitting down on the bed. But this was odd. Aled hadn't said anything about it the night before. In fact, he had said he didn't expect to hear until sometime today. Wasn't it a bit early for telegrams to be flying around? Unless of course the information had been waiting for him when he returned home last night. But it wasn't something she could discuss with Anderson without giving herself away.

'I hate hanging around with nothing to do,' Anderson said, glancing out the window. 'This really is a one-horse town. How do people stand it?'

'Most sensible people are still asleep, Anderson. Besides, it's winter, it's freezing, and no one with any sense goes out unless they must,' she said.

He threw her an amused glance. 'Let's hope there is no more snow today. I'd hate for that shipment to be post-poned.'

'Well, if there is no panic, perhaps you could give me a chance to get dressed? We can discuss a plan after breakfast.'

'I've already eaten,' he said, heading for the door. He stopped just in front of her. 'Come to my room in an hour and we can finalise the arrangements for this evening,' he said, before leaning over and ruffling her hair.

For several minutes after he left, she sat still, her breath coming in short bursts. The intimacy of his gesture had caught her completely unaware. No, no, she was reading far too much into it. He was in a playful mood, excited at the prospect of action at last. Yes, that was it. Nothing more to it than that. Nothing at all. So why was she trembling?

17

It was ten to six and already dark outside. Anderson was pacing up and down in the army command hut situated in the front compound of Glascoed. Now and then, he would peer at his watch or stop and look out the window facing the entrance.

'Where the hell is Thomas?' He threw his hands up in the air. 'He should be here by now.'

Sarah was standing just inside the door and shrugged. 'Maybe he was delayed in work or got stuck in the snow. The weather may have been worse in Cardiff.'

It had been snowing all day, on and off, and the last snow shower had added another few inches to the already deep drifts. The road up to Glascoed had been tricky to negotiate. Anderson had driven their hired car far too fast, and they had skidded several times in the icy conditions. Her remonstrations fell on deaf ears. He prided himself on his driving skill, declaring it with a grin when she had cried out yet again and asked him to slow down.

'No one else has ever complained, sweetheart,' he had said. 'You should see the roads back home in winter. This is easy.'

It took great restraint, not to mention fear for her safety, not to thump him.

The hut was freezing. Sarah stamped her feet, hoping to get some warmth into them. Even with two pairs of socks on, the cold seemed to seep into her boots.

The door to the hut opened and Captain Hart, who was in charge of the grenade convoy, entered.

'Well?' he asked her.

'It doesn't look like Mr Thomas is going to make it, I'm afraid,' Sarah said.

'He could still appear, Captain, give him a few more minutes,' Anderson said coming over to them.

'I can't delay, Anderson,' Hart said, shaking his head. 'We have to leave now.' He walked back out the door.

Anderson rolled his eyes heavenward. 'It's not like I didn't try. Guess we will have to manage without him.'

They followed Hart outside to where three delivery trucks from the factory were lined up, along with two jeeps and an army truck.

'My job is to get those to Bristol this evening,' Hart said, giving Anderson a sour look. 'I don't answer to MI5. As it is, I'm not happy about you lot sticking your noses in.'

The captain had already made it clear he thought their assertion that the IRA intended to hijack the grenades was daft. It was common knowledge the shipments were heavily guarded. Any attempt to ambush would be suicidal, in the captain's opinion. In the end, Anderson had phoned London and eventually the order had come through to Hart to take it seriously and allow the three MI5 officers to tag along. Hart, clearly peeved, had grudgingly agreed. Thomas not showing up made them look a bit foolish, but there was no way the army or Glascoed were going to cancel the shipment just because he had failed to appear.

The captain strode off, commanding his men to get ready. As they watched, the engines of the delivery trucks were started, and the soldiers boarded the escort vehicles.

Sarah shrugged at Anderson. 'It's not going to make much of a difference if he isn't with us, now, will it?' she asked.

'No, but he is supposed to be in charge of this operation.'

'Guess you'll have to do the honours, then,' she said with a smirk.

He treated her to a scathing glance. 'Huh!'

'Well, are we to get into the truck or not . . . boss?' she asked.

'I guess so, Irish.' Anderson rolled his shoulders and walked away in the direction of the truck.

As she followed, her eyes adjusted to the gloom, and she realised it wasn't entirely dark. There was enough moonlight for her to distinguish nearby people and objects. Above, the sky was clear, with a multitude of stars visible. Even the hills in the distance seem to shimmer; pale against the velvety darkness of the sky with their covering of snow. But as she lowered her gaze, she could have sworn she saw a flicker up in the hill to the west. She froze.

'Come on, then,' Anderson shouted to her from behind the truck.

'No. Look,' she answered, beckoning him over. 'Come back and take a look at this.'

'We can't stall any longer. Hart's already mad with us—' he said as he approached.

'Never mind that!' she exclaimed, pointing up to the hill. 'There is something glowing up there.'

Anderson sighed then glanced up to the west. 'It's probably from a house. They've forgotten about blackout.'

'It's too big to be a house light, and it's getting brighter . . . That's a fire that has been lit on purpose!'

'Nah,' Anderson replied.

'Captain Hart?' Sarah called out.

'Sarah, for God's sake,' Anderson muttered.

'What is it now? We have to go. Immediately!' Hart barked as he walked over. With a scowl, he crossed his arms and stood in front of her.

'Captain, you have to see this. You know the area well; are there any houses up on that hill?' Sarah asked, pointing up to the light, which was now growing brighter.

Hart turned his head, then froze. 'No. It's farmland.'

Sarah grabbed his arm. 'Exactly. There shouldn't be any light up there. Look! There's another one over there,' she gasped, pointing north. 'That can't be a coincidence, surely? Those are markers.'

'Bloody hell, Sarah, you're right,' Anderson exclaimed. 'There's only one reason someone would set fire to beacons. Someone is guiding in a plane.'

'A bomber?' Sarah asked. Anderson nodded, his face now tight with tension.

'Then an attack is imminent. We've got to get those bonfires out,' Hart said in a strangled voice. He glanced down at her. 'Well spotted, miss. If we were on the road, we would never have noticed those.' He moved away quickly. 'Sergeant! Ring through to the manager's office. Tell him we have a situation. The convoy is cancelled and get those air-raid sirens going. Scramble the crews to the anti-aircraft gun positions.'

'Yes, sir!'

Suddenly, everyone was running around them. Sarah looked up at Anderson. 'They're gonna need help putting out those fires, Anderson.'

'Absolutely. I'm game if you are, Irish.' Anderson grabbed her hand, pulling her over to where Hart was still issuing orders. 'Hart, we want to help.'

The captain looked at them for a moment. 'Great. I'm putting a couple of teams together to go and sort those out.'

'I think you'll need three, sir,' Sarah said. 'Another one has been lit to the east.'

Everyone swung around. Flames were all too visible on the hillside up to their right.

'Bugger! Any pilot worth his salt will be able to triangulate and pinpoint us,' Hart said. The captain scanned the courtyard. 'Here, you can go in this one, Miss,' he said, striding over to where the first convoy jeep was parked. He yelled out for four soldiers to get in too. 'Anderson, you go in the next one.'

'Right-oh,' Anderson said, disappearing inside the second jeep.

'You take the bonfire to the east and get that bloody fire out as quick as you can,' Hart instructed the driver of Sarah's jeep.

★ ★ ★

Fifteen minutes later, the jeep skidded to a halt. Sarah released her grip on the metal frame of the vehicle and opened her eyes, which had been squeezed shut for most of the terrifying journey. Several times, they had gone into a skid. How the driver managed to keep them on the road, she wasn't sure. Why did men have to drive like lunatics?

They clambered out and gathered in a circle at the front of the jeep. The soldiers had their rifles at the ready.

'Right, lads, we're going to make our way up as quickly as possible, but try to keep low. We may be sitting ducks in these dark uniforms, but there's nothing we can do about that now,' the driver said. 'There could even be enemy up there ready to ambush us. Spread out across the field before you advance. If they fire on us, retreat to here. We may need to find a less direct route up. Not ideal, obviously. Time is of the essence. Any questions?'

'No, sir!' was the chorus.

'OK, lads, you know what we have to do.'

Sarah watched as the soldiers clambered over the wall and scattered.

'I'm Frank, miss, best you stay with me and keep a few paces behind.' He frowned down at her.

'OK, let's go.'

Sarah followed Frank over the wall and landed knee-high in snow. Within seconds she could feel the legs of her siren suit becoming damp.

But it was slow going. If she lifted her head, she could make out the dark shapes of the other soldiers against the snow as they moved forward. But she soon discovered it was quicker if she kept her head down and only stepped in Frank's footsteps. The only sound was the scrunch of their footsteps. After a few minutes, she stopped to draw breath and looked up the hill. With dismay, she saw the bonfire was now a roaring blaze. They really needed to speed up.

And then she heard it. The drone of an engine. She grabbed at the back of Frank's jacket. 'Stop!'

But he had heard it too and was scanning the sky. So were the searchlights down at the plant. The beams were slicing through the darkness, moving quickly, trying to locate the plane. It was getting closer.

'There it is. A bloody Jerry plane coming in from the south,' Frank said. The drone grew louder as the plane flew down the valley. An ominous dark bird in the night sky. To Sarah's dismay, the searchlights kept missing it. 'Come on,' Frank urged. 'The others are nearly there.'

From up ahead, minutes later, they heard a shout of 'all clear!' from one of the soldiers. At least they weren't going into an ambush. Sarah, breathing hard, paused and looked up ahead. The others had reached the bonfire. She could see them silhouetted against the sky. In the distance, Sarah could hear the air-raid siren blaring down in the plant. The bomber swooped low. Sarah and Frank flung themselves down into the snow as it swept over them. Sarah felt the rush of air and almost panicked. The searchlight swept across their field, desperately trying to follow the plane's path. The guns pounded, the light from the shells lighting up the sky above her. But then, to her horror, she saw the flap on the undercarriage open. Bombs dropped from the base of the plane. They were too late. Jerry had found the target.

Beside her, Frank scrambled to his feet, cursing, and ploughed ahead. She followed, her heart beating so hard she thought it would burst from her chest. She was back in No. 18, the walls tumbling down around her. Maura crying out . . .

She had to shake the memory off. She had to keep moving forward.

Another burst of anti-aircraft fire, then an almighty bang burst around them. Sarah turned to see flames licking upwards, but she couldn't tell if the bomb had hit a building within the plant as it was in total darkness, except for the searchlights around the perimeter. It was certainly close.

The last few feet of the hill were steep. As she drew level with the others, she followed their example. Scooping up handfuls of snow she flung them onto the flames. It seemed hopeless. She could smell petrol. It would take a heck of a lot of snow to put the raging fire out.

'The beacon to the north has gone out. Come on, lads. Put your backs into it!' Frank yelled.

Sarah looked. Sure enough, only the beacon on the far side of the valley was still alight. The bomber engine could be heard again, coming closer. They all looked up as it glided past.

Another payload was dropped.

With renewed purpose, Sarah bent down, scooping up as much snow as she could, and flinging it onto the flames. They kept at it for what felt like an eternity, but gradually the wood began to steam and hiss as the snow did its work. As the flames died, black, choking smoke rose into the night sky.

Exhausted, they all dropped to the ground. They might have succeeded in putting out the fire, but the damage was done.

As they watched, the other beacon went out and the bomber slowly turned once more, dipped its wings as if to mock them, before heading south and out of sight.

18

By the time Sarah arrived back at the Glascoed plant, the all-clear siren was sounding. Her heart sank to see a fire crew busy putting out the flames on several buildings as their jeep swept through the gates. But to her relief, most of the bomb damage was on the western side of the site and mostly on or near the perimeter.

Sarah shook hands and bid farewell to Frank and her other companions before making her way back to the hut. The others weren't back yet, but she knew they wouldn't be long. She waited at the window, watching the glow of the fire, which was visible above the roof of the opposite building. A small crowd of workers had gathered in the courtyard. Sarah hoped no one had been killed or injured in those buildings, but it didn't look good for anyone who might have been caught out by ignoring the air-raid siren.

A few minutes later, two jeeps drove through the gates,

pulling up in front of the hut. Anderson and Hart climbed out of their respective vehicles and for several minutes, they stood, heads together. Sarah's irritation with Anderson returned. Why weren't they discussing things with her? Anderson was doing this deliberately. Leaving her out. Isolating her. And he had dared to preach to her about teamwork.

Miffed, she sat down with her back to the window. Now that her adrenaline levels had reduced, she was suddenly weary. Much to her surprise, she started to tremble. The incident with the bomber up on the hill had stirred some disturbing memories. Memories that most likely would keep her awake tonight when she finally got to bed.

Anderson entered the hut alone. 'Ah, you're back. Are you OK?' he asked, coming across the room to where she sat.

'Fine,' she said. 'You?'

He leaned against the edge of the table. 'Yeah, but you do know there will be hell to pay over this. London will not be happy. The good Captain Hart is going mad. Can't understand how his anti-aircraft guns didn't bring that Jerry bomber down.'

Sarah shrugged. 'Lack of practice?'

Anderson whistled. 'I hope not for their sakes. He's fit to kill 'em, either way. Can't say I blame him. There was only one plane.'

She nodded. 'And how come no one here at the plant noticed the activity up on the hill? It must have taken a while to build those bonfires.'

Anderson gave a grim nod. 'Unless our IRA friends had hidden the stuff close by and waited until dark to make them. There could be farm buildings up there. In winter, the farmers probably don't go up there much.'

'I suppose you could be right. What worries me is that this suggests the republicans are working closely with Berlin, not just a handful of local crackpot fifth columnists.'

'That's for sure. They would have had to be in radio contact to pull this stunt off tonight.'

'Do you think an Abwehr agent could be here in Wales?' Sarah asked.

'It's possible . . . I suppose. Aren't your father and his friends facilitating the travel plans of these guys both in and out of Fishguard?'

'Possibly,' she ground out. 'Tonight certainly has all the hallmarks of my father's warped logic. It was probably his idea that the IRA would guide that plane in.'

Anderson quirked his mouth, then rubbed his chin. 'If I ever meet the guy—'

'You'll have to get in line. I'll be at the top of that particular queue.'

'Fair enough.' To her amazement, a smile played about his lips. Was he at last beginning to trust her? 'Right. I better ring London and make a report.'

'What are you going to say? We don't know for sure what occurred tonight. We can't even be sure the grenades were ever a target.'

'What do you mean?' he asked.

'Well, I think we can agree that what happened only makes sense if the IRA and the Luftwaffe were in contact and working together. But what was their objective? Was it to facilitate a bombing raid or had they two aims in mind?'

Anderson nodded. 'I see what you're saying. The grenades

for the republican boys and a nice munition factory target for the Luftwaffe. Killing two birds . . . isn't that the expression?'

'Exactly.' Sarah continued: 'It's rather clever, really. If the convoy had left on time, the beacons would not have been spotted by us, and possibly not by anyone else here at the plant until it was too late. We would have driven into whatever ambush they had planned, and they would have hijacked the shipment.' She paused for a moment, trying to sort out her tumbling thoughts. 'Or perhaps they hoped the bombing raid would pull the army escort back to Glascoed, leaving the convoy vulnerable.'

Anderson grimaced. 'Either way, a win–win situation, leaving the IRA and Jerry very happy indeed. At least we scuppered one part of that plan.'

'Yes. Surely Everleigh can't lay the blame on us for this. We couldn't have known this was what was planned,' Sarah said, suddenly jaded.

'Yes, but there must have been whispers. Someone always talks. Why didn't Aled pick up on this and more importantly, why didn't he turn up this evening?'

An awful thought struck Sarah. 'We know the republicans are aware they are under surveillance after the murder of that other agent. Nigel, wasn't it?' Anderson nodded. 'Maybe Nigel talked before he died and they know Aled is MI5 too and have decided to . . .'

'Neutralise him?' Anderson cursed under his breath.

'Yes. We need to warn him.' Heart pounding, she stood. 'We need to get to Cardiff.'

Anderson's expression was grim. 'Agreed. Let's just hope we're not too late.'

★ ★ ★

Two hours later, they pulled up in front of the address headquarters in London had provided for Aled. It was a quiet suburban road in Cardiff. Middle-class, and the kind of street and house you would expect a bank manager to call home.

An ARP warden walked past, stopped, and retraced his steps to stand beside their car. He played his torch into the car, peering in at them. Sarah stared back, raising her brows. The warden touched his cap and walked on.

Aled's house was shrouded in darkness, the same as every other house on the street. The driveway was empty. 'What do you think?' Sarah asked. 'His car isn't there. Looks very quiet. I suppose his father could be at home.'

Anderson leaned across her and gazed up at the house. He was so close she could feel his breath on her cheek. As he drew back, their eyes met. Sarah looked away first.

'There's only one way to find out, Irish,' he said, opening his door.

As they got closer to the front door, Sarah could hear a radio. 'Someone's in,' she whispered.

Anderson knocked on the door. A minute later, they heard a bolt being drawn. Sarah could just make out Mr Thomas senior's face in the gap as the door was opened slowly.

'Is that you, Aled?' a worried voice asked.

'No, Mr Thomas, it's Aled's friends, Mr Fisher and Miss Cavandish. We met you a couple of days ago at Newport station,' Anderson said.

'Oh yes, I remember. The Yanks,' he said, opening the door a little wider.

'We were wondering if Aled is home, sir,' Sarah said.

'No. I was sure it was him knocking. He knows I put the bolt on when it's late,' he answered. 'You better come in.'

Mr Thomas shut the front door after them, twitched the curtain back in place over the front door and switched on the hall light. He pushed his glasses up his nose as he regarded them.

'Have you any idea when Aled might be home?' Anderson asked.

'No. It's not like him to be so late,' the elderly man said with a shake of his head.

'Would he not ring, sir?' Sarah asked.

Mr Thomas smiled. 'We don't have a phone. I won't have those infernal machines in the house.'

'Perhaps we could wait with you, sir?' Anderson asked.

Mr Thomas's eyes strayed to a clock up on the wall. It was almost ten o'clock. 'I usually retire about now.'

'It's very important we speak to him, Mr Thomas,' Sarah said, smiling encouragingly.

Mr Thomas hesitated, then his shoulders sagged. 'Very well, best you come into the sitting room.'

The room was small but comfortable, with the remnants of a fire in the grate. Sarah was thankful for the heat, even though they had stopped briefly at the hotel to change out of their wet clothes. She still hadn't warmed up completely.

'Would you like some tea, my dear?' Mr Thomas enquired.

'Oh, that would be lovely, sir,' she replied, 'why don't I give you a hand.'

Mr Thomas nodded and headed back out into the hallway.

'Stall him as long as you can. I want to look around,' Anderson whispered to her, his eyes flicking towards the stairs.

'Will do. Good idea,' she replied.

Sarah followed Mr Thomas down the hallway to a glass door. The kitchenette was tiny, with a small table and two chairs taking up most of the space. She watched as Mr Thomas filled the kettle. 'Is it unusual for Aled to be out this late?' she asked.

Mr Thomas paused with the kettle in his hand. 'Yes, and he never said he had anything on this evening. He always tells me so that I don't worry about him.' Then he frowned. 'Mind you, he was very late last night.'

Sarah smiled guiltily; that was because Aled had been kind enough to drive her back to Newport. 'I see. Does he say where he is going on the nights he ventures out?'

Mr Thomas frowned as he lit the gas, then looked at her over the rim of his glasses. 'No, why would he? I don't pry into his private life.'

'Of course not. It's more that it might help us find him if we knew the places he liked to go.'

Mr Thomas cast her a worried glance. 'Do you think he is in trouble?'

'No, sir. I'm sure he's just been delayed somewhere.' Mr Thomas grunted. 'And he went to work at the usual time?' she asked.

'Yes, I waved him off at half-eight, same as usual.' He pointed to a cupboard behind the door. 'You'll find the cups and saucers up there . . . Miss?'

Sarah lifted down three of each. 'Catherine, sir, Catherine Cavandish. Would he normally take the car to work?'

'Oh no, it's my car, you see. No, he usually walks or gets the bus into town. The bus stop is at the bottom of the hill,' Mr Thomas said, pouring the boiling water into a teapot.

Sarah heard a creaking floorboard above and cringed, but

Mr Thomas appeared not to notice. Anderson needed to be more careful. Perhaps the elderly man's hearing was as bad as his sight. Mr Thomas rinsed out the pot and spooned in the tea.

'But he took the car today?' she probed.

'Yes, said he had an errand to run at lunchtime. Sometimes he must visit other branches. He is a manager, you know,' he said, his eyes shining with pride. He turned back to the sink and poured the rest of the water into the teapot. 'Now, where is that tea tray?' He rummaged around beside the sink and pulled out a wooden tray. 'Ah! Here it is.' His face fell. 'I'm sorry. I didn't know I'd have guests. I don't even have a biscuit to offer you.'

Having not eaten since lunch, Sarah was disappointed, but she forced a smile. She felt sorry for him. He did look worried about Aled and her own concerns for Aled's safety were growing by the minute.

'Not to worry, Mr Thomas. Tea is perfect. We don't want to put you to any trouble, sir.' Sarah hid a smile. Anderson never drank tea; only coffee. Well, he'd just have to suffer it for once. She took the tray from the elderly man and arranged the dishes on it as slowly as she dared. With relief, from the corner of her eye, she saw Anderson slip down the stairs, a dark shadow through the glass door as he went back into the sitting-room.

'Why don't I carry this for you?' she offered, picking up the tray and walking slowly up the hallway.

For a quarter of an hour, Sarah tried to make polite conversation with Mr Thomas. He was clearly tired, wanted his bed and wanted them gone. Anderson didn't help. With a grimace, he gulped down the tea then sat there throwing her glances heavily laden with . . . well, that was just it. She had no clue what he was trying to convey. Had he found something significant while snooping? She returned his glare and turned to their host.

'It's getting late, sir, and I'm sure you wish to retire,' she said.

'I do indeed, young lady.'

'Perhaps you could ask Aled to leave a message at our hotel in the morning, just to reassure us he got home safely.'

Mr Thomas rose from his chair with a grunt. 'Yes, yes, I will tell him. He'll be sorry he missed you, but I'm sure he will be home soon.'

The front door was shut firmly behind them.

At the bottom of the driveway, Sarah grabbed Anderson's sleeve. 'What the hell was all that about?'

'Dearest Sarah, I was hoping you would pick up the hint. I was trying to get us out of there. We have a problem.'

'Yes, we certainly do,' she replied. 'I have a bad feeling about this. I think they have snatched Aled. How on earth are we to find him?'

'I'm not so sure.'

'Oh! Why is that?' she asked, glancing at his profile as they settled back into the car.

'I did a quick search of his bedroom.'

'Yes, I heard you,' she sniffed. 'Luckily, Mr Thomas didn't.'

Anderson huffed. '*And,* I found something.'

'Well, spit it out, what did you find?'

'A wireless set in a suitcase, shoved into the back of his wardrobe.'

Sarah frowned across at him. 'I suppose he needs it for contacting London.'

'It's a *Jerry* wireless set.'

Stunned, Sarah could only stare at him. 'What? Are you sure?'

'Positive. The markings and model number all point to it. They use the format SE, followed by a number.'

'You've seen one before?' she asked, her heart sinking.

'I've seen pictures of them. The "S" stands for *Sender*, the German for transmitter and "E" stands for *Empfänger*, which is receiver. Aled Thomas is a German mole.'

'Bloody hell!' Sarah exclaimed.

Anderson gave a mirthless laugh. 'My thoughts exactly.' He started the engine and pulled out into the road.

'But that means we have been compromised. In fact, all the agents in Wales have been.'

'He will have blown our cover, for sure,' Anderson said. 'Damn!' He thumped the steering wheel.

'Thank goodness he doesn't know my connection to Da.'

'Are you sure he doesn't?' Anderson asked.

'Yes, Everleigh advised me not to say it to anyone . . . well, except you, as we are working together.'

'That's something, I suppose. But, if your father found out what you are doing, how would he react?'

Sarah gulped. 'Badly.'

'OK, we need to get to a payphone. All our Welsh colleagues will have to be warned. We don't want them to be picked off by your dad's chums.'

Sarah's stomach turned over. What if they were too late? 'There.' She pointed to the far side of the road. 'That's a call box.'

Anderson pulled over and jumped out. Sarah followed and stood at the open door.

'I can't see the stupid dial properly,' Anderson grunted. He handed her a box of matches. 'Here, light one of these.'

Sarah took a quick look to make sure there were no ARP wardens about before she struck a match and held it up while Anderson dialled HQ. 'Yeah, reverse charge, operator. Thank you,' Anderson said, raising a brow at Sarah.

Sarah blew out the match and leaned in, trying to hear.

Anderson went through the security checks and asked to speak to Everleigh. He grunted. 'I understand that, buddy, but this is extremely urgent. Yes, I do know what time it is,' he grunted again and shook his head at Sarah. 'I'm telling you he needs to be contacted and . . . OK, I'll wait.' Anderson covered the receiver. 'I think they are ringing through to him now.'

'He must be at home,' she said. He nodded.

'My number?' Anderson asked, throwing a frantic glance at Sarah. 'One moment.'

Sarah lit another match and held it close to the phone. 'OK, here it is . . . 8 9 7 7 . . . Cardiff. And he'll ring me back straight away? Good, we are standing by.' Anderson put down the receiver. 'I need a cigarette.' He pushed past her and walked across the pavement to a boarded-up shop front. Cupping his hands, he lit up.

The shrillness of the phone ringing made Sarah jump. She grabbed the phone. 'Hello?'

'Sarah? It's Everleigh. What's happened? Did you find Daffodil? Is he safe?'

'No, sir. But we did find something at his house which is causing us considerable concern.' From the edge of her eye, Sarah saw Anderson stroll back over. He leaned against the door frame and nodded to her to continue, and he took a long drag from his cigarette.

'Sir, is the line secure?' Sarah asked.

'It is.'

'Wales is compromised, sir. Daffodil is in the enemy camp. We found an enemy wireless set at his home.' There was silence at the other end of the phone. 'Sir, did you hear me? Do you understand? You need to put out a warning as soon as possible.'

Everleigh coughed. 'Yes, I understand. This was not the news I was expecting.' She could hear the strain in his voice.

'No, sir. What should we do?'

'Best you come back to HQ as soon as you can get a train.'

Sarah grimaced.

'What did he say?' Anderson asked.

She covered the receiver. 'Says we have to go back to London.'

Anderson shook his head and took the phone from her. 'Sir? Anderson here. Look, sir, we know some of the people involved in this. While the trails are fresh, why not let us continue? Yes, of course I understand how dangerous it will be, but they'll expect us to hightail it home to regroup. Sarah feels the same way, sir. We've come too far to drop this now.' Anderson wiggled his brows at her and grinned. 'I agree. That would be best, and the quicker the better, sir. Yes, sir, of course. We will contact you in the morning. Good night.'

'Did he agree?' she asked.

'Kinda,' Anderson said, 'He is going to contact Special Branch straight away to round up McGrath and Evans.'

'Probably too late, though,' Sarah said.

'Of course it is; like Thomas, I'm sure they had an exit plan in place. Goddamn it! I can't believe Thomas betrayed us.'

'Neither can I. He seemed so trustworthy.' Sarah felt a fool. Thomas could so easily have handed her over to McGrath in Cardiff. Eventually, she would have to confess to Anderson about that little jaunt. He would not be pleased.

'Now, I don't know about you, but I'm flat-out tired. Let's get back to Newport. We can form a plan of action in the morning.'

'Will it be safe? They could be waiting for us.' She shivered, and it wasn't just from the cold night air.

Anderson put an arm around her shoulder as they walked to the car. He walked her round to the passenger side and opened the door. 'Guess it's best you sleep in my room tonight, Irish. I'm the only one with a gun.'

19

Sarah slept fitfully for part of the journey to Newport, and by the time they arrived back at the hotel, it was well past one on Friday morning. The front door was locked, and they had to rouse the night porter to gain entry. Grumbling under his breath, the porter went behind the reception desk to get their keys.

When he turned around, his lips were a thin line of disapproval. 'You appear to have post, sir,' he said, handing Anderson an envelope.

'Thank you,' Anderson replied, tucking the pink envelope into his pocket. But not quickly enough. Sarah caught sight of the handwriting. It was from the same woman as last time. She'd put money on it. It made her uneasy again about Anderson, especially coming so soon after discovering Thomas was a traitor. Could she trust anyone?

The night porter dismissed them with a grunt and a brusque good night.

'You Brits sure know how to make a customer feel good,' Anderson said as they climbed the stairs.

'I'm not a Brit, as well you know.'

'Oh, so you are saying I'd get a better welcome in an Irish hotel?'

Sarah had to laugh. 'Not at one in the morning, no.'

Anderson halted at his door and unlocked it. With gun drawn, he ducked in and did a quick scan of the room while she watched from the doorway. When he came back out, he told her: 'In you go. I'll check your room to see if it's safe. Won't be a minute. Close the door after me. I'll give two sharp raps when I'm back.' With his pistol raised, he headed off down the corridor.

Sarah waited anxiously, suddenly conscious of being alone, tired and scared. A few minutes later, she was relieved to hear the two knocks on the door.

'It's clear,' he said, on entering the room. 'Get your stuff together and get back here quick as you can. I'll keep watch in the doorway.'

Sarah scooted down the corridor and into her room. Heart thumping, she tossed her belongings into her suitcase. She pulled up short. Anderson had shoved the pillows down under the covers to make it look like she was in the bed. Unsettled, she scurried back to Anderson and immediately tackled him about it.

'Why? I reckon those lads might want a little target practice if they show up.'

Horrified, she stood staring at him. 'You *do* think they are going to come after us.'

He shrugged. 'Who's to say. Don't fret about it. Close the door, Irish. I'll take the chair,' he said.

Swallowing hard, Sarah replied: 'That's hardly fair.' However, she eyed the bed with longing. She was so tired.

'Hey, sailors learn to sleep anywhere. I'd recommend staying dressed in case we need to depart unexpectedly. Throw me one of those pillows. Best get some shuteye. Tomorrow will be a busy day.' He settled down in the chair by the window and covered himself with his overcoat. His pistol was next to him on a small table. He followed her gaze. 'Just a precaution, in case of any nocturnal visitors, lacking manners.'

Sarah sat down on the bed. 'I don't know if I will be able to sleep.'

He sniffed. 'Come on, Sarah. I know you are braver than this. You're overwhelmed. I get it. A lot happened today. It's my nature to be cautious, that's all. Always best to consider the worst-case scenario and be prepared.'

'Yes, of course. That is sensible. But I'm still finding it hard to believe Aled is a double agent.'

'Well, doll, that wireless set would not be there in his room unless he was. I just hope we can limit the damage.'

'I wonder why he did it,' she said.

Anderson scoffed. 'Money or ideology; it hardly matters. What does matter is that he played us, and I don't take kindly to that. For his sake, our paths better not cross again.'

'Yes, my own feelings are similar.' An awful connection clicked. 'Anderson, if he is a fifth columnist or even an Abwehr agent, then he must have betrayed that other agent, Nigel. The man who took the photographs of McGrath and my father. The man who Aled claimed he found with his throat cut.'

'Yep. In fact, I'd say our friend Aled did the cutting.' He

gave a wry laugh. 'He must have been livid the roll of film found its way to London before he could intercept it.'

'It's hard to imagine he is that cold-blooded and to think I trusted him.' She frowned. 'I'm puzzled, though,' she said. 'Why did he give us the correct information about that shipment of grenades? He could just as easily have given us a different date. He knew we trusted him and were unlikely to check.'

Anderson gave a little shrug. 'Perhaps he suspected I might just check. It didn't matter anyway. He knew we would be sitting ducks for that bomber coming in. He never intended to show up to Glascoed to help us. I'd say he left work at lunchtime, or maybe he never even bothered to go to work but made straight for Fishguard.'

'You think he has already left for Ireland? But if he was the one with the wireless, surely he would have had to have been close by to Glascoed to let the plane know when to come in?'

'Not necessarily. You're assuming he's the only Abwehr agent in Wales with a wireless set. Most likely it was someone else guiding that plane in. He knew if things didn't go as he wanted, we would rumble him when he didn't show up and would start investigating. I reckon he was gone already.'

'Leaving that wireless behind was a mistake, then.' Sarah gnawed on her lip. Aled's betrayal was difficult to come to terms with. 'If we hadn't found it, we would have continued to assume the republicans had got their hands on him and we would be frantically searching for him.' She sat up taller. 'We would have walked straight into their trap.'

'But only if we had a trail to follow. It's much simpler than that, my dearest Sarah. They know who we are and where we are. He didn't need to set a false trail and a trap at the end of it, though I'm sure the thought of us dashing in like the cavalry to save his sorry ass must have amused him.'

'He has betrayed us then,' she said gloomily.

'I don't doubt it, Irish,' Anderson replied. 'I believe he just didn't care. He knew he had enough time to leave the country. Think how happy his Abwehr handlers must be with him with that bombing raid on Glascoed pretty much a success. He will be welcomed back to the Fatherland with open arms.'

'At least the bombs dropped only damaged one unit, and no one was killed or injured. However, whatever way you look at it, it paints a terrible picture of Thomas. Everleigh must be furious.'

'Yeah, someone playing him at his own game of double cross,' Anderson snorted. 'That's gonna hurt, for sure.'

'But if Thomas is as bad as you make out, why didn't he hand me over the night of the meeting?' The words were only out of her mouth when she realised she had given herself away.

Anderson sat up straight, his coat slipping to the floor. He glared at her. 'What meeting? What are you talking about?'

Her heart sank; she would have to confess after all. 'OK. Don't get mad with me, but I went to one of those fascist meetings with Aled.'

'You did what?' he shouted, now red-faced.

She held up her hands. 'Sorry, look, I thought it was a good idea at the time.'

'So, that's where you went on Wednesday. I thought that cinema story was a bit off.' Anderson shook his head, breathing hard. 'I don't believe this! Why didn't you tell me what you were up to?'

'I . . . well, I wanted to speed things up. I hoped I'd find some clue to help me locate my father or that I'd recognise one of his cronies at the meeting. You only seemed interested in your assignment at Glascoed.'

'That's pathetic, and you know it, Sarah. You deliberately left me out. We are supposed to be a team.' He thumped the arm of the chair. 'How can I trust you, if you do things like this?'

'Yes, I know. It was stupid. I'm sorry. I won't do anything like that again.'

Anderson exhaled slowly. 'And did you?'

'Did I what?'

'Find any clues?' he growled.

'No. But Jenny McGrath did show up when the meeting was over.'

'What? And you didn't think that was significant enough to pass on to me?'

'There was nothing to tell. All I can confirm is that she was there, chatting with some of the local nationalists. We passed her in the hallway as we were leaving, but she didn't recognise me, I'm sure of it. I took care with my appearance and Cardiff would be the last place she would expect to see me; I'm not a total idiot.'

'That's a matter of opinion!'

Sarah smarted, but she was on the back foot. 'Don't be mean, Anderson. That Evans fellow from Glascoed was at the meeting and the leader of the group, Bennett, also lingered after the meeting. It looked as though they were hanging on to meet Jenny. I tried to eavesdrop on the meeting, but I was discovered and had to scarper rather quickly.'

Anderson blew out a slow breath. 'You were nearly caught?'

Sarah shrugged. 'I had my excuse ready for my presence and I was believed. But Aled was very reluctant to get involved in my plan.'

The blaze of anger was all too evident in Anderson's face. 'Hardly surprising now we know he is one of them.'

'But he could have given me away, and he didn't,' Sarah said.

'Yes, because he knew their operation would be carried out this evening . . .' He glanced at his watch. 'Actually, yesterday now. Anyway, he couldn't jeopardise that by showing his hand. If something happened to you, he knew I'd act.'

'Really? What would you have done?' she asked, deeply curious.

He frowned at her as if she were stupid. 'I'd bring in Special Branch, of course, to round them all up. He couldn't risk that. He needed us to believe he was MI5 until the attack on Glascoed was over.'

'Yes, I suppose so. And now he has disappeared, there can be no doubt,' she muttered. 'I feel sorry for his father.'

Anderson cast her an impatient look. 'Don't be. For all we know he could be a Nazi too. Some of these Welsh seem to be obsessed with nationhood. Fascism is only an idea or two away. Wasn't the old man spouting Welsh at us?'

'Why are you so suspicious of everyone? You can't equate speaking one's native language to being a fascist. No, you can't really believe that. Mr Thomas appeared perfectly normal to me,' she said.

'And you are such a great judge of character, Sarah.'

That was a little too close to the bone. She shrugged. 'Anyway, aren't you Yanks always bleating about how great your nation is?'

'That's different. It is!' He laughed and suddenly the tension in the room dissipated. She sagged with relief. 'Sarah, you are far too innocent for your own good. Now, is there anything else you need to confess?' She shook her head. 'Good. We can talk more in the morning. Now, for the love of God, go to sleep! I'm exhausted.'

'OK, good night.' She switched off the light. Fully clothed, she lay on the bed with just a blanket over her. Her muscles ached with tiredness, but she suspected sleep was far from near. So much had happened today. She stared into the darkness, reliving that crazy scramble up the hill at Glascoed. How clever of the republicans to light those beacons. Such a pity they hadn't been able to put them out before the plane appeared. If there had been any doubt before that the republicans and the Germans were in cahoots, it was as clear as day now. She wondered how long Aled had been working for them and, more importantly, why? He hadn't struck her as someone with strong views but of course, he would have kept that hidden. Anderson's assertion that Aled was a cold-blooded killer didn't sit easy with her either, but it did seem likely considering what they had learned tonight. Just like Captain Northcott, Thomas had projected his false persona with complete confidence. Still, it was demoralising to know she had been duped yet again. Could you trust anyone these days?

But then an awful thought crept into her head. She only had Anderson's word that Nazi wireless existed. What if he had made it up to cause panic? Effectively, they had just dismantled the entire Welsh MI5 network! That would be quite a coup for a German spy.

Sarah broke out in a cold sweat. Surely not! If Anderson was a double agent he could easily have eliminated her by now or handed her over to the IRA. No, she had to believe he was genuine or she would go mad. She couldn't cope with this constant shifting of loyalties ... and possible double cross. War really did bring out the worst in people. It was disheartening, all of this betrayal. Whatever was the truth, she had to stick with Anderson for now. But it would do no harm to keep a close eye on him. She sighed into the darkness. At this rate, working for MI5 was going to destroy her faith in human nature. Trusting anyone was proving to be a fool's game. She needed to be more like Anderson; more detached. Particularly if she were to survive whatever lay ahead.

The only consolation was that the shipment of grenades hadn't fallen into the hands of the IRA. She hated to think what use her father's cronies would have put them to; how many people would have been injured or lost their lives. Ambushing an army-escorted shipment was profoundly risky. Whoever had thought of the distraction of a bomber was a genius. It was the perfect plan, giving both sides what they wanted. Da must be livid, she thought with a shiver. The Germans had achieved their aim, and he had been left empty-handed. God help whoever he might blame for the fiasco. Hopefully, it would be McGrath.

The operation was typical of the IRA. They always went for the small weaponry, easy to carry and hide, as they carried out their guerrilla tactics. And grenades were just the kind of weapon they could use to cause the maximum amount of carnage. They probably wanted them to launch an attack on an army base somewhere. As she had said to Anderson earlier, the operation had all the hallmarks of her father. A wave of rage coursed through her. She went rigid, her fists clenched at her sides. Was there no end to Da's cunning? An awful thought crept into her mind. Was he responsible for turning Aled as well? It would be something he would revel in, with the added piquancy of getting one up on the British establishment, destroying a network of agents and causing panic.

The only good thing was Aled didn't know of her relationship to Da. My God, if Da knew she was alive and here in Britain ready to betray him, he would come for her. In fact, she had no doubt he would kill her. And he would have Jenny McGrath egging him on. However, Sarah still had the element of surprise if they ever came face to face. To them, she was just another MI5 agent.

More than anything, she wanted revenge, even though it was eating her up inside, dragging her thoughts to the darkest corners of her mind. Was there a limit to the amount of grief and anger a person could tolerate before it drove them mad? Was she inching towards insanity? Is that why she had been so reckless in Cardiff? The intrigue and the lies; all of it left her feeling slightly nauseous. But there was a score to settle. And until that retribution was attained, she must carry on.

There had been too many sacrifices, too many lives destroyed by Jim Gillespie. He had to be stopped. Every vile thing he did hung over her too. She couldn't help it; she felt guilty even though she had no part in his schemes. The next few days and weeks would be tough, but if ever she faltered, she only had to think of her little sister, lying in that grave back in Dublin. She dared not think of Paul.

But how on earth were they to find her father? It seemed hopeless. She only hoped Anderson was right and the few clues they had found would lead them to him. A snore broke the silence. *Lucky Anderson, able to sleep*, she thought. She thumped her pillow and turned over onto her side. She listened to his deep breathing and gradually relaxed. Whatever lies ahead, I'll need my wits about me. *And at least this time I'm not alone; I have Anderson on my side*, was her last conscious thought.

Cheerful whistling woke Sarah the following morning. She blinked awake to find Anderson grinning down at her.

'You talk in your sleep,' he said.

She struggled into a sitting position, wrapping her arms around her knees. She narrowed her eyes as she looked up at him. 'What did I say?'

'Most of it was gibberish. Who's Maura? You seemed to be very anxious about her.'

'My sister. I dream about her a lot,' she said.

'Is that the girl who died in the bombing?' he asked with a sympathetic look.

'Yes, she was only seventeen. Sorry, I think the bombing raid yesterday triggered some bad memories.'

Anderson reached out and gently squeezed her arm. 'That's understandable. However, I will have to think twice about sharing a room with you again. You snore as well.'

'So do you, buster.'

'I've never had any complaints,' he answered with a grin.

Sarah felt the colour rush into her face at the implication. God, he was so full of himself.

'Come on. It's seven-thirty. I suggest an early breakfast, a quick call to Everleigh and then we check out of this dump,' Anderson said, stuffing his belongings into his bag. 'I don't feel safe here.'

'Can I just wake up properly first?'

'You're not a morning person, are you?' he said with another grin. Then he cast her a questioning glance. 'Are you all right after what happened last night?'

Sarah was surprised. He looked genuinely concerned. 'Sure, I'm fine. Still a bit shocked about Aled, though.'

Anderson blew out his cheeks and shook his head. 'I have to admit I am, too. Still, at least we were able to warn HQ.'

'And to think we went to Cardiff to try to help him,' she said with a grimace.

'Life would be easier if the baddies wore badges, wouldn't it? Don't feel too bad about it. He fooled us all.' Anderson pulled back the curtains. 'At least it didn't snow last night.' He surveyed the street. 'The car is still there. All appears to be quiet.'

She stretched when she got off the bed. Her muscles felt as though she had gone ten rounds with a prize fighter. She felt grubby, too. She needed a wash and to tidy her hair before putting that blasted wig back on. Opening her suitcase, she rummaged around. 'Bother! I forgot my hair-brush, Anderson. Where's the key to my room?'

'It's on the mantel over there.' He nodded towards the fireplace.

'Won't be a minute,' she said, grabbing the key.

As Sarah came out of Anderson's room, a maid approached from the other end of the corridor. 'Morning, miss,' she said as she walked past. But the maid gave her a look as if to say, why are you coming out of a gentleman's room in such a dishevelled state?

'Good morning.' Sarah hurried to her door and stepped inside. There goes my reputation! After drawing back the curtains, she grabbed the brush from the dressing table and made for the door. But something caught her eye. She stopped in her tracks and looked down at the bed in horror.

There were three bullet holes in the eiderdown.

20

20th February 1942, Newport, South Wales

Sarah gasped. There were singe marks around each bullet hole in the eiderdown. With a trembling hand, she pulled down the bedcover. The three bullet holes continued through the pillows. Two bullets were lodged in the wall opposite.

If she had slept in this bed last night . . .

Anderson appeared in the doorway. 'What's keeping you?' Sarah turned to him, but no words would come.

'You look like you've seen a ghost,' he said with a frown before stepping further into the room.

Sarah took a step away from the bed, beckoning him over.

Anderson froze as he looked down at the bed, before a trail of expletives peppered the air.

Shaking, she asked: 'Why didn't we hear it? We were only two rooms down.'

Anderson put his arm around her shoulder and hugged her close. His jaw clenched. 'Silencer. They'd hardly want to announce their presence. I half expected they would make an attempt.'

'What do we do?' she asked, panic taking hold.

'Hey, Irish, don't worry. I'll get us out of here. We will be OK.'

'But could they still be in the hotel?'

'I doubt it. But we need to leave right now. We can't hide this and as soon as the maid comes in to clean, and she sees this, the hotel will be crawling with police. I don't know about you, but I don't want to have to explain this.'

He grabbed her arm and ushered her out the door and back to his room. 'Quickly, now. Finish packing.'

'Are we just going to walk out the front door?'

Anderson was over at the window, scanning the street below. 'And into the arms of a republican welcoming committee? I don't think so, Irish. We'll go out through the rear of the building. There's an alleyway that runs behind this block.'

'How do you know that?' she asked.

'Why do you think I did that recce on the first day?'

Sarah blushed. He was showing up her inexperience so much, it was depressing. 'Won't they anticipate that escape route?' Sarah asked.

'I'm betting they are keeping watch on the car. They'll expect me to make a quick getaway in that. Don't forget, they think you're dead.'

'Well, that's just lovely!'

'Hey, we have the upper hand for now, Sarah. Let's make the most of it.'

'OK. I'm ready,' she said, closing her suitcase with trembling hands. 'Just give me a minute to get this blasted wig on.'

Anderson was now at the door, drumming the finger-plate with his fingers. 'Sorry, Sarah, but we need to move, now.'

'I'm done, I'm done,' she said, picking up her case.

They hurried down the stairs and waited until the receptionist was busy before taking the corridor towards the back part of the hotel. They passed the kitchen with its delicious breakfast smells, chatter of staff and clatter of cooking utensils. Regrettably, eating would have to wait until they were somewhere safe.

They turned a corner and at the end of the empty hallway there was an open door leading to outside. Anderson gestured for her to wait. He popped his head out the door and looked up and down quickly.

'No one around. Come on, let's go,' he whispered. 'Might be quicker if I take this,' he said as she passed. He grabbed her suitcase from her hand. 'We need to disappear, fast.'

The alleyway ran behind the hotel and the shops along Commercial Street for some way. Luckily, there was no activity in the alleyway as the stores would not open for a couple of hours yet. With relief, Sarah saw the opening onto the street ahead.

'Which way?' she asked Anderson.

'I suggest we head for the train station. Let's take the long route, just in case. We can contact London from there.'

'Do you know the way?' she asked, doing her best to match his walking pace.

'Again, why do you think I did a recce that first morning?' he answered.

'Thank goodness you did.' She hoped he saw that as the olive branch it was.

'Yes. Now you must realise how important it is to do them,' he said.

'Well, I did map the route on the drive from the station to the hotel.'

'That is never sufficient. You need to walk around the area or, if that's not possible, study a map.'

'Don't worry; I won't make that mistake again,' she said, feeling rather glum.

'At least you have some colour back in your cheeks,' he said after a minute or two.

'That was quite a shock, seeing those bullets,' she admitted.

'I guess it must be. It's not pleasant to know there are folk out there trying to despatch you.'

Sarah gave a wry laugh. 'It's not the first time.'

'Really?' He shot a look at her. 'Tell me, I'm intrigued. There was little detail in your file.'

Sarah gave him a brief outline of what had transpired with Captain Northcott in Winchester.

Anderson whistled. 'That was a close shave.'

'Yes, but it happened so fast I barely had time to think. This morning is different. Do you think they knew it was my room?'

'Hard to know. They wouldn't have cared, either way. Just following orders, Sarah.'

'But why didn't they try to kill you?'

Anderson blew out his cheeks and shook his head. 'Maybe they were disturbed. Lost their nerve. Who knows?'

Or, she thought, *they wouldn't kill one of their own.* Shocked by the idea, she almost stumbled. Bloody hell, but she was becoming paranoid. No, this was silly. If he was one of them, he would not be helping her escape.

He came to a sudden halt and looked down at her. 'Are you OK? I would have sorted it out. You don't need to worry about it.'

'I don't doubt you would have if it had come to it. I guess I'm feeling vulnerable, not having a gun myself.'

'Yeah, that was probably my fault. Sorry. I suggested to Everleigh it wasn't a good idea.'

'Why?'

Anderson glanced away. 'I didn't trust you enough. I persuaded him it was sufficient for one of us to be armed.'

'Thanks!' *What a convenient excuse*, a little voice inside her head whispered.

'Hey, I said I was sorry,' he answered.

To Sarah's amazement, his eyes were full of regret. But was it regret for not trusting her or for not having back-up in what might have been a tight situation last night?

'All right. Forget it,' she said. 'Can't be undone.' She thought about it for a second. 'Does that mean you trust me?'

A smile tugged at the corner of his mouth. 'Maybe, Irish, just maybe.' He gave her a gentle dig with his elbow. 'We are in this together now, for better or worse. No more withholding information, OK?'

'Agreed!'

The phone box was situated outside the station entrance. Not ideal, being so public, but speed was of the essence. Sarah looked on nervously as Anderson went through the same rigmarole as the previous evening before he got through to Everleigh on a secure line. With the station being so busy, she hoped it would put anyone off trying

185

to finish what they had started the night before. She kept watch all the same. As she listened, Anderson brought the colonel up to date.

'Did Special Branch have any luck rounding up McGrath or Evans?' He listened for a moment, then shook his head at Sarah. 'I see. That's a pity. I was hoping they might give us a lead if we could get them to talk. I don't believe there is any point in us staying in Newport. A few loose ends, sir, yes. We had to abandon the hire car and the hotel bill. Can someone at your end look after those? Thank you.' There was a pause. 'Yes, sir. At this juncture, I believe how we proceed is up to her. I'll put her on.' Anderson handed Sarah the receiver.

'Sarah, are you all right?' Everleigh asked.

'Yes, sir. A bit shaken but glad to be away from that hotel,' she answered.

'I suppose we should have expected something so brazen.'

'Thankfully, Anderson did, sir.' Anderson raised a brow and smiled back at her.

'I think it best you both return to London immediately,' the colonel said. 'Luckily, we have been able to warn all our agents in Thomas's network. All are safe for now and on their way back to London or elsewhere for reassignment.'

'That's a relief, sir. The IRA acted so fast last night I was afraid they might have succeeded in eliminating some of the others. We couldn't have been the only targets.' She glanced at Anderson. 'The thing is, sir, I agree with Anderson. I'm not so sure about us returning to London. That's probably what they'd expect us to do. I think we could still pick up Thomas's trail. At least we could verify for you if he has left the country. If he hasn't, we can try to track him down.

Either way I think our best bet is to check things out in Fishguard. And, sir, I am hoping it is still possible to find my father if his cell is running that escape route.'

'Unfortunately, Thomas will have told the IRA that we know about the route. They will have closed it down or moved it. I doubt you'll be able to track down anyone involved.'

Sarah sighed. 'You're probably right.'

'However, I can't deny that it would be useful to know where Thomas has gone,' he said. 'And obviously, any information pertaining to your father would be beneficial. Well, Fishguard it is then.'

'Yes, sir. We are already at the station. There's a train in half an hour.'

'Very well. You'll need new identities and somewhere to stay in Fishguard. I suggest you hook up with a friend of mine. He is running a small SOE station there. Let me just check the address.'

Sarah looked at Anderson. 'The colonel has a contact we can stay with in Fishguard.'

'Sarah?' Everleigh was back on the line. 'Yes, they have taken over a small hotel called The Bay Lodge. Shouldn't be hard to find; the locals will know it. I can radio ahead and tell him to expect you.'

'That would be great. Thank you, sir. Could you send us a picture of Aled Thomas as well? It would be useful to have it to show it to people. Most likely, he was travelling under a false name. A photo may help us track his movements more easily.'

'Yes, that won't be a problem. I'll have your new documents and the photographs despatched by train later today. You should get them by tonight,' he confirmed.

'Thank you, sir. What is the station commander's name?' Sarah asked. Anderson raised a brow in query. She shook her head at him and turned away.

'Hinchcliffe. We served together in the last war. He'll see you right,' Everleigh said. Another long pause. 'Sarah, if things get out of hand, there would be no shame in abandoning this mission. These men will stop at nothing to protect their network and we both know what your father is capable of.'

'That's true, sir. But we are forewarned now by the attempt on my life last night, and hopefully they won't take us by surprise again. Whether or not my father is behind this, I am determined to finish the job. I'm only glad Thomas didn't know my true identity.'

'Indeed. Very well. Let me know when you arrive. The SOE station will have secure comms. And, Sarah?'

'Yes, sir?'

'Best of luck.'

21

20th February 1942, Fishguard

Sarah and Anderson's train pulled into Fishguard Harbour station at midday. To her delight, Sarah could smell the sea and hear the lapping of the waves as they disembarked. As the harbour wall was only feet away from the station plat-form, Sarah walked over to the barrier and stood looking out to sea, breathing deeply. After the awfulness of the previous day, the scene had a soothing effect. She had spent the entire journey trying to ignore the horrible, hunted sensation she had felt since discovering the attempt on her life. To think someone had cold-bloodedly gained access to her room with the intent of killing her almost made her falter. Indeed, only Anderson's solid presence was keeping the panic at bay. Except, of course, there were niggling doubts about his intentions. But could she trust her own judgement? Hadn't she been wrong before? She came to the conclusion that she would have to trust him for now.

Completing the mission without his help would be almost impossible.

Fishing boats were bobbing at their moorings in the harbour, and in the distance, Sarah could see a steamer approaching the port. Several more ferries were moored alongside the quay. The seaport was busier than she had expected.

Anderson appeared at her side. 'Charming enough place, I suppose, but let's find this Hinchcliffe guy and get settled in somewhere. I need to catch up on my sleep.'

Sarah glanced at him in surprise. 'I thought you slept OK last night. There was certainly plenty of snoring coming from your part of the room.'

He responded with a dirty look. 'And I could say the same! I woke up a few times. Now I am wondering if it wasn't noise from our would-be assassins that disturbed me. At the time, I put it down to the discomfort of the chair.'

'What happened to *sailors can sleep anywhere*?' she asked with a grin.

'I must be out of practice. Come on; let's find this SOE set-up.'

'Hold up a minute, there's something I wanted to say. Last night could have ended differently. You took on the responsibility of protecting us—'

He threw up a hand. 'There's no need—'

'No, please, there is! Only you stood between us and certain execution if they had chosen your room first instead of mine,' she said. 'I'm really grateful to you.'

Anderson shrugged and to her surprise he looked embarrassed, not meeting her eye. 'I'm a great believer in fate, Irish. Guess our time wasn't up.'

Sarah suddenly felt bad. She really had underestimated

Anderson. He would have attempted to keep them safe if the worst had happened last night. Her doubts about him were silly, surely? And could be explained easily enough.

Following the directions given by one of the train station porters, Sarah and Anderson climbed the hill towards The Bay Lodge. However, only a few yards from the harbour, Sarah gasped and clutched Anderson's sleeve.

'That's Thomas's car, I'm sure of it,' she exclaimed, pointing to a Morris 10 parked up at the side of the road.

'You're right!' Anderson replied. 'Well spotted.' He tried the door. It was unlocked. He slipped into the driver's seat and poked around. 'Nothing!'

'Well, I guess this confirms he did leave from here,' Sarah said.

'Or,' Anderson said, getting out of the car, 'he was happy to leave this here to make us believe that. He may have changed vehicle and be halfway to Scotland by now. We really do need that photograph. I won't be happy until we have a positive identification from someone at the port who saw him board a boat. All right. Let's continue. I'll come back later and give it a thorough examination.'

Ten minutes later, they reached the hotel. Tall, ornate pillars and metal gates stood at the entrance to the grounds. A high stone-clad wall formed the perimeter.

'I wasn't expecting anything this grand,' Sarah said, looking up at the building.

'Let's hope it's more welcoming than that last place,' Anderson quipped.

Sarah laughed and pointed to the sign on the gate. 'Maybe not so welcoming.' The sign said 'keep out by order of the Ministry of Works' and a heavy-duty padlock secured the gates. A few feet away, on the other side of the gates, was a small hut with a man in uniform sitting inside. Sarah waved to him. The sentry nodded back, but immediately reached for a phone.

'Do we climb over?' Sarah asked, half-joking, as Anderson walked down by the perimeter wall, craning his neck to see into the grounds. Moments later he returned, saying: 'No need. Someone's coming.'

A young man in blue overalls appeared. He nodded to the guard and approached the gate. His sweeping gaze sized them up. 'Lieutenant Anderson?' he asked.

'That's me,' Anderson replied.

'May I see your papers, sir, please?'

Anderson pulled out his ID and flashed it. 'I believe we are expected.'

'Yes, sir. I'm Pat Nevis, by the way. I've been keeping an eye out for the train. Reckoned you were on the one that passed a wee while ago.' The lad nodded to the guard, who unlocked the padlock and pulled one gate open enough for them to pass through.

'And you are, miss?' Nevis asked Sarah.

'Sarah Gillespie.'

'Also MI5?' he asked.

'Yes,' she replied, showing him her ID.

'Very good,' he said. 'Welcome to Fishguard.' The guard locked the gate again and took up a position at the hut entrance.

'Can't be too careful,' Nevis said as they walked up the gravel driveway. 'We don't like folk snooping around. Come this way, please.'

They followed him towards the front door, which was

overshadowed by a metal and glass canopy. Before following the men inside, Sarah paused on the steps and gave in to her curiosity, gazing down towards the sea. A ray of February sunshine punctuated the clouds. Where it touched the water, the sea shimmered a deep green. For one brief moment, she was transported back home to Ireland, to Dollymount Beach, and to the last time she and Paul had walked along the shore. It had been one of their favourite spots. Her stomach clenched. It didn't do to indulge such memories. With a sigh, she pulled herself back to the present and followed Anderson and Nevis into the lobby.

'I gather there are no guests staying here,' Anderson was saying as she caught up with them.

'No, sir. We have commandeered most of the place, but due to the nature of our work, it was thought best to close the hotel entirely. We have our own staff looking after the cooking and such. Now, if you'd like to follow me, Hinch is waiting for you upstairs.'

'Hinch?' Anderson queried. Sarah also wondered at the nickname.

The man coloured slightly. 'Oh, sorry, Captain Hinchcliffe. He's our chief. But we don't stand on ceremony here. We're a tight team. Most of us are army engineers and mechanics.'

Anderson shared an amused look with Sarah as they climbed the stairs to the second floor. Sarah guessed that, just like herself, Anderson was dying to know what these people were working on.

The room they entered was extraordinary. Every inch of space was crammed with gadgets and bits of equipment. Sarah could not begin to guess what any of it was for.

Captain James Hinchcliffe stood, hands braced on a table by the window, viewing a map. A tall, thin man, his face was deeply tanned, suggesting a love of the outdoors. His grey hair stood up in tufts as though he were continually running his hands through it. Piercing blue eyes assessed them as soon as he was aware of their presence.

Anderson stepped forward and carried out the introductions.

'Glad you made it. Old Everleigh was in a panic about you two,' Hinchcliffe said, shaking their hands in turn. 'Sounds like you had a close call last night.'

It surprised Sarah that Everleigh had told the man so much. Obviously, he trusted him but was that not foolish given all they had learned in the last twenty-four hours? Even those who appeared trustworthy could be hiding the darkest of secrets.

'Take a pew,' the captain said, clearing a large metal object from a chair for Sarah.

Anderson walked over to the window and peered out. 'Pleasant location, sir.'

'What?' Hinchcliffe asked. 'Oh yes, perfect for our purposes.'

Anderson shared an amused glance with Sarah. 'I imagine this place is usually popular with tourists.'

The captain scratched his head. 'I dare say, but I can't allow 'em to stay here at the moment. We'll be here for the duration of the war, I imagine.'

'What is it you do here, sir?' Anderson asked. 'That's if you are allowed to tell us.'

Hinchcliffe rubbed his chin and frowned at him. 'Research and testing, young man. Let's leave it at that.'

Anderson nodded.

'Now, tell me what exactly you need from us besides a bed for tonight?' Hinchcliffe asked with a smile.

'Firstly, sir, we need to let the colonel know we have arrived safely,' Sarah said.

'That's not a problem. I'll have Nevis do that for you,' he replied.

'Thank you. I assume Colonel Everleigh has told you why we have come to Fishguard?' she asked.

The captain nodded. 'Something about a mole?'

'Yes, sir,' she replied. 'We are here to trace a double agent. It is our belief he has left the country from here, but we need to confirm it. We found his car abandoned on the road from the harbour. If he hasn't left, it suggests he has assumed another identity and moved elsewhere. If that is the case, we need to run him to ground. Do you know who might be able to help us?'

'Certainly; the chaps down at the port authority should be able to assist. It's a busy place, Fishguard, a lot of through traffic with regular ferry crossings over to Ireland to both Rosslare and Cork. Bit of a nightmare if you want to monitor who's arriving and departing. Glad that's not my brief, but I understand those chaps are pretty thorough.'

'Our problem is that this man most likely had false documents of the highest quality,' Sarah said. 'Until his photograph comes through from London, there is little we can do to investigate. We are hoping what we need will be on the next train to arrive from London.'

'Well, the next one is due in late this evening,' the captain replied. 'In the meantime, we can put you up here for tonight. But it can only be temporary. I'd suggest we would need to find you accommodation elsewhere. If you were to remain here, it would look odd and draw attention to you.'

'Yes, it would. Thank you, sir. We are awaiting new documentation as our previous cover stories are no longer viable,' Anderson explained. 'Our mole has seen to that.'

'Those bounders! They really sicken me. Put them up against a wall and shoot the lot of them, I say. Best of luck to you. I hope you track him down. Once your new papers are here, we can make arrangements for you. There is an excellent guesthouse a little further down the hill towards the harbour if you want to play tourist. In the meantime, I suggest you get some rest and a bite to eat here.'

'That sounds ideal, sir,' Sarah said. 'Thank you.'

'I notice your security is tight, Captain. Have you any reason to suspect your activities are being monitored?' Anderson asked.

'Nothing concrete. In recent months we have tightened things up, due in part to MI5's claims that republicans are running amok around here. The locals know we are military, but no more than that. We try to keep a low profile and I'm sure there are many who are curious about us. However, we're not hermits by any means. Friday and Saturday nights usually find us down at the Royal Oak pub. You'd be welcome to join us if you are still around. I can put it about that you are friends.'

'Thank you, sir,' Anderson said, winking at Sarah from behind Hinchcliffe's back. 'I do love a pint of warm English beer.'

But Sarah felt uneasy. What if there were republicans about – wouldn't they be curious about any newcomers? Running a clandestine operation out of the town would make them wary of strangers.

22

20th February 1942, Fishguard

Sarah was assigned a dormer room on the top floor of the hotel. Nevis assured her she had the entire floor to herself; all the men's accommodation was on the floor below. The room was a little dusty, but once she had made the bed with fresh linen and cleaned as best she could, she was delighted to have her own space again. What a luxury not to have to share with Anderson like the night before. Yes, it had felt safe to have him close by and, considering what had occurred, it had probably saved her life. But it had been extremely unnerving, and had felt wrong not only because Paul had passed so recently, but it wasn't something good Catholic girls did! Not that anything *had* happened, of course, or ever would. But she couldn't help dwelling on that notion for a few moments and felt the colour flood her cheeks. *Oh, dear!*

But now what? There was nothing they could do without

Thomas's photograph. It was frustrating to have to sit and wait; she suddenly felt powerless. Might the IRA be in pursuit? Passively waiting to be executed was not a pleasant notion. Sarah longed to act. But what could they do, other than verify that Thomas had boarded a ferry or, if he had not, try to pick up his trail? Unless . . . A mad and dangerous idea began to form in her head. Would Anderson agree to it? She had a sneaking suspicion he just might.

In the meantime, she should get some rest. She lay on top of the bed, trying to relax, but her thoughts were a jumble. If she were honest, she was still a bit jittery after seeing those bullet holes in the linen that morning. Close shaves with death were becoming a little too frequent for her liking. Thank goodness Anderson had thought to make it look like someone was sleeping in that bed, otherwise the assassin might have come to Anderson's room to seek them out. How on earth had they discovered what rooms they were in? Had someone in the hotel been in cahoots? Again, it begged the question why her room was the target, not Anderson's. Wasn't it convenient that no one had attempted to enter his room? No, no, she couldn't let her thoughts stray in that direction. If she couldn't trust him, all was lost, and she might as well pack and take a train back to London.

A few more minutes, and she knew the longed-for nap was elusive. If she could burn off some energy, it might stop her speculating and unnerving herself. After a morning sitting on the train, what she really needed was a brisk walk, she thought. She swung her legs off the bed and stared out the window. The sun was streaming in, tempting her outdoors even though she knew it was bitterly cold out. But a walk by the sea always improved her mood. It wouldn't be a bad idea to get the lie of the land. She had certainly failed in that respect in Newport. To her shame, Anderson had shown far more presence of mind and, as a result, likely saved their lives. Could there be a risk in going out alone? They might have been followed from the station earlier. However, she felt a sudden need to prove herself worthy.

The guard opened the gate for Sarah, wished her a pleasant walk and locked it after her. They really were taking security seriously. She crossed the road and stood for a while looking over the hedgerow, taking in the view of Fishguard Bay below. The sea shimmered blue, green and grey depending on where the sun fell upon it and the town looked quaint from up here, for all the world like rows of dolls' houses. However, her vantage point was exposed and the breeze coming off the sea was sharp, chilling her cheeks with its icy fingers. Perfect for blowing the cobwebs away.

She headed down the hill, her mood lightening with each step. But to her consternation, when she reached the spot where Thomas's car had been, it had vanished. Could Anderson have taken it somewhere? But as far as she knew, there hadn't been any keys left in the car. Unless Anderson knew how to start a car without one. Now, wouldn't that be a useful skill to have?

She continued down to the harbour, retracing their steps from earlier, past the docked boats at the quayside, and headed out towards the breakwater. The structure comprised three distinct horizontal tiers with steep steps cut into them to form stairs. As she drew nearer, she saw a couple of children running along the lower tier, an anxious parent below trying to keep up. Once she was at the start of the breakwater, she could see the lighthouse standing proud at the end. There was a large concrete structure partly obstructing the walkway, close to it. She had no idea what it was and was curious to find out. Either way, Sarah judged the lighthouse to be a ten-minute walk, and as good an objective as any.

As she strolled along, she looked out over the water. It was such a peaceful scene, giving the impression that life was almost normal, with some small boats travelling through the more tranquil water behind the breakwater. Sarah reckoned they were fishing trawlers, their crews swathed in yellow oilskins and thick woolly hats. For several minutes, she stood and watched a ferry heading out towards the open sea. Some of the passengers were on the deck and she wondered if they were nervous as they headed out into the unprotected waters. She still recalled her own crossing of the Irish Sea; the crew and her fellow travellers showing every sign of nerves as tales of attacks on ships were talked about in muted tones. Sarah wondered which route the ferry was taking; Cork or Rosslare? And much to her surprise, she felt a pang of homesickness. How bizarre! That was the second time today the sea had stirred memories of her homeland.

Would she ever return? Maybe someday, when the war was over, it would be interesting to return to North Strand and search out previous friends and neighbours. But the thought left her uncomfortable. She had changed, and what would going back achieve? They were all gone now, those who mattered. Maura, Paul and Ma. Best to remember Dublin as it was during her childhood, unblemished by the realities of war, loss and lies. Yes, she was not the same person anymore. Once Da was dealt with, she could consider the future. That was assuming she survived, of course.

The ferry disappeared behind the breakwater and Sarah continued down the path towards the lighthouse. She had always been fascinated by them, and as a child she had imagined it would be fun to live in one. Da had laughed at her when, only six years old, she had asked if they could have one in their back garden. Romantic nonsense, he'd said. Typical Da. Even when they were little he had constantly crushed their dreams. She wondered if it were possible to see the beam from The Bay Lodge, then shook her head in disappointment. Of course, with blackout, the beam must be switched off as the lighthouse would be far too convenient a landmark for the Luftwaffe.

The yelping of a dog drew her attention to the furthest end of the breakwater. A man stood talking to an elderly couple, the dog at their feet clearly unhappy with the interruption to his walk. As Sarah drew closer, she recognised Anderson. Drat! She felt the colour rush into her cheeks as her stomach clenched. This was ridiculous and of course, now, he would think she had followed him down here. Too late. He had spotted her and waved. He took his leave of the couple and walked towards her.

'Afternoon,' she said, trying for nonchalant.

'Afternoon.'

'What have you done with Thomas's car?' she asked as they fell into step.

'Nothing yet. I was going to look at it on my way back. Why do you ask?'

'It's gone!'

'What?' He came to a stop and stared at her in disbelief.

'I assumed you had moved it,' she said.

'No. It was still there when I passed.' He peered at his watch. 'That would have been about twenty minutes ago.'

'Then who could have taken it?'

Anderson scratched his head. 'Probably whoever was helping him leave the country. Damn! I should have searched it more thoroughly when I had the chance.'

'That confirms the IRA are here, though, doesn't it?' It wasn't a pleasant thought.

Anderson nodded, looking very put out. They walked without speaking for several minutes.

'Hey, sorry. I should have asked if you wanted to come along on a walk, but I assumed you'd had enough of my company in the last day or so,' he said.

'Probably best I don't answer that. Anyway, I thought you were tired,' she answered.

'Nah, wasn't happening. I mooched around a bit, but it made those SOE guys nervous,' he said with a mischievous smile. 'Hinchcliffe *strongly* recommended I go for a walk. As it happened, I couldn't bear the thought of being cooped up all day in that place, so I came down here. The captain's very reticent about his work, isn't he? I'd love to know what they are up to.'

'I suppose he has to be circumspect, and he doesn't know us. We need to be too.'

Anderson quirked his mouth. 'True, but the more secretive they are, the more curious I become.'

'Well, don't upset Hinchcliffe. We do need his help.'

'Don't worry, Irish, I won't blow it,' he replied.

They continued towards the lighthouse. 'You hate being idle, don't you?' she said at last.

'Habit, I guess. On ship, it's always busy.'

'Do you miss being at sea?' she asked.

'I do. There are days I regret joining Intelligence, but it seemed like a good career move at the time. The opportunity to be stationed in London rather swayed it. Little did I realise how complicated life would become. Life on board is much more . . . well, simple, I suppose. You have your duties, and you just get on with them.'

'Not much room for using your brain, though,' Sarah remarked. 'I don't think I would be very good at following orders without question.'

Anderson chuckled. 'That I can believe. But a ship cannot run smoothly if people don't follow orders. The navy is very important, Irish,' he said with a frown, but then he laughed. 'There! You've done it again!'

'What?'

'I don't know what it is about you, but you always manage to get under my skin.'

Sarah couldn't help but grin. 'It's a talent I have perfected in the last two weeks, but I have no idea what has prompted it,' she said airily.

'There you go again!'

She stopped and, hands on hips, she glared at him. 'Seriously, you were so nasty that first week. What did you expect from me? That I would just take it lying down? You don't know me at all, Anderson. You made stupid assumptions based on my nationality and sex.'

He bit his lip. 'OK, I'll admit I probably misjudged you.'

'Probably! Why, thank you!' she replied.

'Perhaps if you were a little less fiery . . .'

'And you were a little less annoying,' she replied, holding his gaze.

He spluttered. 'I can't help it!'

Sarah's irritation fizzled and she increased her pace. They walked on in silence for a few minutes more. Why was it they could never have a conversation without jumping down each other's throats? Their mission might be safer ground. 'Have you given any thought about how to proceed? You see, I've had an idea.'

'Shoot,' he said.

'I was thinking . . . well, I don't know how you'd feel about this, but I think we need to shake things up a bit.'

A brow shot up. 'OK,' he drawled, 'I'm interested.'

'I suggest we try to flush out these republicans into the open. Then we will have a better chance of finding my father. We don't know where they are, but I bet they'd come running if they knew *we* were here. After all, they were mighty keen to find us in Newport.'

'Well, well, Irish, I have to say you surprise me,' he said with a grin. 'I think that is a fine idea, particularly as I don't want to spend more time than necessary in this place. We both have lives to get back to. True?'

'Yes, exactly. I thought that if we ask enough questions at the port and in the town about Thomas, word is bound to get to them,' Sarah said. 'Mind you, setting ourselves up as bait might be considered mad by some people.'

'Yes, but I'm game if you are; it has to be worth a shot. As soon as we have those photographs, we can get stuck in.'

Although her stomach turned, for she was not naive – this would be highly dangerous – being proactive appealed to her. 'OK. Let's do it. Should we try to persuade

Hinchcliffe to let us stay at the SOE station? I'd feel less exposed there.'

'It's too well guarded, Sarah. No, let's stick with the original plan and stay at the guesthouse. They are far more likely to attempt something there. We will be ready for them.' Anderson grinned down at her. 'You have hidden depths, Irish.'

Sarah couldn't help but smile; a compliment from Anderson – perhaps there would be a blue moon tonight!

By now, they had almost reached the end of the break-water. 'Oh, that's what it is,' she said. The concrete bunker she had seen from the far end was a gun emplacement. However, it was unmanned. 'I wonder if they've had to use it. Why would the Luftwaffe bomb here?'

'The harbour is infrastructure. Always in their sights, Sarah. Anything to disrupt us.'

'I suppose so.'

Anderson shrugged and walked on. He climbed up the steps to the first tier at the base of the lighthouse. Leaning on the railing, he beckoned to her. 'We can walk back along the other side of the wall. Great view from up here.'

Sarah clambered up beside him. The Irish Sea stretched out before her. In the distance, she could just make out the ferry she had seen earlier.

'What's that sigh for?' he asked.

She pointed to the ferry. 'Seeing it made me think of home and the life I left behind. I could never have imagined, only a year ago, how my life would change.'

'Or that you would lose so many loved ones?' he asked gently. Sarah could only nod in response, as first Maura and then Paul's features flashed before her. After a few moments, she regained her composure and gave him a somewhat sad smile. 'I have to move forward. We all do. We cannot dwell in the past.'

'Still, it must be hard to be so close to home,' he said, looking out across the water. 'And yet it is out of reach.'

'No more than you, and you must be about four thousand miles from home.'

'At least. I miss my family, for sure, but not home as such. I grew up on a farm, but I always knew it wasn't the life for me. I wanted to travel and see the world. My father didn't take it well when I enlisted. Couldn't understand it. I feel kinda bad for them. My sister went to New York about a year ago, so now my folks are on their own. I left a sweet girl behind, too.'

'But you have Clara now,' she said, watching keenly for his reaction.

His mouth quirked. 'Trust me, no one has Clara. She's as elusive as a butterfly.'

They rounded the corner and started back towards the harbour. Something about his comment didn't ring true to her. If their relationship was so tentative, why did Clara write to him at Newport? With a sinking feeling, Sarah realised she'd have to watch out for any further letters turning up for him. If he gave Clara their new address, it would be something of a red flag and she would have to inform Everleigh.

Here we go again, she thought, *I hate having to second-guess everyone and everything.* Just when she thought she could trust this man, he always said or did something to unsettle her.

And suddenly, she yearned for the tranquillity of the Tracing Room at Supermarine.

23

20th February 1942, Fishguard

After dinner, Hinchcliffe invited Sarah and Anderson to join him and the other officers for a drink. Sarah guessed the room was previously the guests' lounge. It was a large space with comfortable sofas and tables scattered about and one wall was lined with floor-to-ceiling bookcases. Spotting a vacant chair close to the fire, Sarah pounced on it.

Anderson was standing at the bar, chatting away to Nevis. She envied him a little. He had a knack for blending in and talking to people, making them feel at ease. Easy charm. That was his trick, she thought. But what was behind it? It bothered her that she had been in his company all week, but still knew so little about him. Yes, he had opened up a bit about his family this afternoon, but his remarks about Clara were odd. Did his feelings for the woman run deep and, if so, why the flippant comments?

But how he really felt about Sarah was a mystery, too.

He had admitted he had misjudged her, but was that admission sincere? Up to now, she had thought he was dismissive, as if he didn't rate her. But in the last twenty-four hours, something had shifted. She had no doubt his quick thinking had saved her life the previous night. Her lack of experience had been thrown into relief by his adept assessment of what was happening. And he had cared enough to protect her. Mind you, it was likely he just regarded her as a young woman out of her depth, but today she had caught a glimmer of respect, liking almost. He was a hard man to read. Perhaps he didn't like that she was wise to his type and didn't fall for some old patter like some girls did. As it was, she was grateful he'd never tried anything on with her. She didn't need that kind of complication. Paul's death was still far too raw. She kept pushing the memories down. If she didn't imagine what had happened to that ship, she didn't have to accept he was dead. Was it crazy to hope? There was a tiny flicker, and she felt honour bound to keep it alive until such time as they found a body.

Hinchcliffe interrupted her thoughts. 'Miss Gillespie, may I join you?' he asked. 'Oh, I do believe you are lacking a drink? What's your poison?'

Sarah smiled up at him. 'A G&T would be super, sir, thank you.'

'Won't be a jiff,' he said before heading over to where Anderson and Nevis were holding forth amid much hilarity. She was too far away to hear.

Hinchcliffe returned in due course with her drink and pulled up a chair beside her.

'Is your room decent? I'm afraid us chaps aren't great at

keeping the rest of this place in order. No ladies here to tell us off. Do you know, I don't believe I've ever been up on the third floor.'

'It's fine, sir, and lovely and quiet. I managed to catch up on some sleep after my walk this afternoon.'

'Ah! Where did you go?'

'Down to the lighthouse.'

'One of my favourite walks around here. I like to go down when there's a swell. Can be pretty impressive with the waves coming over the wall.'

'I can imagine,' she replied.

'There are plenty of pleasant walks in the area and some dramatic scenery. If you have the time, go up to Fishguard Fort, up on the headland opposite. Fabulous views from up there on a clear day,' he said.

'Yes, I wouldn't mind getting more exercise. I feel as though I have done nothing but get in and out of trains and cars all week. That sounds an ideal spot.'

'By the way, before I forget, that train is due in around ten-thirty this evening. Your documents should be on it. I'll have one of my lads nip down and pick them up for you.'

'That would be wonderful, thanks. We are eager to get to work as quickly as possible before the trail goes cold. And I'm sure you'd like us out from under your feet.'

'Not a bit of it.' Hinchcliffe smiled at her, but his gaze was uneasy. 'However, you will be more comfortable at the guesthouse. Better suited to keeping your cover intact, too. The locals are an inquisitive lot.'

It was obvious from his demeanour Hinchcliffe didn't want them to find out what they were working on in this station. But, like Anderson, that only made her curiosity more intense. Perhaps Everleigh might tell her when they got back to London. Sarah nodded politely and changed the subject. 'I would have thought most of the tourist accommodation would be closed this time of year. Would there normally be tourists here in winter?' she asked.

'I'm not sure; it's my first winter here, but from what I can see, most people time their arrival by train to catch the next ferry. I believe one of the bigger guesthouses down at the harbour is open, but I can't imagine they are terribly busy.'

'Is that where we will be staying?' she asked.

'No. A friend of mine, Mrs Jones, has a lovely place just down the road from here. She will be happy to facilitate you. As I said, it wouldn't be appropriate for you to stay here.' He paused, as if searching for the right words. 'We are extremely busy. So much so, that the days fly by, despite such a long and miserable winter. It was lovely last summer. We used to sit out on the veranda in the evenings with our drinks and listen to the wireless.' He took a sip of his drink. 'So, young lady, Colonel Everleigh speaks highly of you. A rising star, no less.'

'Oh no, sir, my stint in MI5 will be extremely short. I intend to return to my old job as soon as I have completed this mission.'

'And what were you doing before Everleigh sunk his claws in?'

Sarah smiled; never was a turn of phrase so apt. 'I worked as a tracer at Supermarine.'

'Aha! You must know a mutual friend of mine and Everleigh's, Miss Olivia Whitaker.'

'She was my manager.'

'What a small world. I served with Everleigh under the general, her father. A fine man.'

'The colonel spoke of him very fondly . . . and Miss Whitaker,' Sarah said, hoping Hinchcliffe might reveal something of Miss Whitaker's relationship with Everleigh.

'We were all in love with her, you know, your Miss Whitaker. Stunning woman in her youth. I do hope age has been kinder to her than it has been to me.'

'She is a fine-looking lady and someone you would always want on your side. I owe her a lot,' she said.

He threw her a quizzical glance, but she couldn't tell him anything further without revealing Olivia Whitaker was an MI5 agent.

'In those days she was a crack shot and a beautiful dancer, two things us soldiers find hard to resist.' For a moment he was lost in a memory, a smile on his face. 'But as for her mother —' he gave an exaggerated shudder '— she was an absolute tyrant. Everleigh was sweet on Olivia, but Mrs Whitaker did her best to split them up. No young upstart from Yorkshire with no family connections was good enough for her only daughter. Succeeded too, the old bat. Such a shame, you know. They would have been perfect for each other. Well, when you return to Supermarine, please pass on my regards to her.'

'I will, sir.'

'Excellent,' he said, finishing his drink.

'Sir, I wonder if I might ask a favour, please?'

'Certainly.' He smiled at her.

'Would it be possible for me to make a call to London? A friend of mine is ill, and I wanted to check in on her.'

'Of course. There is a phone down in the reception area – in the little back office. You may use that; it's nice and private.'

'Thank you,' Sarah replied.

'Now, if you will excuse me, I'll bid you good night. I need to finish some paperwork. No rest for the wicked, eh? We can talk again in the morning.'

Hinchcliffe was only out the door when Anderson took over his seat. 'Any news on our post?' he asked Sarah.

'He said someone will fetch it for us from the ten-thirty train.'

'Good. Are you ready for another drink?' he asked.

'No, thanks, I'm fine. I want to keep a clear head for the morning. Did you learn anything interesting from Nevis? Anyone I've spoken to is very tight-lipped about what they do here.'

'No, I'm afraid none of my probing bore fruit. But if we are around for a few days we are bound to figure out what they are doing.'

'I doubt it. As soon as our papers are in, Hinchcliffe wants to move us to that guesthouse.'

'That's a shame,' he answered. 'I guess it would be rude to go snooping again.'

'Yes, Anderson, it would!'

A cheeky grin lit up his face.

'So, if our stuff arrives tonight as planned, we can make a start in the morning,' she said, trying to ignore the way his smile made her stomach flip. Why was she reacting to him like this all of a sudden? She didn't even trust him . . . at least, not fully. *Don't you go falling for this man*, she thought. *Life is complicated enough!*

'And we must make as much noise about it as possible,' he said.

'Agreed,' she replied.

Half an hour later, Sarah made her way down to the reception area. She put the call through to Judith's house and waited.

After a few rings, an unfamiliar female voice answered. 'Hello?'

'Hello. May I speak to Judith Lambe, please?'

'Sure, caller. She's in the top-floor flat, isn't she?

'Yes.'

'OK, just hold on a minute.'

Sarah heard the receiver being put down and envisaged the girl climbing the stairs to the top floor.

After a few minutes, a familiar voice came through. 'Hello?'

'Gladys! It's me,' Sarah said.

'Hi! How are you doing? Gosh, it feels like ages since we've seen you.'

'I wasn't expecting you'd be home. I thought you were on the evening shift this week,' Sarah said.

'Had to switch with someone else this evening. Long story. Are you OK?'

'I'm fine, thanks. I was hoping to catch Judith. Is she all right?'

'Yeah, why shouldn't she be? She's not here. Out with himself.'

Sarah had forgotten. This was the evening Judith planned to tell Gerald about the baby. 'She sounded a bit out of sorts when I spoke to her the other evening,' she explained.

'Well, she seems fine to me. Anyway, it's just me and Anne here at the moment. Oh, Sarah, this flat is so much better than Horgan's. When you return, we will have to find somewhere more like this to set ourselves up.'

'Sure. We can talk about it when I'm back in London. Listen, are you certain Judith is well?'

'What a mother hen you are. She's good. Are you taking care of yourself? How's our American friend?'

'Really annoying,' Sarah muttered, 'but I'm keeping him in his place, don't you worry.'

'Ha ha, no better woman than you, Sarah Gillespie. Any idea when you will return to London?' Gladys asked.

'Not at the moment. OK, look, our time is almost up. Say hello to Judith from me and try to behave yourself, Glad. I'll ring again when I get the chance.'

'Right-oh. Bye.'

Sarah hung up. It was disappointing not to have spoken directly to Judith; she was really worried about her. Would her cousin tell Gerald about her pregnancy, as she had indicated, or was she going to keep him in the dark and terminate the baby? Sarah couldn't help it. She had taken an instant dislike to Gerald. Cheating on his wife, no matter what the reason, showed a side to his character she could not stomach. She hated deceit.

24

21st February 1942, Fishguard

Early on Saturday morning, Sarah knocked on Anderson's door. A dishevelled figure, still in his pyjamas, answered after the third attempt to rouse him.

'My God, you look rough,' she remarked, sweeping past him.

'Do come in, Irish. But do you have to shout?' he asked with a grimace, closing the door. The room smelled of alcohol. 'I'll have you know my honour was at stake last night after you retired. Had to show those Brits who could hold their drink.'

'Pity you failed then,' she said, wrenching back the curtains and popping the blackout blind. She pushed up the window to let in some fresh air.

'Hey! It's Baltic!' he objected. He turned away, blinking. 'As always, you are a delight, dear Sarah.' He flopped down on the edge of the bed. 'What has you up so bright and early then?'

215

'It's eight o'clock; not early at all. And we have lots to do today.' He groaned as she handed him the large envelope that Nevis had given her late the previous evening. 'Our express post from London.'

He grunted and pulled out the contents she had already scanned through: a briefing note from Everleigh, two copies of Aled Thomas's photograph, two new passports, one American and one English, two ration books and identity papers in the name of Mr and Mrs Sanders. Lastly, two gold rings spilled out into his hand. Anderson chuckled.

'I don't see what you find so funny,' she snapped. 'This is ridiculous. As if we could pass ourselves off as married.'

'On the contrary,' he said as he finished reading Everleigh's note, 'it's perfect.'

'But on honeymoon!' she exclaimed in disgust.

'Why not? An American officer with his English bride. Love's young dream, in fact. Spending a few precious days together before he goes off to war. The perfect cover and quite romantic, isn't it?' He beamed up at her. 'And the kind of stupid ruse MI5 would propose. Our republican friends will see through it, don't you worry.'

'But it's hardly necessary for us to assume these identities now that we plan to flush them out. Besides, that ginger wig is disgusting!'

'Oh, come on; you were tired of that blonde one anyway, admit it,' he said, handing her the new wig which had been part of the package. 'Have to say, they did an outstanding job on these new papers, considering how short a time they had to work on them.' He glanced over Everleigh's note again. 'Would be a shame not to use 'em.'

'Oh yes, you're finding all of this hilarious, aren't you?'

Sarah said, picking at the wig before dropping it back down on the bed with distaste. There was no way she was ever going to wear it. Anderson shrugged, adding to her irritation. She plucked Everleigh's briefing note from his hand. 'What was he thinking?'

'I think it's a great idea, honey. Remember your vows to honour and obey?'

'Oh, shut up!'

'Is that any way to speak to your husband? Your time would be better spent practising an English accent,' he said, grinning up at her once more. 'Can't have you blowing our new cover.'

'But that is exactly what we *want* to do! Remember?' she said, doing her best not to snap.

His shoulders shook with silent laughter.

Sarah rolled Everleigh's letter up into a ball and chucked it at Anderson's head. He caught it, of course.

'First things first, my sweet; we need to debrief Hinchcliffe, then book into that guesthouse,' he said once he'd finished laughing.

It was an attractive laugh, she had to admit. And she liked the way his eyes crinkled. M*y goodness,* she thought, *this is dangerous territory! He is nothing more than an annoying colleague. If only he weren't quite so . . . attractive. I must remain professional*, she thought, digging her fingers into her palms.

'We can't check in until this afternoon. In the meantime, I suggest you sober up before you make a show of me in front of Hinchcliffe,' she replied, in a much brisker tone than she had intended.

'Yes, dearest wife, whatever you say.' His mouth turned

down at the corners as he slipped one of the rings onto his finger. He held the hand up and did a little wave as she turned and flounced out the door.

By the time they had eaten and said farewell to Hinchcliffe, Sarah was anxious to get moving. However, it was almost ten-thirty before they took the road down to the harbour.

'Are you sure you are happy to tackle the customs guys?' Anderson asked.

'Yes, of course,' she said.

'Let's hope someone recognises Thomas's photograph and wonders why we are asking questions.'

'It is a shame, though, if he got away,' Sarah said. 'He will do a lot of damage to the service if he gets to Berlin.'

'But would he have useful information outside of the network in Wales? I got the impression from Everleigh the harm Thomas could cause was minimal. Particularly as we were able to warn the other agents and get them out. They do their best to keep the agent networks separate for this very reason.'

'Well, I hope you are correct.'

They came to a stop at a fork in the road. A low-rise building further down was the customs office and to the right was the way down to the quay.

Anderson gazed down at the sea for a few moments before turning to her. 'I've been giving the set-up some thought. I reckon for that escape route, for want of a better term, to work best, the republicans must have had an inside man. Half the crews on those ferries and trawlers are Irish.'

'Not all Irish are republicans,' she snapped.

'Stop being so prickly, Sarah. I'm not suggesting they are, but I think it's a possibility.'

'All right, I agree that would make sense. But it isn't necessarily someone on the boats. One of the immigration staff could have been helping them too. Some people are happy enough to turn a blind eye purely for the money.'

'How deep are the IRA pockets, I wonder?' he asked.

'That I don't know. Though they do fundraise in the States.'

Anderson grimaced. 'That's all too true. Off you go, then. I'll meet you back at the SOE station. Good luck!'

Sarah watched him stroll down towards the water. She envied him a little. He exuded so much confidence. She still felt out of her league with all this espionage stuff. Wouldn't it be great if she succeeded this morning? Anderson would have to take her seriously then. She looked beyond Anderson, down to the harbour. The quay was busy with three boats moored. The ferry services ran every day, but she had no idea what volume of passengers passed through, especially this time of year. There also appeared to be an abundance of fishing trawlers coming and going and some of those crews had to be Irish, as Anderson had speculated. Hopefully, someone implicated in the escape route would become concerned at their questions and report it. Although she and Anderson could not control the consequences of that entirely, with luck, it would force the republicans out from the shadows. Sarah baulked at the thought of being confronted by McGrath or Da, but at least this whole mad mission could be wrapped up quickly and the pair would face the justice they deserved.

25

21st February 1942, Fishguard

Sarah waited anxiously in the hotel reception area for Anderson to return. She was unsure if she had achieved anything at the immigration office. Anyone she asked denied seeing Thomas, including a very officious man in charge and two officers who had been on duty the day Thomas most likely left. Hopefully, Anderson would have more success.

To kill some time, she picked up a couple of newspapers from the desk and took a seat at the window. The headline on one caught her eye. 'Darwin Bombed by Japanese'. The whole world was falling into the abyss now. If only there was some good news for a change.

But her mind was only half on what she read and soon her gaze blurred. Usually, she tried her best not to think of Paul, it could only distract her from the job at hand. But today, she longed to look at his picture, to remember his face, his voice or the way his eyes crinkled when he laughed. Was it because she was facing such danger? Could she find comfort in those memories she had been trying so hard to push away?

All she had was one photograph of him, but she now regretted having left it with her belongings in Judith's flat. She longed to be reminded of his face. That picture of him, staring proudly at the camera in his RAF uniform, was one he had sent in his last letter to her before he embarked for America. Perhaps his sister would be good enough to send her a few more if she asked. The idea cheered her up for a moment. But who was she kidding? A photograph could never take the place of a real, live, breathing person. Was she going to end up like some pathetic Miss Havisham figure, mourning the loss of what might have been, even in her dotage?

There was a tap on the window. Sarah jumped, then glowered back at Anderson. He beckoned her outside. She grabbed her coat.

'Well?' she asked when she caught up with him.

'Come down into the garden. Best we talk away from the hotel,' he answered. Intrigued, she had no choice but to follow. What had he discovered?

Through an arched gateway, he led her to a large lawned area, still half covered in snow. He headed for a bench in prime position, overlooking the sea. With a sweep of his hand, he removed most of the snow and sat down.

'Did you have any luck? Did anyone admit seeing Thomas?' he asked.

'No. But only two of the officers who were working on Thursday are there this morning. How about you?' Sarah asked.

'No luck either, I'm afraid. Though they'd hardly admit they were smuggling people in and out of the country to a complete stranger.'

'Well, let's hope we have rattled some cages and that we have done enough to draw attention to ourselves.'

'True. I suggest we stick around for a few days and cover as many of those boat crews as we can tomorrow.'

'And the shops and pubs, too,' Sarah said.

Slowly, he turned to her, his eyes alight. 'Yes, of course. Do you know, I suspect you are enjoying this, Irish.'

'Well, it is certainly different to tracing all day for a living. But have you given any thought to what to do when the IRA turn up? They are unlikely to be friendly,' she remarked with a grimace. 'I'm not even armed.'

'Don't worry. I'm sure that Nevis guy would be game to help out, maybe even Hinchcliffe. I get the impression life is monotonous and their experiments are proving troublesome. They are mostly army chaps and champing at the bit for some action. Nevis said he'd be in the local pub this evening. We could sound him out then. Maybe we could let it slip that we are using false identities when we are there. You know what these local pubs are like. Any small piece of juicy gossip will be around the town in no time.'

'Sure,' she replied. But her insides turned to lead. What a terrifying idea, but he was right; they had no other option, no matter how vulnerable she felt.

The guesthouse was halfway down the hill towards the harbour, one of several detached Victorian villas along that stretch of road. Most of them had 'no vacancies' signs up outside. Hinchcliffe had rung ahead and asked his friend,

Mrs Jones, to accommodate them as a favour, telling her Sarah and Anderson were newly wedded friends down from London.

Anderson raised his brows, his hand posed to grab the door knocker. 'Are you ready, Mrs Sanders?'

Sarah checked her ring was in place, made a face, then nodded.

A rotund, middle-aged lady with a beaming smile, who introduced herself as Mrs Jones, answered their knock. She enthused about their arrival and the fact that she had guests in the off-season.

As soon as Anderson said hello, she fell on him, shaking his hand vigorously. 'Oh, just fancy us having an American officer to stay. Wait till I tell my son, William. He'll be ever so pleased.' She sighed. 'You're *most* welcome, Lieutenant Sanders.'

Sarah wondered if she were invisible. The landlady clasped her hands together in delight and smiled up at Anderson. He always seemed to have that effect on women, young or old, Sarah thought with a wry smile.

'Thank you, Mrs Jones. We are mighty grateful you could accommodate us,' he said, exaggerating his accent and throwing his arm around Sarah's shoulders. 'It's all been a bit of a blur for Susie and me. We only got hitched on Thursday.'

Mrs Jones melted. 'Oh, so sweet, just like in the films.' She patted Sarah's arm. 'Aren't you the lucky girl?'

Anderson's fingers tightened on her arm, in warning. Sarah bit back a retort and instead smiled at the woman. 'Yes. I do appear to have scooped the grand prize.'

'As have I,' offered Anderson, but rather lamely. Stamping

on his foot was ever so tempting. Restraining the notion, however, Sarah smiled up into his face.

'Wonderful, wonderful,' Mrs Jones almost sang out. 'We have no other guests so you can have your pick of my rooms, but I might recommend number three to the front. It has some lovely views over the bay.'

Anderson beamed down at Sarah. 'That sounds perfect, Mrs Jones.'

'Off you go, then,' the landlady said with a wink at Anderson.

Resisting the urge to roll her eyes, Sarah headed up the stairs, Anderson following with their bags.

The room was bright and clean with floral wallpaper and some ancient furniture. Sarah avoided looking at the large double bed with its candlewick bedspread in bright blue. The sleeping arrangements might prove tricky. Anderson would hardly offer to sleep on a chair again.

The room, however, oozed old-fashioned charm. There was even a window seat in the nook at the window. If only she were here with Paul, she lamented as she made her way over to inspect the view. He'd have loved it here. Above the bare treetops, Sarah could glimpse sea and sky. Out further, beyond the harbour, she could see white horses riding the waves.

Anderson joined her. 'Nice place,' he said. 'I wouldn't mind bringing Clara somewhere like this.'

How strange, she thought, that he would echo my thoughts. But then an image of Anderson and Clara together, an image she'd rather not indulge, popped into her head. Sarah pushed it aside. 'Do you miss her?' she asked. She couldn't help it; she was deeply curious about his fancy girlfriend.

'I sure do,' he said, a trifle wistfully, she thought. 'Though I'm not sure it's her kinda place. More of a city girl, is Clara.'

'Yes, of course,' she replied, turning away from the window. She opened her case and unpacked. 'I suppose it's just as well she doesn't know about this little arrangement.'

'Oh, I don't know. I don't think she's the jealous type,' he said, sitting down on the seat.

'She has nothing to fear from me,' Sarah said with a scowl, pulling her nightdress out of her case. She squirmed and shoved it under one of the pillows.

'That's such a relief, Irish. I was afraid you might misbehave, cooped up with me here in the honeymoon suite.'

Sarah tilted her head and gave him her best disdainful glare. 'In your dreams, Anderson. Don't you fret. You're safe from me.'

'You are such a spoilsport,' he replied, before treating her to a cheeky grin. 'So, Irish, which side of the bed do you want?'

26

21st February 1942, The Royal Oak, Fishguard

There'll be a hard frost tonight, Sarah thought as she and Anderson walked down the hill into Fishguard. The freezing temperatures made the footpaths treacherous, even though most of the snow had melted. With the streetlights turned off, it was impossible to see the icy patches. At one point, Sarah saved herself from falling by grabbing onto Anderson's arm. After the second time, Anderson tucked her arm through his. She didn't object; it was a nice sensation.

'Sorry,' she said. 'These shoes have no grip.'

'No problem. Clara's the same, fashion before sense,' he replied, patting her hand. 'Better hang on. I don't fancy trying to find a hospital in these parts.'

'You're such a hero, Anderson.'

He sniffed. 'I do try.'

'And so modest. I'm surprised the Navy could spare such a paragon to come to England in the first place.'

'I wondered myself,' he said.

'As a matter of interest, how long have you been here?' she asked.

'Almost four years. It was only supposed to be for two, but I asked to stay on. Just my luck a war had to break out,' he replied.

'Did the lovely Clara have anything to do with you wishing to stay?'

He chuckled. 'She may have . . . or maybe it's the fabulous British weather.'

Why was he always so evasive when he spoke of Clara? Perhaps he was just a private person, which was something of a redeeming feature in her book. They walked on. For once, Sarah felt comfortable in Anderson's presence, although she wasn't sure she liked him any better. It was strange, though. In the past few days, she could look at him without wanting to punch him. Progress indeed. But his attitude to work impressed her, and his restless energy was contagious. All going well, they might conclude this assignment quickly and go back to London. For tonight, however, she didn't wish to dwell on what that would entail. She was looking forward to a relaxing evening.

The pub wasn't difficult to find, for they heard the babble of conversation and hoots of laughter before they rounded the corner onto Market Square. The building was double-fronted with sashed Georgian windows and there was an inscription above the door, but it was too dark to make out what it said. As they entered, a wall of smoke and the fumes of drink met them. The place was packed, giving Sarah a moment of anxiety. But she had no time to dwell on it as Anderson pushed her forward, his hand in the small of her back.

Sarah spotted Nevis, standing at the bar. 'He's over there,' she shouted over her shoulder. They pushed through the crowd.

'Hello, you two,' Nevis said when he observed them. 'It's a good hike down, isn't it? Good for giving one a thirst. What do you say, Anderson?' He slapped him on the shoulder. 'I'm getting a round in. What would you like?' They each gave him their order. Nevis pointed over to the far side of the bar. 'We have a table over there. Why don't you go on over, Sarah? I'm sure Anderson will help me with this lot,' he said, glancing at the drinks lining up on the bar.

Sarah pushed through, weaving her way through the maze of tables. Out of the corner of her eye, she spotted a face which seemed familiar. Another quick glance and she realised it was one of the immigration officers who had examined Thomas's photograph that morning. He looked up, catching her eye, but he showed no sign of recognition. He turned back to the conversation with his companions, all of whom had their backs to her. Must be a local, she thought, and moved on. As she neared the corner, she noticed Hinchcliffe, who smiled and beckoned her over. He shuffled up the bench so she could sit down beside him.

'Is Anderson with you?' he asked, scanning the crowd.

'Yes, he's up at the bar helping Nevis.' She looked around. 'Is it always this busy?'

'Invariably. Worse in summer when you get tourists as well. I usually avoid it then.' He glanced at her hair. 'I think I preferred the blonde.'

Sarah laughed. 'This is the real me. New identity, new look.' She had consigned the ginger wig to the bottom of her suitcase.

'I don't know how you do it. I'm sure I'd mess it up and forget what name I was using.'

'It's certainly not ideal. I was only just getting used to answering to Catherine Cavandish.'

Hinchcliffe tilted his head to look at her. 'I think I prefer it to Susie Sanders.'

'Yes, I don't think a lot of time was spent thinking that one up,' she replied.

'So, tell me, how is the charming Mrs Jones? I hope she made you welcome,' Hinchcliffe said.

'The house is lovely, thanks for arranging it.'

'Not at all.'

'She's very taken with Anderson. Very taken, indeed.'

Hinchcliffe guffawed. 'You must understand, there aren't many Yanks around these parts. She's bound to be—'

'Enamoured?'

'I was going to say star-struck,' he replied with a grin. 'Though I suppose we will see more and more of them in the next few months.'

'They are a ray of hope, sir, don't you think? Not Anderson particularly,' she grinned, 'but we now have a fighting chance to win this war, if you'll forgive the pun.'

'I agree, but we have a long way to go yet. That's why it's vital my work continues to be funded,' the captain said. He paused as if he was going to make another remark, but instead took a sip of his drink. 'And what you are doing is so important too.' Sarah wasn't sure how much Hinchcliffe knew of their mission, but she was pretty certain Everleigh would not have told him about her father. 'How did you get on down in the port this morning?' he asked.

Reluctant to say too much, she shrugged. 'Not much success, I'm afraid, but we will keep trying.'

Hinchcliffe gave her a look tinged with curiosity, but before he voiced it, the arrival of Nevis and Anderson with the round of drinks interrupted them.

An hour later, Sarah excused herself to go to the bathroom. As both cubicles were occupied, she would have to wait her turn. She did a double take at her image in the mirror above the sink, astonished by the white-faced creature staring back. Leaning in closer, she grimaced. How tired she looked, and her eyes were stinging from the smoke in the bar. She removed her glasses and placed them down on the sink before splashing her face with cold water. With a handkerchief from her handbag, she patted her face dry, feeling better already.

She heard the door to the bathroom open behind her and hoped the newcomer wasn't going to skip the queue. Then, to her astonishment, she felt a hand on her shoulder, quickly followed by an arm around the body, pinning her in an iron grip. Sarah struggled, but to no avail. Before she had a chance to cry out, a cloth was shoved over her mouth. A sweet smell flooded her nostrils.

To her horror, the last thing she saw in the mirror, as unconsciousness claimed her, was the smiling face of Jenny McGrath.

27

21st February 1942, Strumble Head, Pembrokeshire

Sarah came to, disorientated and nauseous. Her hands and feet were tied, and she was lying on a hard metal surface. And it was moving. She was certain she was in a vehicle travelling at speed, shaking her spine every time it went over a bump. There was a strong smell of diesel and a hint of manure, which suggested she was in a lorry or farm truck. Raising her head, she squinted, trying to make out if she was alone. It was too dark to tell. She listened intently, keeping her own breathing as shallow as she could. Still nothing. Should she try to sit up or would it be best to conserve her energy for whatever lay ahead?

Blast it! How had they found her so quickly? Her questions that morning must have triggered this. But who was the inside man? Had it been one of those immigration officers or one of the fishermen Anderson questioned? The fact that she had been taken and not Anderson suggested it might have been someone at the port offices. Though it was still possible one of those crew members Anderson had questioned had seen them together. It hardly mattered now, but hopefully Anderson would think along the same lines and investigate. It would be the only way to find any trace of where they might be taking her. But how much time did she have? They could be headed out of town to a quiet spot to finish her off.

And what about Anderson? How long would it take him to realise someone had snatched her? Would he think she had just got fed up and gone back to the guesthouse? If that were the case, it could be hours before he realised the truth. How on earth would he locate her? Her pulse raced and despite the chill, she was perspiring, adrenaline pumping through her. She couldn't fight her way out of this; she had no weapon. As panic threatened to envelope her, she forced herself to calm down and think. *If they had wanted to eliminate me, they would not be taking me on such a lengthy journey*, she told herself. It wouldn't take long to find an isolated place outside Fishguard to carry out a quick execution at this hour of the evening. She wasn't sure how long she had been out of it, but the truck had showed no signs of slowing down in the last ten minutes.

Jenny had recognised her, of that Sarah was sure. That may have saved her. Jenny would not execute Jim's daughter without at least informing him, or was Sarah giving the woman more credit than she deserved? Unpleasant memories of Jenny crept into Sarah's head. At first, when Jenny had started to walk out with Da, she had been friendly towards her and Maura. But her saccharine comments had always rung false to Sarah. She could not warm to the

234

woman. And then, as the weeks passed, the comments turned nasty when their father was not around. Jenny deliberately targeted Maura, who was too timid to fight back because she was terrified of upsetting Da.

One evening, Sarah had lost her temper and told Jenny to stop picking on her sister. That had earned her a slap across the face. With a stinging cheek and tears of pain, Sarah had grabbed a shocked Maura's hand and ushered her upstairs to their room under the eaves. She locked the door. From then on, whenever Jenny was expected, they took refuge there. Da didn't appear to notice anything wrong, or perhaps didn't care enough to do something about it.

After a couple of months, Jenny's visits to the house dwindled, but they didn't dare ask Da about it. After another few weeks, the girls concluded Jenny had either been dropped by their father or had found someone else. They were so relieved they had danced around their bedroom in celebration.

And now, Sarah would have to face the woman again. But, at least, this time, she would be dealing with her on an equal footing, as an adult, not a nervy teenager doing her best to protect her little sister. Hell! There was no comfort in that notion. None at all. If Everleigh was right, and McGrath was Da's second-in-command, she would be a formidable opponent.

Sarah sensed the truck was slowing down, and she panicked, her stomach twisting in knots. Now what?

The lorry stopped.

Sarah heard doors opening, and then there were muffled voices to the right side of the vehicle. She could not make out what was being said, no matter how she strained to hear. Might be best to pretend to be still unconscious. But her thundering heart was making her breath ragged. It would give her away. She took deep mouthfuls of air and slowed her breathing as best she could. She forced her body to go limp.

Sarah heard the door behind her head open, and she felt a blast of cold air on her skin. Sarah could smell the tang of sea air, and in the distance, she could hear waves crashing. They must be somewhere along the coast, but in which direction had they travelled? East or west from Fishguard? She had no idea.

'Looks like she's still out for the count,' a male voice with a Welsh accent said. 'What do you want to do? Leave her here until the morning?'

'No, don't be daft.' It was Jenny. 'Pull her out and we can put her in the barn on the other side of the courtyard.'

'Then what?' he asked.

'Nothing tonight. I need to contact Jim up in Liverpool and tell him what a nice surprise we have in store,' Jenny said.

The man laughed. 'I'd love to see his face when you tell 'im.'

'Hmm,' was Jenny's response.

Two hands grabbed Sarah under the armpits and pulled her out. The next thing she knew, she was flung over the man's shoulder. She opened her eyes a tiny bit but could barely see anything other than the outline of the truck as it receded into the darkness, and the rough ground the man was walking on.

She heard a grunt from Jenny and what sounded like a door scraping along the ground.

236

'All right, Luke, put her down on those bales in the corner,' Jenny ordered.

'Right-oh,' he replied.

Sarah was dumped none too gently. A musty, grass-like aroma rose around her. It must be a hay-barn. But there was another smell. Animals. Sarah heard a match ignite and was aware of brightness close to her face.

'What if she wakes during the night?' the man asked.

'Don't worry about that,' Jenny said with a laugh, 'plenty more of this stuff.'

Sarah heard the pop of a cork and seconds later she was breathing in that same sweet smell as before.

And once more, oblivion.

A crowing rooster woke Sarah the next morning. To her surprise, someone had thrown a blanket over her. But she lay for several moments, staring up at the rafters of the barn, totally disorientated. Slowly, the events of the previous evening crystallised in her mind. She tried to sit up, but her hands were still tied and were now frozen. Taking a deep breath, she wiggled herself up into a sitting position against the bales.

The barn was huge, draughty and cold. On the far side, looking over a fence, several pairs of large brown eyes were watching her. Cows. She wrinkled her nose. No wonder there was an earthy smell. Behind her, bales of hay were stacked almost to the ceiling. The earthen floor was covered in scraps of hay and what she assumed was animal feed. The barn door was closed, and no doubt locked. For some strange reason, the Iron Cross Mrs Twohig had given her in Dublin all those months ago popped into her head. If ever she needed some luck, it was now. Pity it was lying at the bottom of her suitcase in Judith's flat. Pity *she* wasn't back in Judith's flat!

There was daylight seeping through the gap under the barn door, but Sarah had no idea what time it was. Using her teeth, she yanked back her sleeve, but her watch had stopped.

Sarah heard the bolt pulled on the far side of the barn door. She braced herself, catching her breath. But it wasn't Jenny. The man's face was familiar, though. Luke Evans. To her surprise, he was carrying a cup and a plate of bread and butter.

He approached her with a wary gaze. With a grunt, he placed the food and drink down beside her, then turned away.

'Hey! Can you untie my hands? How am I supposed to manage with them like this?' She held up her bound hands and shook them.

Luke turned towards her, his mouth quirked unpleasantly. 'Just manage. I'm not risking untying you.'

He left, bolting the door behind him. What a friendly chap! Oh well, it had been worth a try, she thought as she manoeuvred her hands around the cup. Strong, hot tea. Better than nothing. Her stomach growled in agreement. At least they were feeding her. That had to be a good sign, surely? You'd scarcely feed someone if you were about to put a bullet in their head.

Sarah had barely finished her meagre meal when the barn door opened once more. This time it was Jenny. She was dressed in a long wool coat and a multi-coloured woolly hat, gumboots on her feet.

Sarah glowered at her. 'Playing at being a farmer, Jenny?' she asked. 'It suits you. Particularly the aroma – eau de cow, is it?'

Jenny stopped a yard away. 'You always were a cheeky madam,' she replied with a sniff. 'You won't be half as cocky when your father gets here. He won't be best pleased to discover you've betrayed your country and are working for the Brits.' She almost spat out the words.

'I don't quite see it that way. I have scores to settle. Joining MI5 was a means to an end.'

'My God, you admit it so casually. Working for MI5! He will be apoplectic.' Jenny shook her head.

'How is my dear father? Will he be here soon? I've rather a lot of questions to put to him,' Sarah said.

'Is that right,' McGrath asked, half laughing. 'Such as?'

'That's between him and me, McGrath. I don't answer to you or your kind,' Sarah snapped.

'What kind is that then?' Jenny asked, stepping closer.

Suddenly, Sarah felt reckless. What had she to lose now? She couldn't physically hurt McGrath, but she could humiliate her. 'Oh, you know, traitors, Nazi collaborators, and general scum of the earth.'

Jenny stepped forward and slapped her face. 'You're very high and mighty for someone about to meet her maker in the not-too-distant future.'

Sarah wiggled her cheek to ease the sting. Then shrugged. 'Are you brave enough to make that kind of decision, McGrath? Da might not take kindly to you taking matters into your own hands. I hear you are answerable to him. Haven't you already botched up badly? That Glascoed raid was a disaster. I'd say you need to keep in his good books.'

McGrath glared back at her. 'That wasn't down to me. The Germans only sent in one bomber, and they mistimed it all. And as for your hide, do you really think he cares about you and that other little whiny brat? What's her name . . . Maura?'

McGrath's reference to her sister only made Sarah's anger burn more brightly. 'I'm sure he doesn't,' Sarah bit out. 'Why else would he have scarpered to England and left me and Maura for dead? I know him better than you, though. He does care about reputation. Even the IRA has a moral code. It might be slightly warped, but it exists. Da is all about ego.' Sarah caught a glimmer of doubt in the woman's eyes. 'So, when does he arrive?' Sarah asked. 'You'll be delighted to hear I plan on staying for the family reunion.'

Jenny laughed. 'Don't worry. You won't miss it. I guarantee it. He'll be here later today.'

'Tell me, was the raid on Glascoed your idea? Pity about those grenades, Jenny,' Sarah said. 'I'm sure you planned to put them to good use.'

McGrath flinched. She had hit a nerve. 'We have other sources,' she growled.

'And dear Aled, how is he? Did he make the ferry on Thursday? I suppose he is happily ensconced in Berlin by now and being wined and dined by his Abwehr handlers.'

'You ask a lot of questions.' Jenny crossed her arms. 'He was a useful mole while it lasted. Aled served his purpose well, and we got him out, yes. I suppose MI5 know about the Fishguard route?' Sarah nodded; there was no point in denying it. 'We suspected as much, and when you showed up yesterday morning asking about Aled, our suspicions were confirmed.'

'Humour me, McGrath, who told you about me?' Sarah asked.

Jenny shook her head. 'I will not tell you his name. The man is still useful to us.'

'I see. But you'll have to stop using that route. Does that mean you will have to cease helping all those traitors escape? I'm sure your friends in Germany will be disappointed. It's all falling apart, isn't it?'

'Pah! They have only ever let us down. Jerry has been using us. They don't understand our position at all,' McGrath sneered. 'But we don't need Jerry any more.'

'Well, I can't say I'm sorry to hear the beautiful friendship is over,' Sarah replied. 'The IRA is becoming more and more isolated, McGrath. De Valera has incarcerated most of your buddies at the Curragh camp. Your support has shrunk to nothing back home.'

'Shut up! You don't know what you are talking about,' McGrath exclaimed, her fists clenched at her sides.

'Then why are you so worked up?' Sarah asked.

McGrath's face flushed with colour. 'Bloody traitors everywhere! Even the Vichy!'

'What?' Sarah was astonished. What could she mean? What did the French have to do with it?

But McGrath's expression closed down, the colour draining from her cheeks, her eyes burning with fury. For a moment Sarah thought she had pushed her too far; that she was going to strike her again. Sarah braced herself.

But instead, McGrath stalked out, leaving Sarah shaking. And it wasn't from the cold.

28

22nd February 1942, Strumble Head, Pembrokeshire

I bet Anderson would have a plan if he found himself in this situation, Sarah thought, as yet another hour crawled past. Cold and hungry, she had wrapped the blanket around her body as best she could. The rain was beating against the side of the barn, only adding to her maudlin mood. The waiting was awful. She had felt brave when she was angry facing McGrath, but then the fear took over as soon as she calmed down. She was proud she had held it together enough to give the vile woman as good as she got. But Da would be a different story.

The last time she had seen him was the evening of the bombing in North Strand. She had been all excited, eager to get out of the house to meet up with Paul. They were going dancing in town. Da had been sitting over a cup of tea in the small kitchen overlooking the back yard. She had popped her head in the door to tell him she was off.

He had grunted in response. 'I suppose you still want to traipse out to Howth tomorrow. Bloody daft idea.'

'Please, Da. It's a bank holiday weekend, and it's to be a nice day. Maura is putting a picnic together,' she'd said. 'We rarely do anything as a family these days.'

He had looked up at her then, his face creased in his habitual scowl. 'And where are you off to tonight? I hope you're not seeing that idiot from the bicycle shop.'

'No, Da,' she had lied. 'I'm meeting some friends from work. See you in the morning.'

And that had been their last conversation.

Ever since Everleigh had informed her Da was still alive, she had regularly practised what she would like to say to him. Well, scream at him, if she were honest. But now that the confrontation approached, she couldn't remember any of the crushing remarks and pithy one-liners that came so easily to her in the middle of the night. She was floundering in emotion, and she hadn't expected that; thought she had hardened enough over time to carry this off. But then, Da was the chink in her armour.

The problem was Maura was prominent in her thoughts. Her terrified face as she had pleaded with Sarah to keep them safe that night haunted her. It was a brutal last memory to have, and yet it stayed with her as if Maura's ghost could not find peace until Da answered for his actions. That longing for revenge had been all-consuming for Sarah, and now that her chance to confront Da was at hand, she was overcome with sadness. But she had already sacrificed so much, and it was unlikely another such opportunity would arise. She had to focus on Maura's needless death and the fact that Da hadn't tried to help them that night after the bombs fell.

Sarah was no fool. She worried about how Da would react when he saw her. Would Jenny have forewarned him she was alive, or was he only expecting to confront a captured MI5 agent? Did he know or care if she were alive, anyway? She doubted he would have cared enough to check last summer. And even though Maura's death had been in the newspapers, would he have bothered to find out?

The bolt on the barn door shot back and Luke appeared in the doorway. She treated him to a baleful glare. He responded in kind.

'Where are we?' she asked as he walked up to her.

'Somewhere safe. The middle of nowhere. Your friends won't find you here,' he answered with a smirk.

'I'll have you know they are more resourceful and determined than you give them credit.'

'Then how come the cavalry hasn't arrived yet?' he asked with a laugh. 'Stick out your legs.'

'Why?' she asked. She didn't like the look in his eyes.

Evans held up a knife. 'I need to untie them.' Sarah watched as the knife sliced through the rope. 'Stand up,' he demanded, tucking the knife into his belt.

A wave of light-headedness hit her as soon as she was upright. She sat back down. 'Give me a minute, please,' she said. 'I'm dizzy.'

'Hurry up; I don't have all day.'

Sarah got up more slowly this time. Evans grabbed her by the arm and marched her out of the barn. Sarah took in her surroundings quickly, as she had trained to do. It was a vain hope, but just in case the opportunity to escape arose, it would be good to know the lay of the land. Beyond the holding, the land sloped down to a lighthouse. A patchwork of fields fringed by hedgerows stretched down towards the sea. There were no trees in the bleak landscape. All disappointing. No natural cover if she bolted for it, and no other houses were in sight that might offer refuge. The truck, which she assumed was used the night before, was parked at the edge of the courtyard they were crossing. And there in the far corner were the burnt-out remnants of a car. Sarah reckoned it was Aled's Morris 10. A dilapidated stable block bordered the far side of the yard, the brickwork exposed and crumbling and the wooden stable doors hanging from their hinges. A farmhouse was at the far end. They were heading for the back entrance.

Once inside, Luke pushed her ahead down a narrow hallway. Somewhere in the house, a wireless was playing. It sounded like a news bulletin. Evans pulled her to a stop, opened a door and shoved her inside onto the floor. By the time she had regained her feet, the door was locked. She heard Luke's footsteps fade into the distance. She hammered on the door in frustration and shouted. There was no response.

Turning around, she surveyed the room. There was a single bed along one wall and an ancient-looking wardrobe. Otherwise, the bedroom was bare. She checked the window. It was locked and partially boarded up on the outside with only a small gap at the top giving her a glimpse of an overcast sky.

There was nothing for it but to sit and await her fate.

The key turning in the lock woke her up. Daylight flooded in from the hallway as she struggled to sit up; the sudden brightness hurt her eyes.

Jenny and Da stood in the doorway.

'So, it's true, then. You *are* alive,' Da said, shaking his head, his eyes wide in disbelief.

The harsh tone and broad Cork accent triggered a galloping heart. Sarah stared back at him in shock.

Nine months had passed since she'd seen him. He still had that distinctive mop of greying hair he could never tame, the same cynical gaze from those green eyes. But physically he had changed, and it shocked her. His clothes hung loosely on his frame, and his face, with sunken cheeks, was almost beetroot red. The lines around his eyes were deeper. Da looked tired and ill.

'Why didn't you believe me?' Jenny asked him.

Da inhaled, crossed his arms and leaned back against the door. 'Wishful thinking, Jen. That it has come to this: that a daughter of mine would work for the Brits!'

'Yes, it's shameful,' Jenny chimed in, hands on hips and a smug expression on her sharp features. 'But don't worry, Jim, no one but me and Luke know. The boys in the unit won't hear about this from me.'

Da gave her the side eye. 'You can go, Jenny.'

McGrath's face fell, and she grabbed his arm. 'Jim, don't let her *plámás* you. The little bitch has given me nothing but backchat.'

'I said go!' Da shouted, shaking off her hand.

'Call out if you need me,' Jenny said, her face flushed with angry colour. 'I'll happily sort her out for you. It would be a pleasure.' Then she stomped off, but not before throwing a malevolent glare at Sarah.

Da continued to block the doorway. Sarah had to dismiss any idea of making a run for it. But of more concern, she

247

had no doubt Da was in a rage. His relaxed stance was deceptive, but his colour was high, and his craggy brows were drawn together. It was a ferocious expression she had encountered many times before. And it never ended well for whoever was on the receiving end.

With a muttered curse, Da smashed his fist into the wall, making Sarah jump. His mouth was working as if he couldn't get the words out. 'You have betrayed me,' he growled, 'in the worst possible way.' Despite her insides having turned to liquid, Sarah raised a brow and remained silent. 'What is worse, you have betrayed your country!' he bellowed.

Sarah had anticipated he would be angry. There was little hope she'd get out of this situation alive. No matter. She had wanted this opportunity to confront him, and now she had it. She had to make the best of the situation.

'That's not how I see it, Da. And what about *your* deceit and betrayal? Leaving me and Maura for dead. Tricking us all into believing you had died on Newcomen Bridge. What kind of father does that?' The words spilled out, thick and fast and full of venom.

His brows shot up, but then he wasn't used to backchat from her. 'There is a higher calling than family, especially when there is a war on.' Da ran a hand through his hair. She noticed it shook.

In that moment, she was overcome with hatred. She despised him for what he stood for and for what he had done to the family. It was his fault she was no longer the young woman with the happy-go-lucky attitude. That version of Sarah Gillespie was gone forever. And it was all down to him.

'Higher than Maura, your flesh and blood?'

He pointed a shaking hand at her. 'That was not my fault. Those bombs were dropped in error. They thought it was Belfast.'

'Nonsense! I can't believe you're making excuses for them,' she said, her anger flaring up even more. 'They killed your daughter and destroyed our home. It was sheer luck I was rescued, not that you'd care. You did nothing that night to save us. After that first bomb fell, you could have come back to the house. You could have checked we were unharmed, taken us to safety.'

Da shook his head. 'No, no, the first bomb landed in Summerhill. There was no need. It was far enough away from North Strand. I knew you were OK.'

Sarah could not believe what she was hearing. She rose from the bed. 'Maura was a timid creature; that you *did* know. She was petrified, Da. And she *died* in a state of terror. How does that make you feel? Um?' Sarah took a step towards him. 'And do you know what? Even after the bombs started falling, all she kept asking about was you. Were *you* OK? Should we try to find you? I made excuses for you. I lied to her. Told her you were on your way, that we would see you at any moment, when I knew you were more likely in the pub.' Now Sarah was standing right in front of him. 'As the walls of No. 18 fell, crushing her to death, all she was thinking about was you.' Although her hands were still tied, she prodded his chest with her fingers to emphasise her words. Probably not a wise thing to do, but hadn't it worked wonders on Anderson?

To her amazement, Da flinched and took a step back. His cheeks were now an even angrier red. 'The cause needed me here. I was offered the chance to head up a unit again. Don't you realise what an honour that was? The fight for freedom must continue.' His voice was raspy. Was it emotion? Regret for what happened to Maura? No. She realised there was no regret, only warped obsession.

However, to show no sorrow for his young daughter's death wasn't a good sign. Was he that dead inside? Suddenly, she felt foolish. There would be no reasoning with him, and she wondered what she had hoped to achieve by confronting him. She had always suspected he was delusional, but she had never considered that he might just be plain bad. It wasn't a happy conclusion to reach, for it meant his intention was most likely to silence her. Permanently.

With a weary sigh, she ground out: 'Ireland is a free state. It's over, Da. You and your crazy friends need to realise that.'

'It's not over while Ireland is still part of the Commonwealth: still tied to the apron strings of oppression. And what about the North of Ireland?' He paused, his breathing heavy. 'Until we are a united nation, we will never stop. There was nothing more I could do in Ireland. They needed me here. I was prepared to make that sacrifice.'

'Sacrifice! How dare you! Me and Maura, we were the ones who made a sacrifice by staying in that bloody house with you after Ma died. The way you treated us was shameful. And poor Ma. She didn't deserve the life you gave her either. She lived in fear of your fists, no more than me and Maura.'

His brows rose in astonishment. 'Does a man not have the right to say what is right or wrong in his own home?'

'Expressing yourself with your fists is not the same thing, Da. And don't talk to me as if you are some kind of martyr.

You jumped at the opportunity to leave behind your responsibilities. Off you went on a little adventure with no thought for the devastation you left behind.'

'You are twisting it for your own ends,' he spat at her.

'Really? But you see, I know the real reason you went. Special Branch in Dublin was closing in on you. If you had stayed you would have been interned at the Curragh, like all the other lunatics.' Sarah gave a mirthless laugh. 'You're a coward! Plain and simple.' Riling him up was dangerous, but she couldn't stop. All those months of pent-up anger were spilling out.

Da's eyes widened, and he spluttered, 'Those lunatics you refer to are my colleagues: every one of them a true Irishman, a soldier of Ireland, not like those gombeens sitting in Dáil Éireann. They're in Churchill's pocket. But I know what my duty is,' he roared. Da paused all of a sudden, trying to catch his breath, leaning against the doorframe. When he spoke again, his voice was hoarse. 'I always knew you weren't a republican, but, my God, what a shock to discover that you are a traitor to the country of your birth, to our family name.' His gaze bore into her. 'You're no daughter of mine.'

'Don't worry; the feeling is mutual.' She almost spat the words at him.

Sarah could see the veins at his temple bulging. He was really worked up now. 'I should have known,' he snarled. 'You were always a secretive little thing, but working for the British is the ultimate betrayal. Why would you do it?' He looked genuinely baffled.

'It's quite simple, Da. Revenge. Anything I can do to hurt Nazi Germany I will do with pleasure. They murdered Maura and Paul and destroyed my home. The only good

251

thing to happen was your supposed death. Shocked, Da? Did you think I would be prostrate with grief for you? Ha!' She laughed, but it was without humour. 'If you hadn't tricked us into thinking you were dead, Uncle Tom would not have offered me a home and the chance of a new life here in this country. How ironic is that? Guess what, Da? I now have a loving family who care about me and want me to be happy. They comforted me in my grief, shared it even.'

'Tom Lambe is an idiot,' Da groaned. 'God help you!'

'He has been more of a father to me than you ever were,' she hissed.

Da glowered. In that moment, she realised her father's treachery had been a blessing. Suddenly, her anger evaporated, and she was calm. 'Now that I think about it, I'm glad you left, or I might never have met them. When I got out of hospital, I was struggling with my grief for you and Maura. My God, I was such a fool! I mourned you as best I could. Paid for your burial and a new inscription on our gravestone and all the while you were here, alive and collaborating with Jerry. But do you know what the worst thing is? I buried a stranger with Ma and Maura. A stranger, Da, and it's your fault!' She poked him in the chest once more. 'I hate you and everything you stand for,' she hissed.

His eyes blazed in response and then, suddenly, his expression turned blank as he gasped for breath. He staggered across the room to the bed.

'What's wrong with you?' she asked.

He waved a hand in dismissal. 'Nothing!' After a moment, he appeared to catch his breath. 'I left because it was too good an opportunity. A soldier must always be prepared.'

Sarah shook her head in disbelief. He was so indoctrinated he couldn't see how pathetic and awful his rhetoric sounded. 'I suppose you thought it was so clever, tricking everyone into believing you were dead, and at the same time you managed to wash your hands of us. And you wonder why I'm working for MI5? When they told me you were alive, I jumped at the chance to track you down. I'm your daughter, whether you like it or not, and you owe me an explanation. And let me tell you, nothing you have said justifies what you have done.'

'I only answer to the Army Council. I don't have to justify my actions to you,' he said, his eyes mocking her.

'And I can't make you, but when MI5 track you down, and they will, you will have to answer to them. They shoot traitors, Da. They probably wouldn't even bother with a trial.'

'I'm not afraid of death,' he replied. 'It would be an honour to die for Ireland.'

Sarah closed her eyes for a moment. There was no reasoning with him, she realised that now. 'You wouldn't *be* dying for Ireland. You'd be shot because you are a traitor, a Nazi collaborator, and a worthless human being.'

Da struggled to his feet. After a moment, whatever ailed him appeared to have passed. He straightened up. 'You have no idea of what matters in this world you have entered. If you are to survive in this game, daughter dear, you need to be more realistic. Most of all, you need to harden up.' He cast her a pitying glance while a cold smile formed on his lips. 'I can't believe you are naive enough to trust the Brits, and as for MI5, why it's riddled with double agents. In fact, most of the Allies are.'

253

She suddenly felt ill. 'What do you mean?'

What could Da know? Had Aled Thomas accused someone in particular, someone working back in headquarters? Then she recalled McGrath's remark about the Vichy.

If she were to get more information out of him, she'd have to bluff. 'Oh, we know about the Vichy.'

Da's head snapped around. 'What? You can't! I only found out a few days ago.'

'Our intelligence is better than you think. Anyway, why would a Vichy spy be of concern to you?' she asked, her curiosity now thoroughly peeked.

Da's eyes narrowed and for a moment he just stared at her as if trying to make up his mind. 'Because they are located in London, in the Free French headquarters, and they are selling secrets to everyone, the Brits included!'

29

Sarah's mind raced to understand the implications of what he had just said, but more importantly, why would he reveal this to her?

'How do you know about this?' she demanded.

'Aled Thomas boasted about it to me. A Nazi sympathiser working in Whitehall was feeding information to Berlin through him. The source of the intelligence was de Gaulle's HQ in London.'

Sarah was stunned. There had to be a catch. 'Why are you telling me this?' she asked.

He gazed at her for a few moments, and she wondered if he was regretting his words. But it was good to see that he had calmed down a little. His colour was less alarming and his breathing less erratic. Sarah reckoned his years of smoking and heavy drinking were finally catching up with him. Not that it mattered to her. Oh, no, she had no feelings for him at all.

Again, that calculating smile of his. 'You're rather fond of revenge, are you not? Let's say it's a family trait,' he said.

'I don't believe you. You're just trying to stir up trouble.'

'Oh, it's true, dearest daughter, I saw some messages Aled forwarded to his handler in Hamburg,' he said. 'And the beauty of it is, the Brits don't have a clue who the source of the secrets is.'

'But you have been collaborating with Berlin—'

'That arrangement has ceased,' he replied sharply. 'It was no longer working. The Army Council has decided to withdraw our co-operation.'

'Why, what happened?' she asked.

Da let out a slow breath. 'They have reneged on their promises, time and again. They promised us guns and money, and in return we were happy to continue carrying out mischief here in Britain for them. But only a token number of the guns were delivered and very little money. In the last few months, several of our operations have been compromised. Too many for it to be just bad luck. Somewhere along the chain, someone is selling information to Special Branch. I want the whole rotten network taken down.'

The irony, she thought. Da getting all moral. 'Treacherous lot, those Nazis!'

'You can be as sarcastic as you want, Sarah, but the fact remains that if they do eventually win this war, the republican movement will have some hard decisions to make. I don't trust them, but there are some higher up who think a deal could be done. I do not wish to work with them again, however. The final straw was that raid on Glascoed. We were left a laughingstock.'

'And yet you facilitated Aled Thomas escaping the authorities.'

Da shrugged. 'I liked him. He provided me with a lot of useful information. Besides, we had a deal. More to the point, he upheld his part of the bargain. After he dealt with that agent who had taken photographs of me and Jenny, he got very jittery. When he came to me, he was certain he had been compromised. He suspected something big was going to happen, and he needed to get out. Anyway, the arrangement was that we would give him false travel documents and safe passage out in return for the list of names of the MI5 agents in his network. He handed the list over before he boarded the ferry. But somehow those agents were warned. By the time I sent out teams to deal with them, they had vanished. Thomas may well have double-crossed me because of a late stab of conscience. Can't trust anyone, it would seem.'

It's probably best I don't tell him that was my doing, she thought. 'I still don't see why you are telling me any of this?' she asked, half dreading the answer. Was he telling her this because it didn't matter, as she wouldn't have a chance to act on it? But why hadn't he just walked in and shot her, or got Jenny or Evans to do it? It wasn't making sense.

'I have a proposal, Sarah.' He paused and drew his hand across several days' growth on his chin. 'Well, it's more of an order, really. I am willing to spare your life on condition you plug that bloody leak.'

Sarah stared at him for a moment as if he were mad. Then she laughed. 'You want to use me to get revenge on Jerry?' She was incredulous.

'Good men of mine are in prison because of that

257

network. That Vichy spy is selling secrets to all and sundry. An entire cell in London has been taken out. Do you remember Mick Malone?'

'Yes, I do,' she said. She remembered the man well. He had turned up at the door of No. 18 on several occasions, looking for Da.

'Well, he was the commander of that unit and he and his entire cell disappeared overnight. God knows where they are and what will happen to them.'

'And you believe this Vichy spy sold them out?'

'I'd stake my life on it. The real scum are those who will sell information to the highest bidder. They have no loyalty. Greed is the only thing driving them. I don't know which of them is worse, the Vichy or Abwehr agents, but both treat us as insignificant. After all we have done for them. Now my unit is discredited, and I've been summoned before the Council to answer for that Glascoed fiasco. Turns out that is the last straw for those I answer to. I had plans for those grenades. Damn right I want revenge . . . and I'm sure you wish to live.'

Sarah sat down on the bed. Her hands were trembling, so she clasped them together. Was he really going to let her go? Then she glanced at him. He was deadly serious.

'I do,' she answered, but her mind was racing. She didn't trust him. Was he setting her up in some way?

He began to pace the floor. 'I haven't been the best father, I'll admit that.' He stopped for a moment and gave her an odd look. 'But I have my convictions and have always been true to them. Honour is everything, Sarah. No one will ever be able to say Jim Gillespie betrayed the cause.'

'Da, that's not quite true, now, is it? I know you were in the British Army during the Great War.'

The vein in his temple stood out once more as he glared down at her. 'Who told you that?'

'Uncle Tom,' she answered.

'That bloody man! Yes, all right, I did join up in 1914. I was desperate, young and naive. I wanted adventure and to get away from the squalor of the Dublin tenements. Turned out not to be such a great experience.' He gazed off into the distance, suddenly looking his age. 'I have done things, bad things, Sarah. Some of them justified, others perhaps less so. But I have always upheld the republican values.'

'Da, I'm not interested. I've had to listen to this guff for years. I don't agree with your views and never will. However, I will act on this information. I just . . . well, I'm finding it difficult to believe you would help the British by exposing this network.'

'You underestimate my desire for revenge. I'm not helping the Brits; I'm punishing Jerry. Those sodding Germans want it all their own way and have dropped me in it. I may lose my command over that fiasco. All my work will have been for nothing. But don't you worry, my dear. I haven't suddenly fallen in love with the Brits. We have plenty more mischief in the pipeline for them.'

'I don't doubt it.' She sighed. 'Would you not just give it all up, Da? At your age you should be thinking about taking it easy.' Everleigh would kill her if he found out about this suggestion, but he was her Da, after all. 'Look, Da, please take my advice. Take Jenny and go to Lisbon. Get lost on the Continent somewhere. Disappear.'

Da began to laugh. 'You're something else. Only minutes ago, you were telling me you hated me and now you want to save my hide!'

Sarah wanted to wring his neck; he was so frustrating to deal with. 'I see. You won't be happy until you are a martyr; until generations to come sing about you in the pubs of Ireland.'

'What a lovely thought! Yes, I'd be happy with that, Sarah. What is life but a fleeting moment? At least I have made a mark.' He grinned at her, his green eyes twinkling. 'I've spent my entire life fighting; I'm not going to stop now,' he said. 'But you must promise you will do this for me.'

'Yes, but not for you, let me be clear, but because you are right. That network needs to be shut down. I foresee one difficulty, though.'

'What?' he asked, his eyes narrowing.

'I'd need some kind of evidence or a name, anything to convince my superiors that the information is valid.'

'Very well. It was some time ago that Thomas referred to all of this.' Da rubbed his chin and squinted. 'There was one name he mentioned. It is something like Manet or Mazet. I don't recall exactly. My understanding is this person works closely with de Gaulle and has been passing information onto the fifth columnist in Whitehall as well as half the other spies in London.'

'And this material was being relayed to Berlin via Aled.'

'Precisely,' Da said. 'But of course, with Aled's departure that will cease.'

'They could find another wireless operator,' Sarah suggested.

Da looked down at her as if sizing her up. 'They could, but word is they have been instructed by Berlin to neutralise de Gaulle and dismantle their network. I think that is what really spooked Aled Thomas into leaving. I don't want those bastards disappearing into the woodwork. I want them caught and made to face the Brits' idea of justice, which I have on good authority is a noose or a bullet.'

Sarah blew out her breath. It was audacious: assassinate de Gaulle! Clearly, the general's rallying cries to the French people were worrying Berlin. 'Have you any information? When is this planned? Who is going to kill him?'

Da shrugged. 'All I know is that it is imminent, hence Thomas's quick exit from the country.'

'But is it safe to rely on Thomas? He may not have been telling the truth. Can we really trust the word of someone who is happy to act as a double agent and sell out his entire network?'

Da pursed his lips. 'I don't see why he would have lied about it. Now, do you promise to pass this information on and act on it?' he asked.

To her astonishment, he held out his hand.

Sarah stared at it. Was this just 'business' or was it an olive branch? There could be no emotion attached to this, for the sake of her sanity. How would she explain this to Everleigh? She was supposed to be tracking Da down and handing him over, not agreeing to work for him . . . with him . . . whatever the hell she was agreeing to. However, she was outnumbered and unarmed. She could hardly frog-march Da and his chums to the police station in Fishguard.

Besides, another opportunity to strike a blow against the Nazis was too good to pass up. Right now, Da seemed the lesser of the two evils. With luck, she might be able to track him down again and finish her mission. But time enough to figure it all out. *At least I'll live to see another day.*

She raised her tied hand up. 'Best you untie me,' she said.

He pulled a knife from his pocket and slit the rope binding Sarah's wrists.

They shook hands.

30

22nd February 1942, Strumble Head, Pembrokeshire

'Luke will drive you back to Fishguard,' Da said. 'Don't return here trying to find us, and remember, if you fail to do what you have promised, you will answer to me.'

The way he said it made her shiver. She knew exactly what he meant.

A shout rang out. It sounded like McGrath. Da spun round as Jenny crashed through the doorway. Her eyes were wild, her cheeks pale.

'Luke has spotted activity up on the hill behind, Jim. We've got to leave here right now. We can't afford for you to be caught.'

The colour rose again in Da's face. 'You assured me this place was safe.'

'It is . . . was . . . Why did you insist on coming? You should have let me deal with her. You were always too bloody emotional about those two brats.'

Sarah almost laughed aloud; he only ever cared about himself. And right now, he looked as though his stress levels were rising rapidly. Who was out there, causing this panic? Could it be Anderson?

Da turned on McGrath. 'Shut up, Jen! Can't you do anything right? How in God's name did they find this place so quickly?'

'I don't know. No one knows we are here.'

'Well, that can't be true; someone must have told them,' Da yelled.

Jenny was breathing hard, and she wouldn't meet his eye. 'All right. I had to tell McGregor, the immigration guy, where to find us if anyone came snooping around. There's no phone in this place. So, he came here at lunchtime yesterday to warn us about her,' she said, pointing at Sarah.

'Mother of God, woman!' he exclaimed. Sarah thought he was going to throttle McGrath in his fury.

Jenny must have thought the same for she blanched even more. 'No one else, Jim, I swear. No one else knows about this place. We've seen no one around here all week,' McGrath pleaded. 'I'd never have willingly put you in danger; you know that. I don't know how they found us, but you can bet it's all her fault,' she said, glaring at Sarah. 'So, what are we going to do about her? I thought we'd agreed on a plan. I can do it now and quickly if you don't have the stomach for it. We really do need to leave straight away.'

'No, I've changed my mind. We're taking her with us,' Da replied. Then he grabbed Sarah's arm and pulled her off the bed.

'What? You can't be serious, Jim. Have you gone soft in

the head?' Jenny shouted as she followed down the hallway to the back door. 'She'll be nothing but a liability.'

Da ignored her. 'Luke!' he bellowed.

The Welshman appeared in a doorway behind them. 'Yes, Mr Gillespie?'

'How many of them are there?'

'I dunno. There's a car parked at the top of the hill. Can't see anybody near it though. They could be making their way down on foot.'

'Get my car ready, then. We're not hanging around to find out.'

'Yes, sir. I'll just grab my rifle.' Seconds later, Evans appeared again in the hallway, a rifle slung over his shoulder. He pushed past them, then out the door into the courtyard. A minute later, Sarah heard an engine starting up. They moved up to the back door. Da took a quick peek out and turned to Jenny. 'Best you go in the front with Luke. I need to keep an eye on this one in case she gets any ideas.' Da looked down at Sarah. 'We'll go in the back.'

'Don't try anything. I'll sort you if he won't,' McGrath threw at Sarah with a grimace before slipping out the door. Sarah watched from the doorway as Jenny ran across to the car.

But she never made it. A shot rang out, reverberating around the courtyard.

Da cursed as Jenny fell to the ground. Her body convulsed once, then lay unmoving. Sarah could see the bloodstain spreading rapidly on Jenny's jumper. It looked as though she had been shot through the heart. A precision shot. Could it be Anderson out there?

Frantically, Da waved at Luke to bring the car nearer to

the door. The Welshman revved the engine and swung the car closer to the house, skirting around Jenny who remained motionless on the ground.

'Shouldn't you try to help her?' Sarah said, gesturing towards McGrath.

'Too late. She's beyond help,' Da answered grimly. Much as she disliked the woman, Sarah was appalled by Da's lack of human feeling.

But as she began to remonstrate with him, another shot was fired. The bullet shattered the windscreen of the car, just missing Luke. He pushed out the cracked glass, which was now obscuring his view. 'Hurry up, Mr Gillespie!' he yelled to Da. 'They're extremely close.'

Sarah weighed up her choices. Should she make a run for it once outside the door, or try to escape back through the house? There was a risk that whoever was shooting might not recognise her. It wasn't far off dusk now, the light fading rapidly. She couldn't be certain it was Anderson out there, even though the precision of those shots suggested it was. She hesitated, undecided.

But it was too late. Da tugged her by the arm and dragged her out the door.

Another shot was fired, bouncing off the bonnet of the car.

Now in a cold sweat, Sarah scanned the area, trying to see where the shots were coming from. But whoever was out there was well hidden. However, the only possible hiding place was a hedgerow about thirty feet away from the end of the courtyard.

'Keep in front of me,' Da hissed in her ear as they edged towards the car. Using Sarah as a shield, he wrenched open the rear door then pushed her inside. He climbed in after her. 'Go, Luke, for God's sake!' he shouted. 'And give me that rifle.'

Evans handed the gun back over his shoulder to her father, then stepped on the accelerator. The car lurched forward, sweeping past the stable block and out of the courtyard, onto a dirt track.

The hedgerow loomed ahead. Suddenly, Sarah spotted a familiar face jutting up just above the hedge. Her heart began to gallop. It *was* Anderson. As they got closer, he jumped up and took aim at the driver. Sarah saw the gun fire. She cried out a warning and ducked.

But it found its mark. Luke cried out then slumped back, letting go of the steering wheel. The car hurtled forward, hit the ditch side-on and spun before it came to a stop, one wheel in the ditch. Sarah hit her head on the front seat as she lurched forward from the impact. Dazed, she thought she could hear shouts and running feet. With a groan, she pulled herself up into a sitting position. Beside her, Da was gasping for breath, his hands braced against the back of Luke's seat.

'Da, were you hit?' she asked.

But he didn't respond. She shook his arm. 'Da!'

She drew him back against the rear seat and was shocked to see he was deadly white, sweating profusely and clutching his chest. *It must be his heart*, she thought.

Her door was yanked open. It was Anderson and behind him was a particularly grim-looking Hinchcliffe. Before she could protest, Anderson pulled her out and marched her over to where Hinchcliffe was standing.

'Stay here, Sarah,' Anderson said. 'I'll deal with him.'

'No; you don't understand. He isn't well,' she replied, but he walked away. 'Stop!' she cried, now terrified that Anderson was going to do something rash.

'Let him do his job, Sarah,' Hinchcliffe said. She tried to break away, but he held on to her arm.

Meanwhile, on the far side of the car, Nevis opened the driver's door and yanked Evans out, dumping him on the ground. Luke cried out in pain; he was still alive.

From where she stood, Sarah could see into the back seat. Da's distress appeared to have eased a little. He shifted position slightly, but he was still having trouble breathing.

'Anderson, help him out of the car. He needs to get to a hospital,' Sarah called out.

Anderson cast her a frowning glance then stepped closer to the car, his gun raised. 'Gillespie,' he called out, 'get out of the car. Nice and slow and don't try anything.'

Da's head swung round towards Anderson, but his eyes fell on Sarah. For an instant, he held her gaze. Then he gave her a quirky smile. It terrified her. He was up to something. Slowly, he reached over and picked up Luke's rifle from the seat, then brought it around so that it was aimed at Anderson.

'Drop it!' Anderson shouted.

Da smiled at Sarah once more, his finger moving towards the trigger. 'Don't, Anderson!' she cried out, trying to slip out of Hinchcliffe's grip, but he was too strong for her.

Anderson raised his gun. He was aiming for Da's head; it all seemed to be happening in slow motion. This was horrific. She knew Da was deliberately goading Anderson into shooting him. He was crazy enough to want to make the ultimate sacrifice.

She squeezed her eyes shut and heard the report of the gun.

When she opened her eyes again, Da was slumped over, blood trickling down from his temple.

31

22nd February 1942, Strumble Head, Pembrokeshire

Sarah trudged back to the farmhouse as if in a daze. She needed to be alone to sort out her feelings, her thoughts, perhaps even her wits. In the distance, she could hear the bell of an emergency vehicle. She paused and looked across the hillside. A police car was winding down the track. She couldn't face them; not right now. How could they explain what was going on without revealing who they were and under whose authority they had acted? Anderson would have to contact Everleigh straight away to sort it out. For now, though, the others could deal with the awkward questions.

She rounded the corner and halted at the sight of Jenny McGrath's body lying on the cobbles of the courtyard. She had almost forgotten about her. Sarah shivered but felt little sympathy for the woman. After all, Jenny had been rather keen to eliminate *her*. Still, McGrath looked so vulnerable lying there. It wasn't right.

Sarah skirted around the body, doing her best to avoid looking at the blood. She dashed into the house, hoping to find something to cover the corpse. She grabbed the blanket from the bed in the room in which they had held her. That would do. Back outside, she threw it over McGrath's body and crossed herself. And because it felt the right thing to do, she said a quick prayer. But then, as the adrenaline of the last fifteen minutes gradually seeped away, her limbs grew heavy, and her head began to pound.

She needed to sit down, and she needed to think.

There was little choice but to go back inside the house and wait for the others to finish up whatever they needed to do. At the end of the hallway, she found the kitchen, which overlooked the front of the farmhouse. She stood at the window for a moment, then turned away. The police and her rescuers were standing over at the crashed car. A heated discussion was taking place, with Anderson gesticulating at the car. Sarah groaned. No doubt the police would want to question her too when all she wanted was to shut out the world. Forget everything that had happened. Move on. That was how she had coped before. That was how she managed to put one foot in front of the other each day rather than dwell on Paul's horrible death. Surely, it would work again.

There were the remains of a fire in the grate, and she gravitated towards it as if by instinct. She sat down, hunched over with her arms wrapped around her body. She gazed into the embers, as her throat tightened with pent-up reaction. She needed the release of tears, but they would not come. For a few more minutes, she tried to let go but there was nothing: no emotion. What was wrong with her?

Should she not be distraught after witnessing her father's death? The man who died twice! They could put that on his new gravestone. Except, of course, it wasn't in the least bit funny. Had she become as unfeeling as Da? But perhaps it was shock, and maybe numbness was better, anyway.

She was adrift, trying to grasp the implications of what had occurred. One thought, however, echoed over and over in her head: *all my family are gone now. I'm totally alone.*

'Sarah, there you are. Are you all right?' It was Hinchcliffe. 'A terrible situation. I'm so sorry it had to end the way it did. Anderson has told me that man in the back seat of the car was your father.' He came across the room, deep concern on his face.

She could only nod.

'My dear girl, you've been through a lot. But don't fret. We have convinced the police that they can wait and question you tomorrow. Anderson is going to take you back to Fishguard in our car. Nevis and I will stay here to sort things out with the police. We know the local sergeant well, so we should be able to smooth any ruffled feathers. The police have radioed for an ambulance for that other scoundrel. He's still alive; bullet went into his shoulder.' The captain squeezed her arm. 'Come on, lass, you look done in.'

The journey back to Fishguard passed in silence. Sarah, desperately trying to hold it together, kept her gaze firmly out the window. It was almost dark now, the scenery a blur of shadows and shifting shapes. When they pulled up outside the guesthouse, Anderson turned to her.

'Are you OK? Would you prefer we went somewhere else? I could grab the bags and we could head for Cardiff.'

'No,' she replied. 'Here is fine. I just need some sleep.'

Anderson quirked his lips and gazed at her, his eyes full of concern. For a moment, she thought he was going to comment, but then he sighed and turned away. For several minutes, he didn't move, just stared out the windscreen into the blackness beyond. At last, he said, 'I'm sorry. You shouldn't have had to witness that.'

'He gave you no choice,' she said in a somewhat strangled voice.

Anderson reached across and touched her hand. 'No, he didn't, but all the same, I wish the outcome had been different. Come on, let's get you inside.' He glanced up to the front door. 'I need to warn you. I'm not sure what kind of reception we will receive. Explaining our absence might be tricky. I didn't come back here last night.'

Mrs Jones answered the door to Anderson's knock. 'Goodness,' she exclaimed, 'I've been anxious about you two, especially when you didn't come back here yesterday evening. I said to my William, that couple are in trouble, we should contact the police.'

'Sorry, Mrs Jones,' Anderson replied. 'We were down in the Royal Oak and by the time we finished up it was extremely late. We didn't wish to disturb you, so we stayed over with Captain Hinchcliffe and eh . . . we were out all day today hiking and sight-seeing. I'm afraid we forgot about the time.'

'I see,' she said, but her expression was puzzled as she closed the door. Then she looked at Sarah and exclaimed in horror, her mouth opening and shutting several times as she scrutinised her.

'What happened to you, Mrs Sanders?' she asked. Mrs Jones continued to stare, her eyes travelling down Sarah's crumpled and stained clothes. 'Were you in an accident, pet?'

'Yes, a slight mishap, Mrs Jones, when we were hiking, but nothing to worry about,' Anderson jumped in. 'All Susie needs is a good night's sleep. Isn't that right, honey?' he said with a meaningful look. Sarah managed a smile and nodded.

'What happened to you? Did you have a fall?' Mrs Jones persisted.

Sarah was floundering and threw a beseeching glance at Anderson.

'If you could put the kettle on, Mrs Jones, I'll fill you in,' Anderson said smoothly. 'Don't be concerned. Everyone is absolutely fine, and Susie will be right as rain in the morning. Nothing a good night's sleep won't sort.'

He turned and winked at Sarah. 'Off to bed with you, honey. I'll follow up in a while.'

Too tired to argue, Sarah guessed he would come up with some plausible excuse to cover the situation, but at this moment she didn't care. A long soak in the bath, bed and the noth- ingness of a deep sleep were foremost on her mind. However, when she opened their room door, it was in total darkness, the blackout blind pulled right down. It felt claustrophobic, her old fear of the dark sending quivers down her spine. She dashed to the window and jerked the blind up, then the window. A blast of freezing sea air blew in, almost numbing her face. But she needed to feel alive and desperately wanted to shake off the pall of death and the image of Da's final moments. Sarah sat down on the window seat and gulped the fresh air as if her life depended on it, her hand clasped over her mouth, for she feared she might cry out or, worse, be sick.

For about ten minutes, all she could do was sit there, taking deep breaths. Eventually, she was calmer and capable of noticing her surroundings. The night sky was clear enough for Sarah to make out the shape of the lighthouse in the distance.

Was what happened today even real? Any of it?

She felt detached and uncertain. Yes, Da was dead. There could be no doubt. How much havoc the last nine months had wrought. At that moment, it felt as if it would take a lifetime to heal. And, as much as she had despised Da for all he had done, she was sorry his death had been so demeaning, even sordid in some ways. He had orchestrated it by pushing Anderson into reacting in the only way he could. But hold on. Did Anderson really have to shoot to kill? She shook uncontrollably. The implication of that notion was too awful to dwell on.

It was several minutes before she could think clearly again. She didn't understand why she was hurting so much. The first time Da had supposedly died, she had been relieved. What had changed? Was it that faint connection they had made this afternoon when Da had charged her with exposing the leak in the French camp? Surely that wasn't enough to mend a lifetime of hurt and the betrayal of nine months before. It wasn't as if she could ever forgive him for that. And although it was the right thing to do, he only asked it of her for his own purposes. But perhaps Maura would have forgiven him; maybe that was what was troubling her. Her sister had never questioned Da's actions, just accepted him as he was.

That smile Da had offered her just before the end: what had it meant? Had it been an apology that she had had to witness his death or was it more of a *'you see, I'll dictate how I die'*? She suspected it was the latter. His health was failing, that was obvious, and the authorities were closing in. And probably the worst problem for him was being in trouble with the Army Council over the Glascoed raid. Of course, he also wanted to avoid the ignominy of a trial. Far better the glory of dying in the heat of battle, as he would have seen it. Anderson had unwittingly granted Da's wish to become a martyr for the republicans.

As Sarah was dozing off, two hours later, she heard muffled voices downstairs. Minutes later, the door of the room next door opened and closed. Sarah wondered sleepily if Mrs Jones had new guests. Then, about five minutes later, the door to her room opened slightly and light from the hallway fell on her face.

'It's all right, Anderson, I was only half asleep,' she said, pulling herself up into a sitting position. 'You'd better close that door; I left the blackout blind up.'

He pushed the door over and chuckled. 'Are you telling me you're afraid of the dark, Sarah Gillespie?'

'Yep! Terrified.'

'And there I was thinking you were the bravest girl I knew.' He took a step closer. 'I'm sorry; I didn't want to disturb you. I wanted to sneak in and grab my toothbrush. Mrs Jones offered me another room to avoid waking you up.'

'Guess you failed, huh?'

'Yeah . . . Are you going to be OK?' he asked, standing at the end of the bed.

'Sure. A bit shaken and . . .' She trailed off.

'Of course. You must be. I ran up to the hotel and put

a call through to Everleigh. Of course, being Sunday, he wasn't there, so I left a message to assure him you were well. I also mentioned that your father was dead. Sorry, I'm not sure whether you wanted to do that yourself. Anyway, we should talk to him directly in the morning. I'm not sure what he will want us to do now.'

Sarah felt her throat tighten up. 'Thank you, I couldn't face telling him, not just yet. It's all still too raw.'

'Look, I'm really sorry the way things turned out. I couldn't believe they acted so quickly and had the nerve to snatch you from right under our noses. I should have been more observant.'

'Don't beat yourself up; I was taken by surprise, too. I guess we both let our guard down.'

'That's for sure. But I want you to know, I really wish the outcome had been different, but your father gave me no choice, Sarah, when he pointed that rifle at me. I had to shoot.'

'I know. But you need to understand it was what he wanted,' she replied.

'What?' he exclaimed, his expression appalled. 'Why on earth?'

Sarah gave him a half-hearted smile and sagged back against the pillows. 'Pig-headedness and the glory of dying for the cause.' A look of distaste crossed Anderson's face. 'Sorry,' she said, 'I'm totally exhausted. Let's talk about this in the morning. Right now, I need . . . well, I'm not sure quite what I need.'

His expression softened. 'A stiff drink? A hug?'

'I don't imagine Mrs Jones keeps any intoxicating liquor in her house,' she replied.

'Guess it will have to be a hug then.' She couldn't see

his face clearly, but she could imagine the way his mouth quirked when he was amused. And it sent tingles through her. Anderson came around to her side and sat down close to her. 'Hey! Why are you crying?' he asked, peering into her face. 'I thought you hated that man.'

Sarah sniffed. 'I did . . . but . . .' She trailed off, floundering even more and desperate for comfort. 'You must think I'm mad,' she whispered.

'Only slightly,' he replied. He shrugged. 'And no more than usual, Irish.' He pulled her into an embrace and rested his chin on her head.

She breathed in the citrus scent of his cologne and relaxed into his shoulder. He was stroking her back, and it was so soothing.

Slowly, she felt the tension leave her body as she relaxed. She had forgotten how lovely it felt just to be held. The bleak thoughts drifted away. Then Anderson muttered something into her hair.

'What did you say?' she asked, raising her head, keenly aware of his closeness.

'I said, I wish I could make things OK. You've been through so much already,' he said softly.

For a second, she froze, staring back into his eyes, as if hypnotized. He would only say that if he cared. And how her heart soared at the thought! How had she not realised her feelings for this man before? Had her grief blinded her to the possibility of finding happiness again?

He broke the spell by drawing back. 'Anyway, I should go. You should get some sleep.'

'I'm wide awake,' she whispered. 'And I don't want to be alone, Anderson, not tonight.'

'Sarah? Are you sure?'

'Never more so.'

When his lips found hers, it seemed the most natural thing in the world.

32

23rd February 1942, Fishguard

Sarah woke to the sun on her face as it streamed in the window. There was even a hint of warmth to it. Through the windowpane, she could see a sky streaked with gold and pink-tinged clouds, a glorious early spring sunrise. Facing death really made you appreciate the little things, she thought dreamily. For a minute or two, she lay totally relaxed, drinking it in until reality came crashing down. Last night, she had slept with Anderson! Slowly, with her heart pounding, she turned over. She hadn't imagined it; it was true! Anderson was asleep on his stomach, his arms tucked under the pillow, his face within touching distance. And naked as the day he was born. Just as she was.

Disbelief quickly followed panic. Her heart faltered. She had betrayed Paul in the worst possible way. He had been a faint memory last night, barely considered. Grief, distress or whatever the hell she had been feeling last night were no excuse. What was worse was Anderson had pulled away after that first kiss and she had pulled him back, eager for more.

And she couldn't deny she had enjoyed every single minute of it. Unlike her, Anderson was most definitely experienced. She felt the heat rise in her face as she recalled his touch on her skin; the way he had ignited such longing in her she thought she would die. She had fallen asleep in his arms afterwards, sated and happy.

And she hadn't thought of Paul at all, consumed only by a desire so strong it had scared her. It had been a wonderful release, yet it should have been Paul, *not* Anderson, who had helped her find it. But the dead give little in the way of comfort, a small voice in her head said, making her squirm even more. She should have been more careful. If she were honest, for days past, Anderson had been in her thoughts, and not in ways related to their work. The physical attraction had sprung out of nowhere, but she hadn't even tried to resist it. She groaned softly. What the hell was she going to do?

Anderson's eyes flew open, and he smiled sleepily. 'Morning.'

She could only stare back at him in dismay.

He raised a brow, reached out and caressed her cheek. 'What's wrong?'

She clutched at his hand and pushed it away. 'We shouldn't have—'

A flicker of annoyance crossed his features, but then he smiled. 'A bit late for regrets, Irish. I didn't hear any complaints last night.'

'Don't be horrible,' she replied, and his smile faded.

'Anderson, you know very well what I mean. You have a girlfriend who trusts you.'

He raised himself up on his elbows and looked down at her with a frown. 'You really are quite the innocent, Sarah. And I'll have you know Clara and I aren't joined at the hip. In fact, I know for certain she has many—'

'I really don't care about Clara; that's your problem,' she cut in.

'I don't know what you're upset about. You're a free agent.' He gave her an odd look. 'Or am I competing with a dead man?'

Sarah gasped. How could he be so mean?

He turned away abruptly but not before Sarah caught the flash of hurt in his eyes. 'Goddamn it, woman, I didn't exactly force myself on you last night,' Anderson snapped before sweeping back the blankets. 'Best we get dressed and get out of this godforsaken hole of a town. I intend to be on the first train out of here this morning.'

She watched him dress, gnawing her lip, torn between shame and a tug of desire. It took some effort to push down the tantalising memories from the night before, especially seeing his body in daylight. He was tanned and toned, an athlete's body. She suddenly recalled the feel of the muscles on his back moving under her hand.

A wanton: that's what you are, Sarah Gillespie, was the thought floating around in her head. *Your mother and sister are turning in their graves.*

Anderson closed the bedroom door none too gently with a muttered 'See you downstairs'. Her reaction upset him this morning and she could understand it. But it was surprising. Had she hurt him? So much for the man's tough image and the smart remarks. But did Clara mean nothing to him? *Surely he could not prefer me to that vision of loveliness.* This was confusing. He must be more sensitive than he looks. Not that it mattered. At all. *Did it?*

But it was lowering to have to admit there was some truth in Anderson's words. If she had really loved Paul so much, how on earth had she let last night happen?

After a hurried and silent breakfast, they paid their bill and bade farewell to Mrs Jones before traipsing back up the hill to The Bay Lodge. The sentry waved them through at the gate and they found Captain Hinchcliffe sitting in the reception area, poring over a newspaper.

'Morning, you two,' he greeted them, jumping up. 'How are you, Sarah?'

'I'm fine, sir, thank you. May I ring Everleigh to report in?'

'Certainly,' he replied, waving her towards the office. She didn't fail to miss the concerned glance he threw at Anderson, who just shrugged.

Once the door was shut, Sarah leaned against it and sighed. Anderson was in a snit and hadn't spoken a word to her all the way up the hill. It was fair to suppose he was regretting last night as much as she, now. *Another mess of your own making*, she thought. *Bloody hell, girl, you really are an idiot. Even grief was no excuse. Let's be honest; you wanted last night to happen.* She sighed again. Gladys would have a field-day when she heard about this!

She could hear the murmur of the men's voices through the door. Were they talking about her or what happened out at Strumble Head?

Right! Let's get this over with.

Everleigh's voice came through loud and clear when the connection clicked in. 'Sarah! Thank goodness you are safe and well. When Anderson rang in and told us you had been taken, we were extremely worried. I was so relieved, when the news came in that you were alive and well.'

'Thank you, sir. It wasn't a pleasant experience. Unfortunately, we let our guard down. And, sir, I'm sorry about my father. I know you wanted him taken alive.'

'No, no, don't be concerned. From what Anderson told me, it couldn't be helped. But, I would like to offer my condolences to you. I know you didn't have much of a relationship with him, but he was your father.'

Sarah gulped. 'Thank you, sir.' She hesitated. Something about her father's death worried her. What she was about to do felt treacherous, but no matter what had happened between them, a question mark hung over Anderson.

'Sir, there is something I need to brief you about and it's pretty urgent, but I'd rather not do it over the phone. We will get the next train back to London. Could I meet you later this evening, alone?'

'Alone?'

'Yes, sir, I think it's best I discuss this information in private . . . without Anderson.'

There was a long pause. 'Very well, I will wait in the office for you,' he replied. 'And Sarah, regarding your father, I think it best he and McGrath are buried quietly in Cardiff, no fuss. There is a Catholic plot in Cathays Cemetery. I'll make the arrangements with the local police in Fishguard. We will move the bodies to the hospital in Cardiff to await interment. I'd imagine the funeral can be held at the end of next week.'

'Thank you, sir,' she said. 'That would be best.'

'I'll see you this evening, then,' he said and rang off.

Sarah replaced the receiver and leaned against the desk. She was shaking. She wasn't sure how she felt about Da being buried with Jenny McGrath, even if they deserved each other. What would the family think? Should she even tell them? Perhaps it was best they believed he died back in Dublin and was buried with Ma and Maura. This whole sordid affair was best forgotten about as quickly as possible. But what was she to do about the stranger buried back in Dublin instead of Da? Imagine that conversation with the graveyard authorities. She shuddered. She had enough problems at this moment without worrying about that.

'If we hurry, we can catch a train in twenty minutes,' Anderson said to her as she rejoined them out in the reception area.

Hinchcliffe jumped up from his chair and came across to shake her hand. 'It was a pleasure to meet you, Sarah. You don't need to worry about the local police. I've sorted things out with them regarding what happened out at Strumble Head.'

'That is kind of you, sir, as we need to get back to London as quickly as possible. As regards my father, Colonel Everleigh is already making arrangements for his funeral.' From the corner of her eye, she noticed Anderson flinch and look away. 'You've been very kind, and I wanted to thank you again for helping yesterday, I'm very grateful to you and Nevis.'

'My pleasure, young lady, I'm just sorry the way things worked out.' He turned to Anderson and held out his hand.

'Well, young man, it was good to meet you and best of luck. Well, to you both, really. This bloody war isn't over yet, but if we have the likes of you two working so hard to root out the enemy, it will help.'

33

23rd February 1942, Enroute to London

Sarah sneaked a peek at Anderson from under her lashes. Seated opposite her in the train compartment, she was sure he was only pretending to be asleep. It was only the two of them, but she guessed the train would fill up once they got to Cardiff. While they still had the compartment to themselves, she wanted to make amends for earlier.

'Anderson?' She nudged his shin with the toe of her shoe.

He opened one eye. 'What?'

'Don't be so grumpy. I know you're not really asleep.'

'I was,' he replied with a glare. 'What's so urgent that you have to disturb my beauty sleep?'

'Oh, come on; stop punishing me,' she said, hoping to coax him into a better mood. 'I'm sorry for this morning, all right? I . . . I was, well actually, I don't know what I was . . .' she trailed off as she blushed. Damn!

'Uncaring and a little unpleasant?'

'Yes, you are right. I didn't handle things very well. But, you see, I've never done anything like that before,' she said in a small voice.

Anderson laughed and shook his head.

'What?'

'Irish, you are a witch!'

'And you are not very chivalrous,' she snapped.

'*Touché*!'

He grinned at her. And it was disconcerting the effect that had. She turned her gaze to the scenery to hide her embarrassment. 'I was upset and . . . thank you . . . for trying to comfort me.'

Anderson leaned forward and grabbed her hands, forcing her to look at him. 'Trying? Let's at least be honest. This connection we have has been building over the last few days, but I don't want you to think I took advantage. My intention last night was to leave you in peace.'

'I know, and you are right; I have felt that connection too. I guess I feel guilty because of Paul . . . what if he is still alive? I have betrayed him.' She had to swallow hard a few times to prevent the tears that threatened.

Anderson's brow puckered as he released her hands. 'I would imagine, Sarah, that if he were alive, they would have found him by now.' He grimaced and cursed under his breath. 'I'm not trying to be cruel, and I don't want to dash your hopes entirely, but you must see how unlikely it is. The poor guy would not have wanted you to become a hermit, Sarah. None of us know what's round the corner these days. Grab happiness, comfort or whatever it is you need and keep moving forward.' Anderson sat back, but he was still frowning at her.

Taking a deep breath to calm herself, she struggled to find the right words. 'I loved Paul so much and imagined my future with him. It's hard to let go of that.'

'You're still grieving, but you will have to let him go, in time,' he replied, but his voice was full of sympathy. 'When you are ready to pick up the pieces, let me know.'

Sarah stared at him in disbelief. He wanted a relationship with her. 'What about Clara?' she asked.

'That's complicated, Irish, that's all I can say for now,' he replied, shifting in his seat. His expression closed down completely.

'OK,' she said, now more curious than ever. He had closed the subject firmly, and she suddenly felt awkward and scrambled for something to say, to keep him talking. She had to find a safe topic, fearing she might plunge him back into a bad mood. 'You never told me what happened on Saturday evening. When did you realise something was wrong?'

Surprise flashed across his features for a moment. 'Yeah, of course, we never got round to talking about it. Well, when you didn't appear after about twenty minutes, I became uneasy. I walked around the pub but couldn't see you, so I asked the woman behind the bar to go and check the bathroom. She came back to say it was empty. Hinchcliffe and Nevis thought it was funny, that you had probably had enough of our boisterous nonsense and had returned to the guesthouse.'

'If I had left, I would have told you beforehand.'

'That's what I said to them. Eventually, I persuaded them to help me search. It didn't take long; the pub was crowded but small. In the end, I popped my head into the ladies' bathroom and spotted your glasses on the sink. I knew then something had happened.'

'Gosh, yes! I'd forgotten about them. I'd left them on the sink while I splashed my face,' Sarah replied. 'Before I knew what was happening, Jenny was right behind me. It was too late to try to disguise myself. She recognised me instantly and grabbed me so quickly I didn't have time to think. Jenny knocked me out by holding a cloth, soaked in something horrid, to my face. I passed out almost immediately.'

'It was probably chloroform,' he said.

Sarah shrugged. 'I don't know. The next thing I knew, I came round in the back of a truck, travelling at speed. I assumed they were taking me somewhere out of town to finish me off.'

'That must have been terrifying,' he said.

'It was! So, what did you do when you realised they had taken me?'

'It was impossible to talk in the pub with the noise, so I persuaded the others to come outside. Once we were out of earshot of the pub, I told them about your father and the possibility that someone had kidnapped you. Of course, they laughed it off. Nevis told me to go back to the guest-house and sober up.' Anderson grimaced. 'I didn't take that very well. We almost came to blows and Hinchcliffe had to intervene.'

'Oh!' Sarah exclaimed. That was rather gallant of Anderson, she thought. 'Then what?'

'We spread out to see if we could find anyone who might have seen something suspicious. I wasn't hopeful as it was pitch dark and the streets were almost deserted.

However, I did find a couple of ARP wardens around the town. One remembered seeing a truck heading out, but he couldn't give me any details about it. At that stage, I knew there was nothing we could do until daylight. We headed back to the hotel. To be fair to Hinchcliffe, he became very concerned. Even Nevis admitted it didn't look good. Anyway, I sent a message to London, which they promised would be passed on to Everleigh first thing. Then, we sat up till the early hours, trying to come up with a plan. But I knew there was a good chance that our questioning that morning had triggered your abduction. Straight after breakfast, I went down to the harbour. There were no ferries docked, so I went to the Immigration Office and sought that Inspector Stewart you had spoken to.'

'Not a particularly friendly sort,' she said.

The corner of Anderson's mouth twitched. 'True. It took some persuading. Eventually, he agreed to let me talk to the two officers.'

'That was lucky that they were on duty again,' Sarah said.

'I don't think they would agree with you, Irish. I may have been a little heavy-handed.'

'What do you mean?' she asked, intrigued.

'At first, neither of them admitted knowing anything but the short guy with the moustache looked nervous.'

'Yes, I remember him. He kept looking over at me when the inspector was asking him about the photograph.'

'Yeah, well, I soon figured out he was the guy. His name is McGregor.'

'Yes! McGrath mentioned him.' Sarah caught her breath. 'I spotted him in the pub that night. I'd forgotten that. His companions had their backs to me; it could have been Evans and McGrath. What bad luck. McGrath must have been delighted they had found me so quickly. Or could they have followed us down into the town from the guesthouse, if they had been watching it?'

Anderson shrugged. 'No idea, Irish. But I can confirm he is a little weasel. Shifty as hell he was when I asked about you. When he began to bluster, I knew I had my man. Then, once I had him pinned to the wall, he started spilling.'

'You didn't!'

Anderson looked mighty pleased with himself. 'Yep! I reckon Everleigh might get a complaint about it, but I was so riled up, I didn't care. I saw red.'

'I shouldn't admit this, but that was sweet of you,' she said with a gentle smile.

'We're partners. We have each other's backs,' he replied with a frown, as if any other idea was abhorrent to him. 'I'd expect the same from you.'

But his words stabbed her in the gut. Da's warning about double agents in MI5 was still ringing in her ears. Anderson's actions, if viewed in that light, were oddly convenient; focusing in on the immigration officer so quickly. And, if she thought about it, hadn't Anderson encouraged her to question the immigration staff that morning instead of the boat crews? This was horrible. Could she really trust him? Deep down, she knew the answer. She had already kept the information about the Free French situation from him. But she had to be cautious until such time as she spoke to Everleigh. However, if Anderson found out later that she had kept that from him, it would destroy any hope of a relationship. Yet again, she was being forced into circumstances where she had to lie to people she cared about. And she did care about Anderson, she had to admit. Why did life have to be so complex? It was like the Northcott affair all over again.

'Anyway,' Anderson cleared his throat and continued, 'eventually, the guy told me where McGrath was holed up. He admitted he had visited her the previous afternoon, as soon as he was off duty, to warn her about you asking questions. A little more persuasion and he revealed your father's organisation was paying him a great deal of money to turn a blind eye to their *special* passengers. I hightailed it back to the SOE boys and told them what I'd found out. Luckily, Hinchcliffe is familiar with the area, and we headed straight out. The rest you know.'

'And the immigration officer; was he handed over to the police?'

'Yes, but I understand he will be passed on to MI5 for further interrogation. I can't imagine he will be treated too kindly after what he has done.'

'No. And I'm sure the republicans will be livid with him too. But they knew they had to close down the route, anyway. Thomas had told them that London knew about it and was monitoring it. My fear is that they might set up something similar elsewhere, just for their own people. Helping the Germans has come to an end but they still want to cause havoc here.'

'That's Everleigh's problem, not yours, Sarah. Did your father admit the IRA involvement in that operation at Glascoed?' he asked.

The train pulled into Cardiff station. Sarah watched the

waiting passengers embark. They were unlikely to be alone for much longer.

'Yes,' she said in a rush. 'He was furious about it. Seemingly, his superiors were unhappy with the outcome and were blaming him. He admitted that relations with Jerry had reached a low point. They are not fulfilling their promises, it would appear.'

'Oh dear,' he said, with a mocking grin.

'Yes, the end of a beautiful friendship. At least something good has come out of this.'

'Just a pity we didn't catch Aled Thomas before he absconded.'

'Or take in my father to face the consequences of his actions.'

Anderson flinched ever so slightly. 'I wish the outcome had been different. All I can say, again, is that I'm sorry.'

'There is no need. Let's not speak of it again,' she answered.

'Thank you. It will be interesting to see what Everleigh has to say when he debriefs us. You could say, Irish, we have failed miserably, but at least we are still alive to fight another day.'

The compartment door opened, and several people entered. Coats were removed and baggage stowed. Anderson met her gaze and winked before closing his eyes once more.

Sarah relaxed back into her seat. The journey ahead would be long. Plenty of time to mull over everything that had happened. It was comforting to know Anderson had had her back, but the problem was, Da's death had once again sown that seed of doubt about him in her mind.

34

It was well past six in the evening when Sarah arrived at MI5. As she stood outside, looking up at the bland exterior of the building, she felt awful. She had parted from Anderson on good terms, and yet here she was possibly about to damage his career based on suspicion and not fact. Still, if she said nothing and it turned out he was involved in the plot and de Gaulle was killed . . .

With a heavy heart, she made her way inside and up to the colonel's office. Miss Abernathy bestowed a flicker of a smile on Sarah as she entered the secretary's domain.

'Good trip?' she asked.

Sarah had to think about it. 'I'm not really sure, to be honest. It was . . . eventful.'

'I wouldn't worry.' Miss Abernathy nodded towards the inner sanctum. 'He's in a good mood. Take a pew, he'll be with you shortly,' she said, before resuming her typing.

Sarah left her suitcase on the chair before walking up to the secretary's desk. 'Sorry to interrupt your work, but I brought this back, Miss Abernathy. Unfortunately, the ginger wig was mislaid.' Sarah placed the box containing the blonde wig down on the desk.

Miss Abernathy's mouth twitched. 'Lost in the line of duty?'

'Yes, you could say that,' Sarah said, trying not to laugh.

'Oh well, not to worry. I'll sort it out,' the secretary replied, her eyes alight. 'There isn't much call for that, em . . . colour anyway.'

The inner office door opened and Everleigh's head popped out. 'Ah! I thought I heard voices. Come in, Sarah.' He patted her arm as she walked past him into his office. 'Miss Abernathy?'

'Yes, sir?'

'You may go now,' he said, and closed the door.

Sarah sat down. Everleigh took his seat. They stared at each other. She wished she were a hundred miles away, and not about to drop Anderson in it.

'We will have a proper debriefing tomorrow, Sarah, with Anderson, of course. But what is it you could not discuss over the phone?'

'I'm sorry about that, sir, but my father told me . . . claimed there were several double agents working within MI5, and not just Aled Thomas, as we discovered. That was the reason I was reluctant to say much over the line, even though it was secure.'

The colonel frowned at her then nodded slowly. 'I understand. Did he give any details?'

'He claimed his source for this was Aled Thomas. Look,

Colonel, my father or indeed Thomas could have been lying. It's also possible my father was trying to impress me or deflect attention away from his own activities, but I cannot figure out why he would do that considering I was at his mercy. That's why I felt it was important I tell you as soon as I could. Just in case there is some truth to it.'

'Yes, you were right to be cautious,' he answered.

'Unfortunately, sir, that's not all. Thomas also told my father about a spy ring operating in London. They were relaying messages to Hamburg through Thomas. If you recall, sir, Anderson found a German wireless in Thomas's bedroom the night we visited his home in Cardiff.'

'Yes, I remember,' he said. 'Go on.'

'Thomas indicated that one of the people in the network was in General de Gaulle's headquarters and was in fact a Vichy spy, feeding information back to Marshal Pétain's agents. That person was also liaising with a fifth columnist, someone high up, in the British civil service. Whitehall was how he put it, sir.'

Everleigh's brows shot up. 'Bloody hell! This isn't good. We need more than that.'

'I'm afraid it gets worse. The network has been ordered to disband. I don't know why; perhaps they fear someone is on to them. My father reckoned that was the reason Aled Thomas left so quickly. Anyway, they are determined to go out with a bang. They plan to assassinate General de Gaulle, here in London. Possibly in the next few days.'

Everleigh sat back in his chair and blew out his cheeks. 'That would be an impressive coup for them, certainly, but there have been no whispers to that effect. I have people circulating in all the places where we suspect agents congregate; pubs and clubs, hotel bars, you know.' He gave a mirthless laugh. 'They say there are more spies than sommeliers in Claridge's.'

'I wouldn't know. It's not somewhere I have frequented, sir,' she replied.

He flashed her an amused smile. 'No, I suppose not.'

'I'm sorry I can't tell you more; that's all I have, sir.'

'It's all a bit vague, Sarah.'

She offered him a bleak smile in reply, but then she remembered. 'Oh! No, there was one name – Manet or Mazet – but my father wasn't sure.'

The colonel rubbed his chin, then wrote the names down. 'I've never heard either name mentioned. I assume that is the Frenchman involved. Very well, I'll contact one of de Gaulle's aides this evening and sound them out. You were right to bring this to my attention. And, Sarah, if any of this proves correct, I'll need you to follow through on this information.'

There goes my escape to Hampshire, she realised with a sigh. 'Could someone else not act on this? I had hoped my job was complete,' she replied. 'My father cannot cause any more harm and his cell is likely disbanded for now. I know we didn't quite achieve what you wanted in Wales, but I don't see what I can do to help in this matter.'

'Yet again, young lady, you underestimate your abilities.'

'No, sir. I'm a realist,' she replied with a smile.

The colonel picked up a pen, twisting it around with his fingers, and Sarah wondered what was going on in his head.

'We are incredibly grateful for what you have achieved and for this new intelligence,' he said at last. 'Your mission in Wales ended as well as we could have hoped. Although, of course, your father's death was unfortunate. I'm sorry you had to witness it. A trial would have been preferable.'

'I think we both know he would have faced execution eventually, sir. He certainly did. His health was failing, and he couldn't bear the thought of being caught and put on trial. The humiliation of it. He goaded Anderson into shooting him.'

'Anderson said as much to me and was genuinely upset, for your sake.' Everleigh gave her a knowing look. 'Have you told Anderson anything about this plot?'

'No, sir. I wanted to discuss it with you first.' She hated to do it, but she had to tell him. Sarah squeezed her eyes shut for a moment.

'Sarah?'

'Sir, it's just something has been bothering me,' she said. 'Well, two things, I suppose.'

'Best you tell me,' he said gently.

'On the one hand, I'm certain my father was happy to die for the cause. He'd already admitted as much, and I know he yearned for that kind of glory.' The colonel's distaste was plain to see in his expression. She hurried on: 'But on the other hand, Anderson knew you wanted my father alive so that he could be questioned, yet he went for a head shot. He had enough time to choose.'

'So, you assert that instead of incapacitating your father, he silenced him.' The colonel sat back with a sigh. 'Hmm, I'm not sure I like what you are suggesting.'

'Neither do I! But we all know Anderson is a crack shot. Why would he execute instead of maim?'

'But, Sarah, if you suggest that Anderson deliberately

killed your father, that implies he feared your father had information that would expose him or someone else.'

'Exactly,' she answered, utterly miserable. 'I can't see any other explanation for it, and I do not wish to believe it's a possibility, but I felt I had no choice but to tell you.'

The colonel exhaled with a grunt. 'Have you any other basis for suspecting Anderson of not being who he says he is?'

'Not really, sir, however, there was something odd. While we were based at the hotel in Newport, Anderson received a couple of letters. I saw one of them, and I'm sure it was from a woman. It struck me as odd, that he would have told this woman where he could be contacted and his false identity. The instructors told me I wasn't to do that.'

'Do you know who the woman is?'

'I'm guessing it's his girlfriend, sir.'

'So, it could have been perfectly innocent?' the colonel said with a raised brow. 'Our Yank is nothing if not unconventional. He has a reputation for being a rule-breaker.'

'Yes. Perhaps I read too much into it. You see, we didn't have the best of starts, but as the days went by and the situations became more complex, we worked well together. And, in his defence, it was his quick thinking that led to my release. If he hadn't found me, I know Jenny McGrath would have finished me off at the first opportunity, when my father's back was turned.'

'Thank you for sharing your concerns. I'm loath to condemn a man on so little, however.'

'As am I!'

'Good. We will give him the benefit of the doubt but keep an eye on him.'

The colonel pursed his lips and said nothing for several minutes. Sarah remained silent, but wished she knew what he was thinking. Everleigh laced his fingers, then looked up, his ruminations complete. 'Sarah, it is a constant worry that we are harbouring double agents, so your father's claims are no great surprise. However, as you say, he could have been stirring up trouble for the sake of it. For now, I will pass this on to my deputy to deal with. However, as for the other matter, the situation with the French is extremely delicate. If anything were to happen to de Gaulle while he enjoys our hospitality, the ramifications would be significant for the Government and the war. If there is the remotest chance that Anderson is involved in any plot, we cannot risk him knowing we are aware of it. Leave this with me for now. We can talk again tomorrow after the debrief.'

Sarah left the office in a despondent mood. She really didn't want to believe that Anderson could be involved in a plot. And yet, there were so many little things that didn't add up. Those letters from Clara, his uncannily apt prepa-rations for an attack at the hotel in Newport, finding that wireless set, Da's shooting, and now his possible involvement in an assassination plot. Could all of those things just be coincidences? She hated thinking like this. Was she becoming paranoid or a just becoming a professional spy? The answer was too depressing to contemplate.

35

23rd February 1942, Paddington, London

An hour later, Sarah pushed open the front door of Judith's building, only to spot Gladys coming down the stairs. Her friend squealed when she saw her and skipped down the last few steps.

Gladys threw her arms around her and hugged her tight. 'You're back! My goodness, how wonderful!' she cried. Then her face dropped. 'Or is this only a visit?'

Sarah laughed. 'No. I'm back for now.'

'I'm so glad to see you, but as you see,' Gladys grimaced down at her uniform, 'I'm on my way to work. Sorry, I must fly. Do stay up until I get home, won't you? I want to hear about all your adventures.' She flew out the door before Sarah could respond.

There was no answer at Judith's flat. After the third knock, Sarah feared there was no one at home. Gladys was so scatty she'd never think to say it. Bother! She didn't have a key. After the day she'd had, this was the last thing she needed.

As she was almost on the point of turning away, a shadow emerged behind the glass. Slowly, the door opened, and a pale face appeared. It was Judith, and she looked dreadful.

'Come in, Sarah. So good to have you back,' she said, opening the door.

Sarah dropped her case and hugged her cousin. 'How are you? You're dreadfully pale; are you ill? I've been so worried about you. The night I rang, you were out with Gerald.'

'Oh, yes, Gladys mentioned you called.' Judith led the way down the hallway to the sitting room. She went straight to the fireplace and poked the coals. Sarah spotted a blanket on the sofa and on the little side-table, a half-drunk cup of tea, its surface scummy as if it had been sitting there for ages. And several crumpled handkerchiefs.

'Judith? What's wrong?' Sarah asked, growing more concerned.

Her cousin looked up. 'Would you like something to eat or a cup of tea?' she asked as if Sarah's question had not registered.

'Sure, in a minute, but first you must tell me what's been going on.'

'Nothing much,' Judith said in a low voice. 'Go and get your food, then we can talk.'

'Well, I must admit, I'm famished. Spent most of the day on the train.' Sarah cast Judith a worried glance. 'Why don't you sit down. I'll rustle up something and bring you a nice fresh cup of tea. Then we can catch up.'

The poker slid from Judith's hand and clattered down

to the hearth. She stared at it for a moment, then walked away. She sank down onto the sofa without a word.

Heart thumping, Sarah threw together a quick sandwich and rustled up two cups of tea. But when she returned to the sitting room, she paused in the doorway. Judith was sitting with her head in her hands. Sarah had a horrible feeling the situation with Gerald had taken a bad turn and her heart filled with sympathy.

She placed the tea on the table beside Judith and touched her shoulder. She seemed to be miles away. 'Is Anne out?' she asked.

Her cousin looked up with a frown. 'Anne? Oh, yes. She's gone home for a few days, and you've just missed Gladys; she's gone to work.'

'I know. I met her on the stairs coming in.' Sarah sat down opposite and balanced her plate of sandwich on her lap. 'Are you OK? You look very glum.'

Judith began to tremble. 'Sarah, I don't know what to do.'

'Did you tell Gerald?'

Judith nodded. 'Yes, on Friday night. He didn't take it very well.'

'I see. I'm sorry,' Sarah said. She jumped up and sat down beside Judith, throwing her arm around her shaking shoulders. 'He's not worth your tears, Judith. You must concentrate on yourself and the baby.'

Judith gulped. 'That's just it, Sarah. There is no baby. I woke up on Saturday with the most awful pain and I was . . . I was bleeding. If there was a baby, I lost it.'

Sarah could have cried. It was devastating news, even though her cousin's pregnancy would have caused a lot of problems. 'Perhaps you were just late, after all?'

Judith gave a little shrug and whispered: 'I don't know. Guess I don't have a problem any more.'

Sarah hugged her again, but she had no words of comfort. Poor Judith would have to grieve not only for that infant that might have been, but the loss of her relationship too. Sarah knew she had been besotted with Gerald. At least now, her eyes had been opened to his true character. *Damn you, Gerald*, Sarah thought, *you never deserved Judith*. She wanted to say it aloud, but she didn't want to inflame an already horrible state of affairs.

'I'll help you in any way I can, Judith. You need not worry; I'll never breathe a word of this to the family. It can be our secret.'

Judith straightened up. 'Do you mean that? That you will help me?'

Something about her tone made Sarah wary. 'Sure, of course.'

Judith jumped up and paced the room, her arms wrapped tight around her body. 'I told him this morning that it was a false alarm, but he finished with me anyway. Told me I'd been careless, and he couldn't risk being seen with me again outside the office.'

'What a bastard!' Sarah exclaimed. 'All he's worried about is his wife finding out. What did you do?'

'Sarah, I was so upset. I fled the office and hid in the bathroom for an hour.'

'Aw, no, Judith.'

A strange look came over Judith's face. 'Don't worry; I've no tears left now. There's only rage. How could I have been so stupid, Sarah?'

'You fell in love,' Sarah replied with a gentle smile.

A pained expression flitted across Judith's face. 'Well, anyway, I went back to my desk, but he mustn't have realised I had returned to the outer office and the door was ajar. I could hear him on the phone. Making arrangements to meet someone. I knew it was a woman. He called her *darling.*' Judith almost spat out the words.

'Bloody hell! He didn't waste much time. But Judith, maybe it was his wife.'

Judith scoffed. 'He never speaks to her like that. Their conversations are clinical and brief. I feel sorry for her now. She's stuck up in Birmingham, the poor woman, while he . . . while he . . .'

'Cheats,' Sarah said quietly.

'Yes!' Judith glanced at the clock. 'He's meeting this new paramour in an hour at Le Coq d'Or. How could he! That's where he used to take *me.*' She stood trembling with rage in front of Sarah. 'I want you to come with me. I think this woman needs to learn a few facts about the charming Gerald Pascoe.'

The taxi dropped them at the corner of Piccadilly and Stratton Street. Judith had been silent for the entire trip, sitting rigid with anger. Sarah was nervous. What was her cousin capable of? Judith was so riled up. Should she let her have her head, or try to calm things down? The trouble was, Sarah had no sympathy for Gerald. In fact, she considered he was due a public humiliation, and Judith certainly looked as though she was going to provide it.

Judith strode down the street and abruptly came to a stop in front of a doorway. It wasn't easy to make out in the darkness, but it appeared to be part of a hoarding-like structure which jutted out from the building halfway onto the path. Judith gave Sarah a fierce and defiant look, then knocked.

A moment later, the door opened. '*Bonsoir*, ladies,' a man gushed, ushering them inside. The place was extraordinary. The structure formed a corridor down to the entrance. It must have been put in place to protect the large windows of the restaurant at street level from possible bomb blast, as well as masking the light from the street, Sarah surmised. Through the large picture windows, Sarah could see the place was packed with diners. She could even hear music in the background, above the chatter.

'Does mademoiselle have a *réservation?*' the man asked Judith in a strong French accent. 'Oh! Mademoiselle Lambe, is it not?' he asked, his voice faltering.

'I'm meeting a friend,' Judith answered, chin up and a dangerous light in her eyes.

The man hesitated, his eyes darting towards the inside of the restaurant. 'And who might you be meeting, mademoiselle?' He side-stepped, blocking their way. 'I believe the party you refer to is not 'ere *ce soir*.'

'Is that so? Well, I happen to know differently,' Judith snapped.

'Miss, I don't want no trouble,' he answered with a glare, suddenly more East End than Saint-Tropez.

Sarah, meanwhile, looked through the window, trying to spot Gerald. She spied him near the back at a cosy table for two, half enclosed by a booth. He was sitting side-on to her, but she recognised his hooked nose and slicked-back hair.

'Do you see him, Sarah?' Judith asked, coming to stand beside her, while the man continued to bluster.

'Yes, see over at the back?'

'Her!' Judith suddenly exclaimed.

At the same moment, Sarah recognised the woman he was with as well. She grabbed Judith by the arm and dragged her back down towards the door.

'Sarah! What are you doing?' Judith yelled at her, trying to pull away. 'I want to confront him. You promised.'

'No, no, Judith, we need to leave immediately,' Sarah answered, grappling with the handle of the door. She frog-marched Judith down the street and around the corner. Once she was sure they were out of sight of the restaurant, Sarah let go of Judith's arm and leaned back against the building, breathing hard.

'You recognised the woman?' she asked Judith.

'Yes, of course. I'd know her anywhere. She's been into the office several times. One of de Gaulle's people. They meet with Gerald quite regularly. She's French, of course, and very sophisticated, and always beautifully dressed. Just his type!' Judith frowned at her. 'But how do you know her and why did you react like that?'

'She's my partner's girlfriend.' Sarah quickly explained about Anderson. 'Her name is Clara.'

'Yes, I know. Clara Mazet. Huh! They are both cheaters then,' Judith scoffed, 'and they deserve each other. But why can't I confront them, Sarah? You promised you were going to help me.'

But Sarah barely heard her as the unfortunate connections clicked into place in her head.

36

24th February 1942, Paddington, London

After several hours, Sarah gave up on sleep. Afraid her tossing and turning would wake Gladys, she pulled the blanket off her bed and dragged it with her into the sitting room. The room was freezing. She popped up one of the blackout blinds, happy to sit in the gloom once she could see the sky beyond the rooftops opposite. In the distance, she could see barrage balloons but did her best not to think about the reason for their existence. Wrapping herself in the blanket, she tucked her feet up under her and tried to sort out her chaotic thoughts.

It had been too late to contact Everleigh when they had come away from Le Coq d'Or. She'd have to get to St James Street early and catch him before the debriefing. At least now they would have something to work with. Everleigh could liaise with his contact to find out about Clara Mazet. It was stupid, really, to have assumed the spy was a man. Yet it was hard to imagine the petite and glamourous Clara was a deadly spy. Could she even be the assassin? If only she could casually ask Anderson if his girlfriend was a good shot! There again, she had messed up by assuming Clara was American. *Some spy you're turning out to be!*

And what was Anderson's role in all of this? She didn't want to believe he was involved, but surely it was too much of a coincidence. Wasn't it strange he had never mentioned Clara was French, and how he was always so coy about his relationship with her? His behaviour confused Sarah. He spoke openly of Clara as his girlfriend, yet he had slept with *her*. Furthermore, he had made it clear he was interested in pursuing their liaison. He kept it well hidden beneath the smart comments, but she sensed he was a decent man. So, none of it made sense unless he really was that good an actor.

She wondered how he met Clara. The colonel had said the diplomatic crowd ran together, frequenting bars and hotels all over the city. Perhaps that was it. Just bad luck, she hoped, and nothing more sinister than that. But, if he were a double agent, he could do untold damage. *And not just to my heart*, she thought, grimacing into the darkness.

Sarah wanted to scream with frustration. Every time she thought she had worked it all out, the doubts flooded in. Could he be involved? It was hard to accept now she knew him better. When they first met, she would have believed him capable of anything. Was her belief in him clouded by that night of intimacy? She had some doubts about why he had despatched Da the way he did, but he had been in a highly pressurised situation. Maybe it was a genuine error of judgement. And surely not enough to hang a man . . .

Now she knew Clara's real identity, it eased her conscience about informing on him. A little bit. No, she had done the right thing. Thankfully, it was out of her hands. It was now up to Everleigh to decide what to do about Anderson.

Well, whatever hope she'd had of going home to Hursley was dead in the water for now. She just knew Everleigh would want her to see this out to the end. His confidence in her abilities boosted her self-esteem, and she suspected he would do his utmost to keep her in MI5 when this was over. Would it really be so bad? Perhaps Gladys was right. Perhaps going back to a sleepy job in a quiet village wasn't realistic, having experienced the thrill of the last few weeks. She had to admit, even when it had been bleak, part of her had enjoyed the intellectual challenge. Trying to stay one step ahead in this game required courage along with some brain cells. How shocked the nuns from her convent school would be if they knew what she was up to. And then Anderson's comment from weeks ago, about hereditary traits, popped into her head. That was uncomfortable. But no, she wasn't like Da. Her moral compass was intact.

And now she had the added worry of Judith. Her reaction to hearing Gerald might be a spy had been unexpected. She wasn't horrified; not even angry. She had been delighted and begged Sarah to let her help bring him down. Sarah had sworn her to secrecy before they got into the taxi home, explaining that an attempt on an important person's life had to be stopped, and that it was possible Gerald might be involved in the plot.

'What do you need?' Judith asked, staring straight ahead. 'If there is evidence at the office, I'll find it.'

'Thank you,' Sarah replied as she made a mental note never to cross Judith Lambe.

Though Sarah doubted Gerald was careless enough to leave evidence lying around, it was worth a try. He might have a legitimate reason for knowing Clara and meeting her. He could be entirely innocent. After all, all Sarah had to go on was her father's claims, and he had not named Gerald specifically.

Sarah woke to someone shaking her shoulder. Bleary-eyed she looked up into Judith's face.

'What are you doing sleeping out here?' her cousin asked.

Sarah sat up, stretched and yawned. 'I couldn't sleep and came out here to . . .' She spotted the time. 'Oh my God! I have a meeting in half an hour.' She threw off the blanket in a panic. 'Sorry, will have to dash.'

'What do I do if I find anything . . . you know?' Judith asked, following her to the bedroom.

'Hmm, OK. Let's meet at lunchtime. The Lyons near your office, say one o'clock?'

'Sure.'

Of course, Sarah was late. Miss Abernathy didn't look impressed as she nodded towards the open door of Everleigh's office, her fine eyebrows lifted in censure. The colonel greeted her with a pointed glance at the clock. Anderson merely grinned at her.

'Apologies, sir, I slept it out,' she said, taking the seat beside Anderson and trying to catch her breath.

'Did you run all the way?' Anderson asked, his mouth twitching in amusement.

'Pretty much,' she answered.

'Shall we make a start?' Everleigh cut in. 'I have a meeting at ten.'

An hour later, Everleigh dismissed them. Anderson made for the door, but Sarah lingered, trying to catch the colonel's eye.

'Are you coming?' Anderson asked from the doorway.

'I'll be with you in a minute,' she said. 'I just have a question for the colonel.'

Everleigh glanced at her and put down the folder he had just opened. 'Very well, Sarah, but make it brief.'

As soon as Anderson had closed the door, Sarah spilled out the previous evening's episode. Everleigh grimaced, muttered something under his breath and drummed the desktop. 'Well done, Sarah. I know of Pascoe, he's high up in the Home Office. The powers that be won't be happy to learn of this. You better be sure, Sarah.'

'It was definitely him, sir, and it does tie in with what my father claimed,' she replied. 'However, Pascoe is a womaniser, sir. He could be innocent, and he has a legitimate reason for knowing her.'

'We can't assume anything at this stage. Right. I'll get back on to my friend in de Gaulle's office and ask him to come over immediately. I will need you to sit in as he will have questions. It will be important to set up surveillance on both Mazet and Pascoe immediately. Hopefully the French will provide additional protection for de Gaulle.'

'But, sir, what about Anderson? Do you think he might be involved given he is Mazet's boyfriend?'

'Honestly? I don't know, but we must be cautious. I'm beginning to think your father's information was reliable. It's just too much of a coincidence otherwise.'

'That's what I thought, sir. My cousin may find something in Pascoe's office to give us further proof of either his innocence or guilt. At least it's worth her trying as we couldn't get access without spooking him. I'm due to meet her at lunchtime to see if she found anything.'

'Can she be trusted?' he asked.

'Judith hates him now, and I don't blame her. He treated her appallingly. She is keen to help.'

Everleigh shifted in his seat. 'Sarah, when someone is that vengeful, they are capable of anything. The last thing we need is her planting evidence.'

'No, sir, I don't believe she would do that. She's hurting, but it's the realisation that she should never have become involved with him that is driving her now.'

'I'm not so sure, Sarah, but I hope you are right and as you say, she is our best hope right now. But she must be careful. We don't know what these people are capable of.'

Sarah sat forward, alarmed. 'Do you think she could be in danger? I'd never forgive myself if anything were to happen to her.'

'I can give you no guarantees, Sarah. You know yourself how dangerous these people often are, particularly if cornered. I'm sorry, but my biggest problem right now is not knowing who the assassin is.'

'Could it be Clara or Pascoe?' she asked.

'Yes, but there could be others embroiled in this plot, too. At least we know there is no republican involvement.'

'Might they hire someone to do it?'

'That is a strong possibility, particularly if Berlin is involved and happy to provide the funds,' he said. 'Special Branch may be able to help us. Their informant network is much greater than ours. I'll have Miss Abernathy get on to them immediately. Well done, Sarah, now off you go. We will talk later.'

For some reason, Sarah found solace in the fact that Everleigh wasn't simply assuming Anderson was the hired gun.

Anderson was sitting with his feet up on the desk when Sarah entered their cupboard of an office.

'What was all that about then?' he asked before she even had a chance to sit down.

'Just tidying up loose ends. I wanted to know when I can leave,' she said, not quite meeting his eye.

'Sarah, I've known you long enough to know when you're prevaricating. Our job together is finished. You can leave anytime you want.'

'Oh, well, he is trying to convince me to stay on. He's desperately short-staffed, as you know.' She sat down.

'You should stay. You're not half bad, Irish.'

'Why, thank you. That's such a great compliment, coming from you.'

'Oh, I'm your number one fan.' Something about the way he said it, and the look in his eyes, made her toes curl. Suddenly she was back in Fishguard in that guesthouse . . .

'So, what are you doing next?' she asked, desperate to change the subject.

Anderson pulled out a cigarette, lit it and inhaled deeply. 'I'm off to SOE for a few months.'

'Do you know where?'

'Somewhere in the country but I can't tell you, sweetheart. If I did, I'd have to—'

'Kill me? Yes, Anderson, I know. You're hilarious. When do you leave?'

'Last I heard – end of the week,' he replied.

So soon? It wasn't what she wanted to hear. She would miss him. But then, if he were involved in the de Gaulle plot, he wouldn't be going anywhere anytime soon. 'So, what will your Clara think of you disappearing off again?'

She watched for his reaction, but he just shrugged. 'I'll find out tonight when I tell her. Hey, as I told you already, we're not joined at the hip. That gal has a lot of fish to fry.'

I bet she does!

Everleigh and the Frenchman were deep in conversation when Sarah entered the room. The colonel made the introductions and Sarah felt the full force of a pair of startlingly black eyes. Henri Vayssière was a short, stocky man and Sarah guessed he was in his mid-fifties. She had no sooner sat down when he bombarded her with questions. It was soon evident that de Gaulle's head of security wasn't entirely convinced a plot existed.

In despair, Sarah looked to the colonel.

'Henri, you know well I would not drag you here unless I was sure about this,' Everleigh said at last.

'But the source of this information. It cannot be reliable. No offence, young lady, but your father was a paramilitary engaged in activities that help only the Germans. I have spoken with the general about this and he refuses to believe it.'

'You must convince him, Henri. For both our sakes. If

anything were to happen to him here in London, there would be hell to pay.'

'Of course, I know this! I am not an idiot. But what can I do? The general refuses to let me increase his protection.' Henri threw his hands up in the air and shrugged.

'Sir, may I make a suggestion?' Sarah piped up. 'If Monsieur Vayssière used his own men, the general would recognise them. But he doesn't know me. Perhaps I could be one of a team to shadow him. If nothing happens, the general will be none the wiser. And if it does, and we stop it, it can only strengthen the relationship between Britain and the Free French.

Henri gave her a sharp, assessing glance. 'This might work, Everleigh,' he said, slowly. 'But it would only be necessary during the day. The general's protection team drive him to and from our offices and his home is well guarded. It is only at lunchtime that the general likes to walk over to the Connaught for lunch. That is when he would be most vulnerable.'

'And what about Mazet, Henri?' the colonel asked.

'Again, she knows all of my officers. If we were to follow her about, she would know.'

'We can't risk that. Very well, I will organise surveillance,' Everleigh said with a sigh.

'Excellent! I knew I could rely on you,' Vayssière said, standing up. He shook hands with both of them and left.

Everleigh sat down, shaking his head. 'Wily old fox! I'd a feeling I'd get lumbered with this entire operation.'

'And the blame if it goes wrong?'

'Oh, yes, Sarah; nothing could be more certain. Come

back in an hour. I will pull some people together.' He glanced at his watch and grinned at her. 'Get yourself down to Farringdon. You'll need to be armed.'

37

24th February 1942, MI5, St James Street

Farringdon was waiting for Sarah and ushered her into his small office beside the shooting range. Sarah could hear the muffled reports of guns being fired. The range was busy today.

'Take a seat, Miss Gillespie, while I get you sorted,' he said. He rummaged around, pulling down boxes, humming under his breath.

Sarah sat down, her chair opposite the open doorway. But she found it hard to relax. She didn't really like the idea of carrying a gun, even less having to use one. Her one brief practice hadn't inspired confidence either – beginner's luck. She could still recall Anderson's disparaging glance and needling remarks. Was it a sign of how desperate Everleigh was that he was allowing her to be part of the team? The other issue was keeping it all secret from Anderson.

But protecting de Gaulle from a possible attempt on his

life was a tremendous responsibility. Thank goodness she wouldn't be on her own. But still, the niggling doubts lingered. What if she screwed it up? Imagine being known as the person who allowed the general to be shot and killed. Her stomach lurched at the thought. Hopefully, the other members of the team were more experienced in this kind of work.

The entrance door to the shooting range opened and, to Sarah's dismay, out walked Anderson. He stopped and frowned when he saw her. If she were supposed to be leaving, she had no reason to be down here with Farringdon. Anderson would pounce on that. Would he come in and demand to know what she was doing? But he seemed to think better of it, nodded to her instead, and left. Why had he been in there? Why the sudden need to practise? *Stop it, Sarah*, she berated herself, *you're reading too much into it*. She hoped she wouldn't bump into him again today.

'Now, here we are, Miss Gillespie. One revolver and a box of ammunition. Sign here, please,' Farringdon said, holding out a clipboard. Sarah did as she was bid. 'How about a little test run?' he said with a broad smile and a nod towards the range.

Sarah was impressed at the speed with which Everleigh pulled the team together. There were four of them, including Sarah: one to keep tabs on Pascoe should he leave his office, one on Mazet, and two to shadow de Gaulle. To Sarah's relief, the colonel said they would rotate roles each day.

'Sir,' Sarah piped up, 'I'm afraid Gerald Pascoe knows me.'

'And what about Mazet?' he asked.

'I don't believe so. The only time she would have seen me was at Paddington station, and I was disguised as Catherine Cavandish. She was some distance away as well, so I doubt she would recognise me now.'

'Very well; Jason, please bear that in mind,' Everleigh said to the tall, thin man standing beside Sarah who had been introduced as Jason White, the senior member of the team. 'I can't stress enough how important this operation is. The political fall-out if we fail doesn't bear thinking about.'

There was a knock at the door.

'Come in,' the Colonel said.

Miss Abernathy entered the office and handed Everleigh a sheet of paper. 'Ah! At last,' he said, as he scanned down the page. 'Monsieur Vayssière has sent us the general's diary for this week.' Everleigh held it out to Jason. 'Best you take this, Jason, as you are in charge of the rota.'

'Thank you, sir,' Jason said, folding and tucking the sheet into his pocket. 'Right, let's adjourn to the room across the way and discuss what we are going to do.'

As Sarah and the team passed through Miss Abernathy's office, Anderson was chatting with the secretary, casual as you please, half-sitting on her desk. He looked up and their eyes locked for a second. Sarah kept walking, cursing under her breath. Was the man following her?

After the briefing with Jason, Sarah went back down to the office, thankful to find Anderson wasn't around. She quickly put a call through to Judith.

'Hello,' Judith answered.

'Hi, it's me,' she said. 'I'm sorry, I will not be able to meet you at lunch. Something has cropped up.'

'Really? That's a shame,' Judith replied. Then she lowered her voice to a whisper. 'I've nothing to report, anyway. All quiet here. He's had meetings all morning in the office.'

'OK, Judith. Look, leave it for today. I don't want you getting into trouble. Got to fly; see you later at the flat.'

'Who's in trouble?' It was Anderson, leaning against the door frame.

'Are you following me around?' she asked, putting down the phone.

'Last time I checked, this was my office as well. And why would I be following you? Though now that you say it, you're acting suspiciously, Irish.' His stare was hostile. 'Everleigh has you working on something, hasn't he? Why won't you tell me? Is it something to do with your father?'

'You shouldn't be eavesdropping, and what's with all the questions?' she asked, playing for time. *Here we go again; nothing but lies, lies, lies.* She hated it. Maybe she could just prevaricate. 'Look, Anderson, I am involved in something, but I'm sorry; I can't say what it is. It will be the same for you when you go to SOE, so don't try that on with me.'

'I knew it. You've been acting strange since your father's death,' he said, straightening up and closing the door. 'Why don't you trust me? How many times do I have to say I'm sorry? OK, I can understand you must hate me for killing your father, but he left me no choice.'

'I don't hate you! That's nonsense, Anderson. I know he goaded you.' She lowered her voice. 'I'd hardly have slept with you if I hated you.'

'Yeah, well, I'm not feeling very loved, right now. I thought we were partners; more than partners.'

Sarah stared at him. Was he being serious? God, she didn't

know how to interpret anything he said these days. 'I thought we agreed not to talk about that . . . about what happened.'

He crossed his arms. 'I don't recall. I think we do need to talk about it.'

Of all the moments to pick. She sighed, looked at her watch and came around the desk. 'Anderson, I have to go now. If you really need to discuss it, let's meet up later.'

His eyes widened. 'OK, then, what about lunch?'

Flustered, she clung to her original – now cancelled – lunch plans. 'Sorry, I can't. I'm meeting my cousin. How about this evening, after work?'

'Sure.'

Sarah was halfway out the door when she remembered. 'I thought you said you were meeting Clara this evening?'

Anderson's gaze was full of mischief. 'Must be my lucky day; she just cancelled.'

38

24th February 1942, Pall Mall, London

It was lunchtime, and the streets were busy, which was going to make their job more difficult. Jason had left Sarah outside the Reform Club while he scooted down Carlton Gardens. From the corner, he could watch for the general emerging from the Free French headquarters. Sarah blew into her hands and stamped her feet. February was still showing its teeth; it was icy cold. Not an ideal day to be hanging around. And what if de Gaulle decided to have lunch at his desk? She would freeze to death.

A couple walked past, arm in arm, chatting away. They seemed oblivious to her, which was a relief. This kind of work was all about trying to be invisible. Sarah consulted her watch. Monsieur Vayssière had said the general always lunched at one o'clock. He was due to leave his office at any minute. At the far corner, she could see Jason turning away out of the wind, cupping his hands. He was lighting a cigarette. When the general appeared, he would stamp it out and that was her signal to step back and wait for Jason to catch up with her while he kept the general in sight.

But it was Clara Mazet who appeared first, walking briskly down Carlton Gardens towards her. Sarah instinctively stepped back, even though she was sure Clara would not recognise her. Clara's expression was deadpan as she walked past on the opposite side, pulling on her gloves. She appeared to be in a tearing hurry. As Sarah watched her turn onto Pall Mall, she felt a pang of envy. Clara's beautiful cream coat fitted her to perfection, and she had a natty matching hat perched on her blonde curls. True Parisienne style, but was it based on the ill-gotten gains from selling secrets? A minute later, Mazet's MI5 tail, Alex, followed, keeping well back from the rapidly disappearing form of de Gaulle's assistant. Sarah's heart pounded. Clara was heading down de Gaulle's route to the Connaught. *Let's hope it's just a coincidence*, Sarah thought.

It was a full five minutes before Jason gave the signal. Within seconds, the distinctive figure of de Gaulle appeared on the opposite pavement, walking up towards Sarah's position. But he had company. M. Vayssière! Sarah was stumped and began to panic. Should they still follow? Perhaps it was normal for them to lunch together, but why hadn't M. Vayssière mentioned it? Heart pounding, she waited for Jason, who caught up with her just as the general and his head of security turned left and away from them.

'Come on,' he said, offering her his arm. 'We must stay close enough, then split up once we get to the end of St James Street.'

'Mazet is ahead of them,' Sarah said.

'Ah! I thought it was her, but I only caught sight of her side-on,' Jason said. 'I wonder if she is up to mischief.'

They kept back about three yards, but the street was becoming increasingly busy as workers spilled out from the offices on their lunch break.

'We need to get closer,' Jason said, increasing their pace. Up ahead, de Gaulle and his head of security were deep in conversation. Sarah kept scanning the public, not really sure what or who she was looking for. If only they knew where Mazet was. She hoped Alex was keeping a close eye on her. Could she be ahead waiting to ambush or was she on an innocent lunch break?

Anticipating that their quarry would turn right onto St James's Street, they crossed the road first. A minute later, the men followed suit.

'Jason, we have to pass our building. Someone might call out to us.' Sarah cast him an anxious glance.

'They know better. Just keep walking, Sarah.'

At the top of St James's Street, Jason halted. 'I think it best we split up now.' He peered around the corner. 'They are heading down towards the Ritz. They'll cross over from there. If you cross here, I'll track them on this side.'

Traffic was heavy on Piccadilly, and it was several minutes before Sarah could dash across to the other side. Through the traffic, she caught a glimpse of de Gaulle's tall form as he walked past the hotel. For a few moments, there was no sign of Jason. A truck and a bus passed and suddenly her view was clear once more. To her relief, Jason was keeping pace. So far, so good.

Sarah walked to the corner of Berkeley Street, constantly scanning faces, her nerves jangling. Having memorised the route de Gaulle usually took, she knew the next section might be where he could be most vulnerable, particularly up at Berkeley Square with the park providing excellent cover for any would-be assassin. She waited patiently as the men crossed over. She would stay on this side of the street for now, and Jason would maintain a gap of a few yards behind de Gaulle and Vayssière. As agreed beforehand, she and Jason would switch sides when they reached the park.

As they progressed down Berkeley Street, the crowd thinned a little. Sarah glanced at her watch. Ten more minutes, and they should arrive safely at the hotel. Then, of course, they would have to wait while the general wined and dined before repeating the whole exercise again.

At last, Sarah caught sight of the park in the distance, but she was astonished. She hadn't been in this area before. Amongst the trees, all she could see were parked trucks and army vehicles. As she got closer, she realised the railings had been removed, and the park had been tarmacked over. There was even a tank, the gun jutting out onto the pavement. Her heart galloped. All those large vehicles were perfect cover for anyone with ill intent.

But she had to slow down, for she was slightly ahead. She dropped to the ground, pretending to tie her shoelace. From the corner of her eye, Sarah saw the two Frenchmen move ahead. Quickly, she rose and crossed over. Now, Jason was behind her and should cross over at any moment.

Suddenly, she heard raised voices coming from behind her.

'Hey! Watch where you're goin', mate! You nearly knocked me 'ff!'

She swung around. A thick-set man with a bicycle was

shouting at Jason, and they were standing in the road. *Damn!* Jason must have stepped out in front of him. The confrontation was getting more and more heated. She couldn't wait to see if Jason could extract himself; she had to keep moving.

In dismay, she discovered de Gaulle and Vayssière were now a good bit ahead, almost at the corner. She'd have to catch up. As she trotted after them, Sarah could feel the weight of the revolver in her pocket, knocking against her leg. The two Frenchmen had reached the corner of Hill Street and she was still too far behind.

Then it all happened too fast.

As de Gaulle and Vayssière stepped off the pavement, Clara Mazet stepped out behind them from Hill Street. Sarah broke into a run, but immediately came to a stumbling halt, her previously injured leg objecting to her pace.

In desperation, Sarah called out a warning.

And Vayssière must have heard Sarah's cry, for he pushed de Gaulle into a doorway and spun around. Clara stood mere feet away from them, a gun raised in her hand, trying to get a clear shot at de Gaulle. Vayssière, however, was shielding him. People started screaming and running. Despite the cramp in her leg, Sarah moved forward, her eyes glued to the assassin's back. Why on earth was Vayssière not armed? She had to do something. With a rush of adrenaline, she pulled the revolver out of her pocket, and aimed. Clara's arm jerked as Sarah's bullet found its mark. Clara cried out, then staggered momentarily before raising her gun again.

Panicking, Sarah pulled her trigger, only for the weapon to jam.

But a shot did ring out!

Mystified, Sarah could only stare as Clara slumped to the ground, groaning. A figure with gun raised stepped out from behind an army vehicle in the park. Sarah gasped and then smiled with relief. How had she not noticed him?

It was Anderson.

39

Later that afternoon, Colonel Everleigh looked up from the papers on his desk as Sarah entered his office. He broke into a grin. To Sarah's surprise, Vayssière was sitting opposite.

'Come in, Sarah, please,' the colonel said, jumping up. Vayssière also rose to greet her.

'Mademoiselle, I am deeply indebted to you. Your quick actions this afternoon saved us from a catastrophe.'

'Thank you, monsieur, but it was my partner who saved the day. My revolver jammed. If he hadn't turned up, Mazet might have succeeded.'

'You are too modest, Sarah,' Everleigh said. 'Take a seat, please.'

'And I must go, Everleigh,' Vayssière said. 'I stayed only to thank Mademoiselle Gillespie. The general was most anxious that his thanks were extended as well.' Vayssière took Sarah's hand and kissed it, then handed her an envelope.

'He has written a personal note to you, as is only fitting. If you are free on Friday, he will host a dinner for you, your colleague Lieutenant Anderson and the colonel in Carlton Gardens.' He smiled down at her. 'You have a bright future ahead of you, I have no doubt.'

'Thank you, sir. That would be wonderful!' Sarah replied.

'*Au revoir*,' he answered, and swept out the door.

'Good Lord! I wasn't expecting that, sir,' Sarah exclaimed.

'On the contrary, you and Anderson saved us from disaster today. It is only right that the French show their appreciation,' the colonel said with a smile. 'However, it has been agreed that the incident will remain out of the public eye. Such an occurrence would shake the public's confidence and damage morale.'

Here was an echo of the aftermath of the Northcott affair, she thought. Nothing changes! 'Very good, sir, I understand.'

'Excellent.' Everleigh sat back and gazed at her for several moments. 'You handled yourself exceptionally well during this entire affair. It was unfortunate that your father avoided justice but at least his cell has been disbanded.'

'For now,' Sarah said. 'I have no doubt someone else will fill the vacuum.'

'That is certainly possible, but it would appear he told you the truth when he said that co-operation with the Nazis has come to an end.'

'I wish that was for altruistic reasons and not just a falling out amongst fellow conspirators.'

'It is the end result that matters, my dear young lady. You succeeded and now we must discuss your future—'

Sarah held up her hand and shook her head. 'Sir, with

all due respect, we had an agreement. One mission and then I could return to my family in Hampshire.'

'And waste all that valuable experience you have gained. Nonsense! I'd give my right hand to have more agents like you, Sarah Gillespie. No, no, there is no shortage of jobs at the moment that you would be perfect for.'

Images of Hursley swam before her eyes but she knew she was being sucked in. How could she return to 'normal' life after what she had been through? How could she leave London . . . and a possible future with Anderson?

'Aren't you even a little curious about what the job might be?' Everleigh held her gaze.

Sarah hesitated; he was manipulating her again, but her resistance was low. After the exhilaration of this afternoon, she knew well normalcy was never going to satisfy her again. 'Very well, sir. Tell me!'

At the end of that very long day, Sarah found herself in a pub, sitting across from Anderson. The rest of the team had drifted off in ones and twos, some going home, a couple heading to clubs. Even Everleigh had graced them with his presence earlier in the evening.

'I thought they'd never leave. Another, Irish?' he said, nodding towards her empty glass, his expression roguish.

'Only if you promise to tell me the truth about what happened today,' she answered with a challenging look.

'Fair enough,' he said, and headed off for the bar.

Sarah sat back, closing her eyes, thinking back over the day's events. As if in a daze, she had advanced to where Clara was lying on the ground. A small crowd had gathered around her. One man was on his knees trying to help her.

In response, Clara let out a stream of expletives. Anderson had only winged her, too, and a nasty dark stain was seeping down the sleeve of her coat from her shoulder where Sarah's bullet had penetrated. Relieved, Sarah skirted around the crowd in time to see de Gaulle and Vayssière disappear around the corner. Well! Was that expediency or the call of an excellent lunch? Lovely! Vayssière was leaving MI5 to clean up the mess. Jason and Alex, Mazet's tail, caught up with her.

'There was nothing I could do to stop her!' Alex explained to Jason. 'She just stood there for ages, smoking and checking her watch. What could I do? There was no sign she was going to do what she did. I thought she was just waiting for someone.'

Jason sighed and shook his head. 'Of course she was waiting for someone, Alex. De Gaulle! That was a close shave. Everleigh won't be pleased with us. Thank God for you and Anderson, Sarah.'

'You're welcome,' the man himself said, joining their little group. 'Just as well I happened to be passing,' he said, winking at Sarah.

'Yes . . .' Jason replied, not looking convinced. 'Right. Best we get her to a hospital and put under guard.'

Soon after, Clara had been carted off in an ambulance with a bobby in attendance, but not before she had directed a tirade of abuse in French at Anderson.

He had waved her off, blowing her a kiss. Sarah had turned away. *Why am I even surprised at his cockiness any more?*

'Hey! I don't usually put ladies to sleep!' Anderson announced on his return.

She opened her eyes and treated him to a withering

glance. Then she noticed the brandy in front of her. 'I don't normally—'

'I know you are a G&T girl, but I thought after the day you've had, this might go down well,' he replied. He held up his glass. 'Cheers!'

'*Sláinte!*' Keeping her gaze fixed on his face, she took a sip. 'Do I have to resort to the rack or are you going to tell me how you just happened to be in the right place today?'

'Luck!'

'Nonsense!'

Anderson got up and moved around the table to sit beside her. 'I'm afraid it's your fault,' he said in a low voice. 'You've been acting so oddly since Fishguard. My curiosity was piqued when instead of packing your bags, you were clearly involved in some operation at Everleigh's bidding. Seeing you with Farringdon confirmed my suspicions.'

'I couldn't say anything.'

Anderson's eyes narrowed. 'Why? Don't you trust me?'

Sarah sucked in a breath. Should she admit her doubt? 'I had information that there was at least one double agent in MI5.'

'And you instantly suspected it was me? Why?' His voice had an Arctic edge to it.

'Unfortunate coincidences,' she replied. 'And I wasn't convinced, but I had to tell Everleigh.'

'What was your source for this intelligence, might I ask?'

'My father.'

'Bloody hell, Sarah. Hardly the most reliable,' he said with a shake of his head.

'Da offered me a deal to spare my life. As well as the double agents, he also said there was a spy ring in London involving a Vichy spy and a fifth columnist in Whitehall. There was a plot to assassinate de Gaulle in the coming days. He was convinced someone in the network was selling secrets to the highest bidder, including exposing IRA cells in London to Special Branch. He wanted me to take the network down. All he had was the name of the French person involved. I assumed it was a man. And of course, I was wrong. It turned out to be Clara.'

'And why didn't you tell me about this plot?' he asked.

'You were her boyfriend, Anderson. Be reasonable – what were we to think?'

Anderson grunted then shrugged.

'Anyway, Everleigh decided to be cautious. I'm sorry. I should have trusted you, but the risk was too high.'

'Ah! Sarah!'

'No, listen a moment, please. I saw the letters you received from Clara when we were in Newport. That seemed very odd. We were undercover; only MI5 agents were supposed to know where we were, and even then, only a handful. And then, in the confrontation with my father, you went for a head shot instead—'

'So that's it.' He twisted around in his seat to stare at her. 'He left me no choice when he raised that rifle, you know that.'

Sarah nodded. 'But combined with the letters . . . all right, I guess I have become paranoid. It's hard to know who to trust anymore. I hate this bloody job!'

'And as soon as we got back to London you ran to Everleigh and told him all of this?' he asked.

'I had no choice. Come on, admit it: you would have done the same in my shoes. Then things got worse when

I discovered Clara's surname was Mazet, where she worked and who she was meeting. I had assumed she was an American, and that you knew or met her at the Embassy. Once we knew who she was, your role in it all came into question, yet again. Everleigh decided to leave you out of the loop. Anderson?'

He sat very still, not looking at her. After a swallow of brandy, he said: 'Yes, Clara has been extremely naughty. But your father was wrong if he thought I was part of their plans. Quite the opposite. US intelligence had suspicions about her for some time. My brief was to run with the diplomatic crowd in town and get close to her. Let me tell you, not as easy as it might sound. It took months before she trusted me a sufficient amount to consent to walking out. Not once did she let anything slip. Funnily enough, around the time I was seconded to MI5, I was on the verge of giving up on her. She must have caught wind of my move to MI5. Suddenly, she was all over me.'

'But what about today?' she asked.

His expression became sheepish. 'I decided to follow you to see what you were up to. It was clear to me, fairly quickly, that you and those others were tailing de Gaulle. It was sheer luck I had skirted around the back of the park and gone further down the square than you had. I had intended to wait behind some of those trucks until you had passed. Imagine my surprise when Clara popped up like that waving a gun.'

'And your instincts kicked in?'

'Um-hm.' He grimaced. 'First time I've had to shoot a woman I was walking out with. Hope I don't have to do that again.'

Sarah tried not to laugh. 'You're going soft.'

'How dare you!' he said, but his eyes were alight with laughter. 'By the way, who was that man with de Gaulle?'

'His head of security,' she explained.

'A brave man to stand up to her like that, unarmed,' he said with a sigh.

'Yes. I thought she'd shoot him to get to de Gaulle. Maybe her heart wasn't really in it.'

Anderson threw his head back and laughed. 'You are such an innocent, Sarah. I think it's what I like about you the most. If she had had a clear shot, she would have done it.'

Sarah looked away, picking up her glass of brandy. 'So, are you really disappearing off to the country?' she asked. Anything to change the subject.

'Yes, indeed.' He nudged her. 'Will you miss me, Irish?'

'Like a hole in the head,' she countered, but inside she wanted to cry. That feeling of being adrift was much stronger today, but she couldn't pin down the cause. Was it Da's death, or Paul's? Or maybe, if she were truly honest, could it be this man beside her? Everything was moving too quickly.

'Has Everleigh asked you to stay on?' Anderson asked.

'Yes.'

'I knew it. He thinks highly of you.' Anderson put an arm around her shoulder and squeezed. 'Let's be honest; you can't really see yourself going back to that humdrum job in Supermarine.'

'I loved it there,' she answered, but even she could hear the doubt in her voice.

'This war doesn't allow anyone to stand still, Sarah. Don't you feel that sense of panic? That today might be your last?'

'I try not to think about that,' she said, making a face.

'Well, yeah. It's kinda scary. But you're a good person, even if you did fall under my magnetic spell.' She shook her head, half laughing. 'And with a bit more experience,' he continued, 'I think you could be a tremendous asset to the secret service. Most of all, you need to move on with your life. Move on from everything that has happened to you in the last year. Sorry if that sounds brutal, but we have to grab happiness when we find it.'

'Are you always this philosophical when you drink brandy?' she asked, when what she really wanted to ask was had he found any happiness with her.

'No. I think it's your bad influence, Irish. In fact, I'm pretty sure you intend to lead me astray completely.'

'Is that so?' she said, sipping her drink demurely as a bubble of excitement did something strange to her stomach.

'The thing is, I wouldn't be averse to helping you in that endeavour,' he said, leaning in close and whispering in her ear. 'My flat is only a block away.' They locked eyes for one brief and intense moment. Then his gaze strayed to her glass. 'I have a bottle of very fine French wine, if you'd care to join me.'

Sarah chuckled. 'Was that not intended for dear Clara?'

He looked off into the distance and frowned. 'Now that you say it, it probably was, but I have it on good authority that she is indisposed for the foreseeable.'

'Has anyone ever told you how charming you are?'

'Only my mother and a few of my aunts. So, what's your answer, Irish?'

40

Judith rushed out into the hall as Sarah closed the flat door. Sarah was tired and emotional, and slightly tipsy. All she wanted was to curl up in bed and welcome the oblivion of sleep.

'Where have you been? What happened today?' Judith asked, almost jumping up and down with excitement. 'You'll never guess! The police came to the office this afternoon and took Gerald away. You should have seen his face. I was never so delighted. They ransacked his office. Lord! There was pandemonium and a huge set-to between the police and our boss. Is it awful that I almost cheered as they dragged him off?'

'No. I'd imagine I'd feel the same if someone had treated me the way he treated you,' Sarah replied. 'Sorry to disappoint you, but it turns out Gerald wasn't the spy after all. Clara Mazet named someone else, and he has confessed. I imagine Gerald will be back in work tomorrow.'

'Oh!' Judith said, sounding extremely dissatisfied. 'Are they sure? I'd hate to think he was getting away with anything.'

'Sorry, it was just an unfortunate coincidence that he was chasing Clara,' Sarah explained.

Judith made a face. 'And what about that French tart? Did you sort her out?'

'In a manner of speaking. You may be glad to learn she was shot and is in hospital. Turns out she is indeed a spy, and a dangerous one too. Luckily, we were able to scupper her plans.'

Judith sniffed. 'I'm not surprised she turned out to be a bad 'un. I always thought she was too good to be true.'

Sarah tried not to smile. 'Now, make me some tea while I freshen up, and I'll fill you in on my day,' Sarah said with a weary smile. Judith's cheerfulness had a forced edge to it, which didn't augur well. Sarah had a feeling she'd be up half the night with her.

When Sarah joined Judith in the kitchen, a half-empty bottle of whisky had appeared. Sarah threw her hands up. 'Honestly, Judith, I've had enough drink for one night, in fact, probably for an entire week. Where's that tea?'

'Suit yourself,' Judith said, picking up the teapot and pouring her a cup of tea. 'But I definitely need something much stronger. Gerald left this bottle here, finest malt, he said, and very, very expensive. He need not think he can show up here again looking for it. I hope he rots in hell.'

Judith's speech was slightly slurred. Sarah suspected her cousin had been drinking for some time. 'Well, he may not be a spy but consorting with one won't do his career much good, I'd imagine,' Sarah said.

Judith's eyes lit up. 'True!'

'Are you going to be OK?' Sarah asked. 'You've had a tough few weeks. Will Gerald's run-in with the police cause you problems at work?'

Judith sighed. 'I'd already asked to be transferred to another position. There were some awkward questions this afternoon after all the drama though.'

'Was it common knowledge, you and Gerald?' Sarah asked

'Yes.' Judith stared down into her glass. 'Many of us socialised together. You met some of them that night at the Mecca. Well, you know what people can be like.'

'Lots of gossip, I suppose. It will pass, Judith.'

'I've taken a long hard look at myself and . . . I'm not proud of what I did. I suppose I got caught up in the glamour of it all. And, he was so convincing. His poor family, though. Any hint of scandal will affect them.'

'I doubt there will be any. The government may hush it all up. It's not good for public morale to have suspicion hanging over anyone in the civil service.'

'I guess not,' Judith said, her voice ringing with disappointment. 'Still, a bit of public disgrace would have done him good.'

'Best to forget him.'

Judith took a slug of whisky. 'I'll do my best, but it might take some time. Now, you haven't told me what happened to you. Why couldn't you meet me at lunchtime?'

Sarah told her about Clara, but only telling her she tried to kill a prominent politician. The attempt on de Gaulle would have to remain a secret, even though it had occurred in broad daylight in front of the public. Everleigh had forbidden the national newspapers from printing anything about it.

Judith's eyes grew wide. 'Golly! Who'd have thought she was a killer? And there was me thinking she was ever so glamorous and sophisticated.'

'According to my partner, Anderson, she is, but also very devious. She has been selling secrets to the highest bidders. Even to the British.'

'War really does bring out the best and worst in some people,' Judith remarked, taking another slug of whisky.

'Actually, Judith, there is something I'd like to tell you, but it must remain secret. It's about my father.' Sarah explained how Jim Gillespie had absconded from Dublin, his activities in Britain and his demise at Anderson's hand.

'Good God! He was alive all this time.' She took a large swallow of her drink. 'Blimey! Oh dear, I am sorry, Sarah. How awful for you. So that's why you had to disappear off.'

'Yes. MI5 wanted him neutralised. I'm not quite sure how I feel about any of it. It was a shock, coming face to face with him again. But oh, Judith! You should have heard the awful stuff he came out with. If anything his crazy beliefs had strengthened. I was so torn for I truly believe he was mad; there is no other explanation for any of it. And then he offered to save my life if I helped to uncover those who had betrayed him. They were planning to kill someone very important.'

'Good Lord!'

'I had little choice but to accept, of course, and if he had not told me of the plot . . . well, all I can say is that it would have caused so much trouble for this country.'

'Perhaps he had a conscience, after all?' Judith asked.

Sarah shook her head. 'I doubt it. He only ever acted in his own interest and now he is dead, I will never know for sure what his motivation was. But I can never forgive him for what he did to Ma and Maura. If he had acted differently the night of the bombing, Maura might still be alive.'

'Does my father know about Uncle Jim?'

'No, and he never can. I am sworn to secrecy and I must ask the same of you. I suppose if he had been caught alive and sent for trial it would all have come out in the press. Maybe it's for the best this way. However, I wanted to ask a favour,' she said.

'Of course, anything, Sarah. Name it!'

'His funeral is next week in Cardiff. Would you come with me? I don't think I could face it on my own.'

'Of course!' Judith reached across and hugged her. 'Poor you. Having to carry all that pain and grief around and not being able to share it. And all of this on top of losing Paul.'

'Losing Paul broke my heart, Judith, but at least I can put Da and his past behind me, now,' she answered. 'And Maura's awful death is easier to bear. At times, it has felt as though Da has been haunting my every step.'

'I understand,' Judith said. 'Don't you worry. We'll give him a decent send-off and then you can close the door on that part of your life very firmly. His actions shouldn't overshadow your life.'

'They won't any more, Judith.'

'Good. Then life can go back to normal. But please don't say you are going back to Hursley. London is full of interesting people. Maybe someday you will find someone special to replace Paul.'

Sarah blushed. 'Well, I may have already. I have to confess I haven't exactly been a good Catholic girl.'

Judith's brows rose. 'Anything you'd care to share?'

At last, Sarah could talk to someone about Anderson. Sarah told Judith a little about the mission, his involvement in Da's death, and how they had ended up sleeping together.

Judith's eyes widened. 'You must have been very vulnerable that night. I'm glad you had someone to give you comfort.'

Sarah felt the heat in her cheeks rise. 'I was in a state, Judith. But the shock of what happened out at Strumble Head opened my eyes. I had been in denial up to then, wearing my grief for Paul like a suit of armour. And here was a living, breathing man who cared. In the end, I encouraged him. It was all my doing,' she said with a grin.

'Good for you! And is there any future in this relationship?' Judith asked, suddenly reminding Sarah of Aunty Alice's tone when she'd question Tom or Martin about something they had done.

'Possibly, I mean we talked about it a little this evening. It will depend on work, and the war to some extent. Neither of us knows where we will be sent next, or at least I don't. He's heading off to another unit and doesn't know when he will be back in London.' She shrugged. 'It will be down to luck. Hopefully, at some future point, we will both be in London at the same time.'

'And would you like to keep seeing him? Is there a future in it?'

'Who knows, Judith, but yes, I do want to see him again. I feel so conflicted about it, though, so guilty,' Sarah said.

'Because of Paul?'

'Yes, it's only been two months. It feels disloyal somehow.'

'But nothing can bring Paul back to you,' Judith said, gently. 'You have to get on with your life.'

'Oh, I will. After the bombing the future looked bleak. The first ray of hope was your family's kindness. And although the past few months have been awful at times, I can now look at the future with a small amount of optimism.'

'Paul adored you and he would have wanted you to be happy. If you think Anderson can bring you that, why not?'

'I like him a lot, Judith, but you know us Catholic girls, always racked with guilt.'

'Then, let us banish it for good. Come on, let's make a toast.' Judith grabbed a clean glass and poured out a finger of whisky and shoved it across the table to her. 'To all the men in our lives, past, present and future!'

'Cheers!'

'What did I miss?' a voice asked from the kitchen doorway. It was Gladys, arriving in from her shift.

Judith poured out another glass. 'Please join us, Glad. We've been putting the world to rights, or to be more precise, sorting out the male of the species. One has been condemned,' she winked at Sarah, 'and the other is a rising star.'

Sarah spluttered with laughter and shook her head.

Gladys threw her clippie hat on the table and plonked down. 'Oh, well, tell me more. I need cheering up because I've just had the dullest shift ever. Not one nice-looking bloke this evening and one creepy chap who kept trying to catch my eye.' Her eyes narrowed. 'So, what kind of day have you two had?'

Judith laughed. 'Dull as dishwater!'

'Boring as hell!' Sarah joined in.

'You two have been up to mischief, I can just feel it,' Gladys said, giving each of them a searching look.

If only you knew, Sarah thought, but she remained silent. Judith attempted to look innocent. Gladys pouted and frowned.

'Drink up, Gladys, we really do have something to celebrate.' Sarah stood up and raised her glass. 'I've come to a decision, ladies.'

'And what might that be?' Gladys asked, her glance flicking between Judith and Sarah. 'We're not going back to Horgan's, are we?'

Sarah chuckled. 'Good God, no!'

'So, what is it?' Judith asked.

Sarah grinned at them. 'You two are stuck with me. I am going to remain working at MI5 and hopefully be based in London.'

Gladys jumped up. 'I knew it!' She turned to Judith. 'Didn't I tell you she'd stay?'

'I hoped she might. And by the way, my other flatmate, Anne, is not coming back to London. So . . .'

Gladys beamed back at Judith. 'Can we share this place with you? I love this flat; it's so perfect.'

Judith nodded. 'I was rather hoping you would.'

Then Gladys came around the table and hugged Sarah hard. 'You won't regret changing your mind. Think of all the adventures we are going to have. London won't know what hit it!'

The End

Acknowledgements

I have been incredibly lucky, for I grew up in a house where books were king. However, it was my father's love of history which resonated with me the most, and although I devoured crime novels as a teenager, historical fiction has always been my 'go-to' when choosing what to read. And my luck has continued in having such a supportive family and group of friends. To Conor, my husband, and my children, Stephen, Hazel and Adam, thanks for putting up with the rushed dinners, un-ironed laundry, and general scattiness! Becoming a full-time writer is daunting and would not have been possible without the encouragement and support of family, friends and work colleagues who urged me to take the leap. I am happy to say I have no regrets.

I would like to take the opportunity to thank one incredibly special lady, Thérèse Coen, my agent. The Sarah Gillespie books are the result of her suggestion that I write a WW2 novel with an Irish perspective. For your continued support, guidance, and hard work, I am extremely grateful.

A big thank you to all the team at Hardman & Swainson. You guys are the best.

WW2 espionage on the Homefront is a fascinating subject. On reading Tim Tate's *Hitler's British Traitors,* I realised it was a font of ideas for a series of novels. When I stumbled in my research, being unable to find out the port used by the IRA for their covert route into Britain during WW2, Tim was kind enough to share his research with me. (If you are interested, the port is unknown as the file which contained this information was destroyed). Thanks are also due to the London Transport Museum who, as ever, are always so quick to respond to queries. This time around it was the layout of Covent Garden tube station's lifts and stairways. A special word of thanks to authors Brook Allen and Judith Arnopp, who kindly helped me with queries regarding Americanisms and the Welsh language, respectively.

Producing a novel is a collaborative process, and I have been fortunate to have wonderful editors, copyeditors, proof-readers, and graphic designers working on this book. In particular, thanks to Radhika Sonagra, Lucy Frederick and Katie Loughnane, my editors, and a special word of thanks to Becci Mansell in PR for her hard work on my behalf. To all the team at Avon and Harper Collins, thanks so much.

I am extremely grateful to have such loyal readers. For those of you who take the time to leave reviews, please know that I appreciate them beyond words. To the amazing book bloggers, book tour hosts and reviewers who have hosted me and my books over the years – thank you.

Last, but certainly not least, I am incredibly lucky to

have a network of writer friends who keep me motivated, especially Sharon Thompson, Valerie Keogh, Jenny O'Brien, and Fiona Cooke. Special thanks to the members of the Historical Novel Society, RNA and Society of Authors Irish Chapters, and all the gang at the Coffee Pot Book Club.

Go raibh míle maith agat!

Pam Lecky, April 2022

A life-changing moment
A heart-breaking choice
A dangerous mission

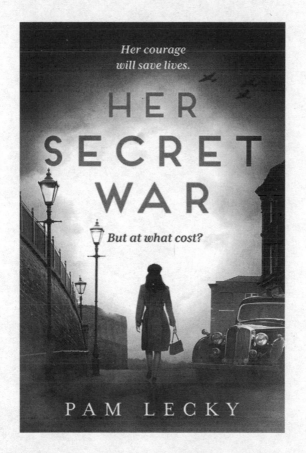

A gripping story that explores a deadly tangle of love
and espionage in war-torn Britain, perfect for fans of
Pam Jenoff, Kate Quinn and Kate Furnivall.

Available now.